DEMON OF LUST

PRINCES OF HELL
BOOK 1

SARA
HUMPHREYS

ALSO BY SARA HUMPHREYS

Amoveo Legend Series:
Unleashed
Untouched
Undenied (free e-short story)
Untamed
Undone
Unclaimed
Unbound (February 2015)

Dead in the City series:
Tall, Dark, and Vampire (Read on for a sneak peek)
Vampire Trouble
Vampires Never Cry Wolf (March 2015)

CHAPTER ONE

Struggling with the skeleton key, Kai swore under her breath as she fought to open the attic door of her grandfather's old, colonial house. Her mouth was set in a firm line as she wrestled with the uncooperative lock and reminded herself it was now *her house*. For better or for worse, the enormous place was now *hers*.

Kai hadn't ever met her maternal grandfather and if it weren't for an old picture her mom kept she wouldn't even have known what Jacob Kelly looked like. Kai's parents were killed in a car crash a couple of years ago, and not only did the jerkoff skip the funeral, he didn't even call. Not a card, a note, a text. Nothing. Not a Goddamn word.

What a prince.

Then about a month ago, Kai received a call from Ben Flaherty. He claimed to be an attorney in Idaho and said that she was the sole beneficiary of her grandfather's estate. At first she thought it was a joke or a scam or something, like one of those emails from the guy in Kenya who said you inherited a billion dollars. But after learning a few pertinent facts, she realized it wasn't a joke.

Ever since her parents died it was like she'd been traveling under a dark cloud of shitty luck. Kai's little tarot shop in New Hampshire went belly up last year, her boyfriend cheated on her—again.

Needless to say, life was sucking in a big, fat way. The only soul in the world Kai could count on was her Siamese cat, Zephyr, and she was a moody little thing. So, when Mr. Flaherty had laid it all out, the inheritance wasn't easy to turn down.

The property was in Bliss, Idaho with a whopping population of about three hundred people, but when Kai heard that Bliss was

1

located in Magic Valley, that was when she knew it was all going to be okay. She'd always been fascinated with all things mystical and, at a young age, had discovered she had a knack for reading people, or more specifically the auras that surrounded them. Tarot cards helped her get a more in-depth reading but, in most cases, she was able to get a solid bead on people by studying the color of their aura.

When she was little, she called it *the glow* and only her mother knew what she was talking about because she could see it too. Kai's dad would chuckle when *his girls* yammered on about auras, inner light and so forth. Kai was relatively certain her father thought it was just a silly game, but she and her mom knew better.

While Kai's mother was happy to discuss it in private, she discouraged the idea of sharing their intuitive nature with other people. So when Kai opened the tarot shop, her mom was less than thrilled and worried that Kai might attract the wrong sort of people—the ones without light.

Her mother, Katherine, called them the Dark Ones and warned Kai they would come if Kai wasn't careful about the kind of mystical practices she dabbled in. According to her mother's stories, the Dark Ones were capable of stealing a person's light—essentially they were soul- stealers. Her mother said that a Dark One could suck the soul out of a regular person, but that it was even more dangerous for people who saw auras or light the way that Kai did.

Kai shuddered but quickly shook it off. She knew her mother was being overly cautious or perhaps just flat out made up these scary stories to keep her from using her powers too freely.

Kai scoffed as she continued to fight with the lock on the attic door. The idea of a person without an aura was ludicrous because it would mean they didn't have a soul. Kai had never met anyone without light. Some people had auras that were darker or murkier than others, but everyone had a glow of some kind because everyone has a soul. Even animals have auras.

Kai let out a short laugh as she adjusted her grip on the iron key. Right now, she'd give just about anything for one of her mother's lectures on the mystic realm... and one of her hugs. The hole in Kai's heart grew smaller with time but there were moments the sadness and grief would surge and threaten to overwhelm her.

Not today. Today she would reclaim this house in her mother's memory and in honor of the twenty-five loving years her parents had shared. Kai had come out here with the intention of clearing the place out and selling it, but once she set foot on the property, something inside of her, that swirling unsettled energy that constantly battled to be let out... stilled.

With a growl of frustration, Kai swiped sweaty strands of blond hair from her forehead.

"Old man," she muttered through clenched teeth as she tried to force the lock. "This door is as stubborn as you were."

Holding her breath, the key slippery in her sweaty hands, Kai leaned her shoulder against the white painted door and in one final effort, the lock gave way with a satisfying *thunk*. Kai let out a sound of relief and gave Zephyr a thumbs up, while, in typical feline fashion she sat in the hallway giving Kai a bored look.

"Well, you could at least give me a small meow or something." Kai said between heavy breaths. "I almost had a stroke trying to get this door open."

Zephyr let out a short mewling sound and promptly began licking her front paw, clearly unimpressed.

"Nice." Kai laughed as she wiped sweat from her brow and tightened her ponytail. "Some help you are. It's just the two of us out here in the middle of nowhere so you better behave yourself or I might let the coyotes get you."

Zephyr meowed loudly and flounced over, rubbing her furred body up against Kai's bare calf.

"Oh, I'm just kidding." Kai scratched the cat's head and brushed the layer of cat hair off her skin as Zephyr trotted down the hall. "Shit, you are shedding like crazy. I can't blame you. It's hotter than Hades in here but something tells me it will feel downright balmy compared to the attic."

As if answering her prayers, a cool breeze from the open window at the end of the hallway wafted over her, providing momentary relief. Kai closed her eyes and reveled in the breeze but as soon as she tugged the attic door open she got a face full of thick, stale humid air.

Kai flipped the light switch on the wall as she tried not to breathe in the stifling air. To her great relief, the bulb dangling at the top of the steps still worked, so at least she wouldn't be stumbling around in the dark. Steeling herself, Kai climbed the creaky wooden steps with a combination of excitement and trepidation.

On one hand, she loved the idea of investigating what hidden treasures might be up there, but on the other, was the irrational fear that the bogeyman was in a dark corner waiting for her.

As Kai gripped the weathered railing, she coughed as dusty air filled her lungs, and reminded herself that the Dark Ones weren't hiding in attic corners. Darkness, true evil, lived in the hidden parts of people's hearts and minds, and that was more terrifying than any bogeyman.

As one Converse-clad foot hit the landing she looked around in awe. The attic was a cavernous space that ran the entire width of the house and it was filled with years worth of stuff. Dust-filled rays of sunlight streamed in from two oval windows, one at either end of the room, and Kai let out an exhausted sigh as she walked around the box-littered floor.

"We've got our work cut out for us," Kai murmured.

Zephyr rubbed against her leg again before trotting off and disappearing into the sea of clutter.

"If you find any mice, please don't behead them and drop them at my feet." Kai stepped over an old, steamer trunk. "It's gross and I'm already convinced of your bad-ass ninja like fighting skills. I don't need any more proof."

Making her way through what looked like a path amid the clutter, Kai opened both windows, which made the space bearable. Between the open windows and the door at the bottom of the steps, a gentle breeze now flowed through the musty room.

Kai glanced over and saw Zephyr lying on top of a box in front of one of the windows, settling in for yet another nap.

"Your mouse hunting skills are rivaled only by your ability to sleep, but I guess that's why they call them cat naps," she laughed. "Don't mind me. I'm just jealous. But as soon as I get through this mess, I'm taking a nap of my own."

Several hours later, Kai had managed to dig through almost every box and pile in the stuffy attic. Most of it was comprised of old clothes, blankets, books and records. There didn't appear to be anything of any real value monetarily or emotionally, and it became abundantly clear she was going to need to have all of it hauled away. Little of it was even in good enough shape to donate.

She'd hoped that there would be pictures of her mom as a little girl, old photo albums or something, but no such luck. Kai chalked it up to the fact that Jacob, clearly hadn't bothered with sentiment.

Her grandmother had died soon after Kai's mother was born and Jacob was so distraught he removed all images of his wife from the home. Kai shook her head as she stood up and brushed dust from the back of her shorts. "Charming."

A sudden gust of wind rattled the window and slammed it shut with a nerve-shattering crack. The sound had Kai jump about a foot in the air and sent Zephyr running for cover beneath a stack of framed prints that were leaning against the beamed wall.

"Holy crap," she said with a laugh. Kai's hand rested on her chest as her heart thundered rapidly. "That scared the bejezzus out of me."

Kai stepped over a few boxes and went to inspect the window, convinced the glass must have cracked from the force of the blow. To her relief the only thing that had come off was a bunch of old white paint chips that were scattered over the blanket where Zephyr had been sleeping.

"Looks like your bed got dirty," Kai said, as she brushed away the flakes of white. She peered over her shoulder at the cat, currently hissing at Kai from her hiding spot. "Don't be pissed at me. I didn't make the wind blow."

Kai turned back and noticed a blanket was covering a small crate. She pulled it off, coughing from a mouth full of dust. Beneath it was a weathered wooden box with faded symbols she couldn't quite make out. The top was nailed shut, which only piqued her curiosity further.

"Leave it to you," she said to Zephyr. "To find the most interesting-looking thing in the whole place. I'm gonna need a crow bar or something to open this one. Come on, girl. Let's get it downstairs."

Kai picked up the box and while it clearly had something inside, it wasn't as heavy as she thought it would be. With Zephyr at her heels, Kai made her way down the steps and breathed a sigh of relief when she hit the much cooler air of the second floor.

Mystery box in hand, Kai trotted down the main staircase, which led to the front entry hall of the old colonial. She passed through the massive formal dining room that looked like it hadn't been used in a century and took her treasure into the sunny country kitchen.

She put the crate on the weathered, butcher-block kitchen table, but as she headed for the mudroom, the sound of a car pulling up the driveway caught her attention. With Zephyr at her heels, Kai went to the front hall and peered through the screen door to see a familiar black Lexus pulling to a stop in the semi-circular dirt drive.

Smiling, Kai pushed open the creaky door and stepped out onto the covered porch to greet Mr. Flaherty. She held the door for Zephyr but the petulant feline stuck her tail in the air and went back inside, clearly uninterested in their visitor. Kai brushed her hands off and trotted down the steps to greet her grandfather's attorney.

Ben Flaherty stepped out of the car and looked even more out of place in this rural setting than his car did. His dark suit and crisp white shirt stood out in stark contrast to the rolling, green fields and red, weathered barn. He was tall, handsome, wealthy and educated. The kind of man she would never in a million years attempt to date because the man was slick from head to toe.

Even his aura was extra bright. Most healthy people had brightly colored auras but his was an almost blinding yellow. She'd never met anyone with an aura that bright other than her own mother. The familiar feel of his aura was probably why she'd felt comfortable with him right off the bat.

His clothes were never wrinkled and so far she'd seen no evidence that he perspired, and at the moment Kai was sweating like a pig.

Mr. Flaherty flashed a big pearly, white grin as he crossed around the front of the car and extended his hand to Kai.

"What brings you all the way out here, Mr. Flaherty?" Kai asked as she shook his well- manicured hand.

"I thought I told you to call me Ben," he said as his aura shifted from yellow to a reddish hue. "Mr. Flaherty was my father."

Kai blushed as his hand held hers a bit longer than a typical handshake.

"Right," Kai said, removing her hand from his. That color change in his aura was a sure fire sign that he was attracted to her and she had to admit, he was cute. "I thought we took care of everything the other day in your office."

"We did," he said as he took off his sunglasses and peered at her with warm, brown eyes. "But since you don't know anyone in the area and you're living out here all alone, I thought I'd pop in and check on you. You look like you've been working hard," he said as his eyes wandered over her.

"You could say that," Kai said, as she self-consciously brushed off her dusty tank top. "I managed to get through most of the house and today I finally tackled the attic."

"Really?" His gaze flicked to the open attic windows and his eyebrows rose. "In this heat? You're a brave soul, Kai Kelly. Find anything of interest?"

"Not really. Mostly old clothes and stuff." Silence stretched out for a moment as he continued to study her. Feeling awkward, Kai jutted her thumb toward the house and squinted against the setting sun. "Would you like to come in for a glass of lemonade?"

"I'd love to but I have to get back into Gooding for a dinner meeting." Ben glanced at his watch and then locked eyes with Kai. His voice dropped to a softer tone. "I'll do you one better, though. How about if you let me take you out for dinner tomorrow night?"

"Uh, sure," she said with a smile. Kai stuck her hands in the pockets of her shorts and instantly felt even more self-conscious than she did before. She didn't own a single item of clothing that would be appropriate for any restaurant Ben would want to go to.

"Did you have any place in particular in mind because I saw a neat looking place in town and I wanted to try it," she said. "Angels and Outlaws. Have you heard of it?"

"Well, sure." Ben let out a short laugh. "But I was hoping for our first date to be somewhere more fitting of a lady. But I want you to be comfortable. So Angels and Outlaws it is."

First date? Kai swallowed the lump in her throat and wrestled with her conflicting emotions. Ben was hot and rich and she'd be crazy not to go out with him. So why was she feeling hesitant?

"Well," Kai began slowly as she tried not to notice the ripples of red in his aura. "I'm a simple girl and if you tried to take me to one of the fancy places you probably had in mind, I'd use the wrong fork or something. A burger joint is fine with me. How about if we meet there tomorrow night around seven?"

"Sounds good to me," Ben said as a smile cracked his face. He slipped his sunglasses back on and walked back to the driver's side of his car. "I'll see you at seven tomorrow and by the way... something tells me you're anything but a simple girl."

Before Kai could respond Ben was in his car and driving down the driveway. As the cloud of dust settled and his taillights disappeared from view, a smile played at Kai's lips. Maybe Bliss wasn't going to be so boring after all?

Kai made her way back into the house and started rooting around in a box of tools that were in the mudroom adjacent to the kitchen. Crow bar in hand, she came back into the kitchen and found Zephyr sitting on top of the box again.

"What's your story?" Kai asked with narrowed eyes as she pointed the crow bar at her companion. "I'll make you a deal. You can have the box but I get whatever's inside."

Zephyr, seemingly satisfied with the arrangement, hopped off the crate and onto one of the chairs. Her large blue eyes stared intently at the box, her curiosity matching Kai's. That phrase *curiosity killed the cat* ran through Kai's mind.

"Here goes nothing," she murmured.

Finding the seam along the top, Kai wedged the tip of the crowbar into the crack and with one big push the top popped open. She did the same thing along two other edges, and when she finally pulled the top off, what she found inside left her stunned.

A stack of old black and white photographs sat inside, and the hauntingly, familiar face of a young woman stared up at Kai through a pair of large dark eyes. Eyes that were just like hers. With shaking fingers, Kai reached in and pulled out the pile of weathered photographs.

She flipped through the stack one at a time and found that every picture was of the same woman. Based on the fifties style clothing and striking resemblance to both Kai and her mother, Kai could only assume this was her grandmother, Kristine.

All the photos showed a smiling, young woman full of life, but it was the last picture that gave her pause.

It was an image of her grandmother with a baby in her arms and Kai was certain it was her mother, when she was an infant. Tears fell freely down Kai's cheeks as she ran one finger over the faded image. Sniffling, she flipped the picture over to see if there was a date and while there was something written, it wasn't what she expected.

My sweet, Katherine. The next Custodian.

"Custodian?" Kai said, confused. Her grandmother was a custodian? "Do we come from some long line of school janitors or something?"

As Kai swiped at her damp cheek with the back of her hand, she spotted a small black bag that had been hidden beneath the photos. She placed the stack of photos on the table and picked up the heavy, worn, cotton bag and felt a lump inside. Kai loosened the drawstring and turned the bag over, emptying the contents into her hand.

A heavy ring made of iron, tumbled into her palm and the metal felt cool against her damp skin. Holding it between her fingers, Kai squinted and went to the light by the kitchen window to try and make out the unusual design on the round face

There were a series of four circles with some kind of lettering evenly spaced between the rings. It was so tiny and worn away by time that she'd need a magnifying glass to get a clue as to what it said. At the center of the smallest circle was what looked like a star and it had some kind of crystal in the middle.

"Why wouldn't Jacob have given this to my mom?" she murmured.

It was beautiful. Not in a traditionally gorgeous and sparkling kind of way, but beautiful none-the-less and it was definitely old. She had no idea just how old but it really didn't matter. This ring obviously belonged to her grandmother and that's what made it valuable.

"Priceless."

Smiling through her tears, Kai slipped the precious ring onto the middle finger of her right hand and found that it fit perfectly. As she held her hand up to inspect her newfound prize, a howling gust of wind ripped through the house and slammed the front door shut.

Kai yelped and spun around to see the pile of pictures blow around the room and flutter to the kitchen floor. Her hands gripped the edge of the counter behind her as she fought to still her racing heartbeat. Zephyr was nowhere to be seen and the only sound was the old, cuckoo clock that ticked loudly on the wall.

She squatted down to pick up the scattered photos and as she placed them back on top of the table, her attention was captured by something written on the side of the crate. As her gaze slid over the words, the little hairs on the back of her neck stood on end. *Custodians of the Light.*

***

The disturbance in the air had been subtle, a quiet rumbling that, at first, Asmodeus mistook for the usual notification of new arrivals. Every day when a new batch of tormented souls arrived, there was a shift in the atmosphere. As one of the seven Princes of Hell and the Demon of Lust, he was responsible for the pathetic individuals who earned their ticket to hell by reveling in lust and desire.

Lust or lusting for someone wasn't evil but, when humans allowed themselves to be corrupted by it that was when the scales tipped to damnation. The souls that landed in his little corner of hell were the worst of the worst.

Rapists, murderers, pedophiles. The humans, who in Asmodeus' opinion, gave lust a bad name and he was more than happy to escort them into an eternity of hell and damnation.

But he could do without the paperwork.

Asmodeus had been overseeing tortured souls in Hell for several millennia and he was growing weary of it. He watched mortals, on many occasions, and envied the life, the freedoms they were given. So when they abused that freedom, there was something gratifying about implementing their punishment.

Lucifer, the leader of all demons, granted them a vacation on earth every one hundred years. However, Asmodeus, much to his dismay, wasn't due for another trip for quite some time. Oh, he'd snuck up there a time or two to help his half-mortal son but he didn't stay long enough to truly enjoy it.

While Asmodeus loved trips to the mortal plane he sure as shit didn't want to get a trip to earth like this. As he walked through the tunnels of stone that led to the mortal plane, he let out a beleaguered sigh.

The first disturbance in the air had been nothing compared to the series of bone shattering sonic booms that rocked the Underworld in nauseating succession. The instant it happened, Asmodeus knew what it was. He'd heard and felt that same ear-splitting sound three thousand years before and, until an hour ago, Asmodeus and the rest of the Brotherhood thought the threat had been eliminated.

Apparently not.

The disturbance in Hell meant that someone had found the Ring of Solomon. The ring had the ability to control all demons and if the bearer so desired, it could be used to destroy them as well. King Solomon had almost done exactly that when the guy had put Asmodeus and the rest of the Brotherhood under his complete control. Lucky for them, one hot summer day, Solomon had imbibed far too much wine and his curiosity got the better of him. He asked Asmodeus what demons could do if they had total power over humans. What powers did they truly possess?

Asmodeus promised to show him, but said he needed the ring and his freedom in order to properly demonstrate. Solomon, drunk as a skunk, handed the ring to Asmodeus, who then promptly tossed it into the sea, releasing the Brotherhood in the process.

They all thought that was the end of it. Not so much.

Someone had not only found the ring but was wearing it and, whether or not they knew it; this individual quite literally could command Hell. Since none of the demons had been summoned, it was a safe bet that the bearer of the ring had zero idea of the kind of power they had in their hands.

However, not wanting to take any chances, Lucifer chose to send Asmodeus and the rest of the Brotherhood up to earth in search of the ring. As far as Asmodeus was concerned it was like looking for a needle in a haystack and could take a century to find it.

They knew was it was somewhere in North America, but they were unable to pinpoint its location. Given the fact that the ring's whereabouts were somehow cloaked, the wearer must be a unique human being indeed.

Asmodeus slipped on a pair of aviator sunglasses as he strode out the mouth of the cave. Wearing jeans, a white t-shirt and motorcycle boots, he placed his hands on his hips and let out an exasperated sigh as he surveyed the area. Idaho. Of all places, he gets to start his search in Idaho.

There were several direct portals to Hell within the continental United States. Los Angeles, Houston, Las Vegas and New York City, just to name a few, but one of them was deep within the caves of the Craters of the Moon. The four hundred-acre lava field was one of the only places on earth that actually resembled the Underworld but it wasn't exactly a bustling metropolis.

Although, given Asmodeus' weakness for the company of women and pleasures of the flesh, he wasn't terribly surprised that he pulled this particular location. Having fewer ladies around meant fewer distractions and he knew that was exactly why Lucifer stuck him way the hell out here.

Great. He gets an extra chance to enjoy the mortal plane and Lucifer puts him in one of the most desolate places in North America.

"What a dick," Asmodeus murmured as he squinted against the light of the setting sun.

Welcome back to earth, Lucifer's voice touched the collective consciousness of the Brotherhood. *Based on various disturbances in the energy fields, I have sent the six of you to the locations the ring is most likely to be. Additionally, there are certain individuals located in these areas that are descended from unique bloodlines and are the most probable candidates to be in possession of the ring.*

Something glinting in the distance caught his eye. Asmodeus grinned when he saw the black and chrome motorcycle waiting for him by the edge of the deserted highway.

I'm not completely cruel. Lucifer's voice floated around Asmodeus with his usual air of self-importance. *You have each been provided with a mode of transportation and a duffle bag with money and some clothing. There is also a paper with the names and locations of the individuals you should be looking for. They're listed in priority order for your convenience.*

You're a real prince, Asmodeus interjected. *I'm sure this all looks very convenient from your corner office in Hell.*

Stop whining, Asmodeus. Lucifer's voice, edged with boredom filled his mind. *You haven't even thanked me for the motorcycle.*

Asmodeus stopped dead in his tracks and dug into the pockets of the Levi's he was wearing. His smile broadened as he pulled out the keys to the Harley Davidson and started walking again toward the bike. Lucifer might be a son of a bitch, but he had his moments. "Not bad," he murmured. "But you're still a dick."

Yes, I know. Arrogance dripped from Lucifer's every word but as the Demon of Pride and leader of the Brotherhood, it was of little surprise. *We have two immediate problems, other than the obvious.* Asmodeus tried to keep his attention on Lucifer, instead of the gorgeous bike. He ran his hands over the smooth curve of the handles as Lucifer's deep, gravelly voice touched the collective minds of the Brotherhood. *Since we haven't been able to pinpoint the exact location of the ring, my concern is that has something to do with whoever is wearing it and you all know how much I loathe not having all the information. Secondly, if you'll recall, the ring cannot be taken from its owner, it has to be given to one of you willingly.*

What if the guy wearing it befalls some kind of horrible accident? Falls off a cliff? Runs into a bullet... or my fist? Satan's voice cut into the conversation and Asmodeus smirked as he walked around and appraised the bike. Satan was the Demon of Wrath, loved mayhem and was the biggest troublemaker in the bunch. *Can we take it if he's dead?*

Yes, Lucifer responded. *But you know full well that we can't harm an innocent, so I suppose you'll just have to play that part by ear.*

Asmodeus opened the duffle bag that was strapped to the back of the bike and pulled out the paper. He perused the list of names and the one at the top grabbed his attention immediately. Kai Kelly— Bliss, Idaho. His lips tilted as he folded the paper up and stuck it in the back pocket of his jeans. Kai was a woman's name, wasn't it?

What makes you think it's a guy? Asmodeus asked as a grin cracked his face. *Could be a lovely lady and wouldn't that be far more pleasant?*

13

Well, shit. Mammon's irritated tone cut into the conversation. As the Demon of Envy he was always feeling slighted and as though he somehow got the short end of the stick. *If it is a chick and Asmodeus finds her first, he'll spend a month in bed with her before he gets the ring. I don't know what part of the continent you guys got, but I'm stuck in Alaska and I'll bet the ring is nowhere near here. Brother, if it is a broad then do us all a favor and get the ring before you fuck her.*

Whatever, man. Belphegor's bored voice interrupted them. *I'm in no rush. I haven't been to earth in a long time. You know all work and no play makes the Demon of Sloth a dull boy.*

Mammon, Asmodeus responded playfully, *if I didn't know better I'd say you were jealous.*

Screw you.

No thanks, brother. Asmodeus' laugh, deep and loud touched their collective minds. *You're not my type.*

If you're all quite finished. Lucifer's voice, sharp and curt, cut off any further banter. *You will get the ring by whatever means necessary. However, Mammon raises an interesting point.*

A heavy silence hung as they waited for Lucifer to continue.

I'm concerned the six of you may succumb to temptations and find yourselves distracted from your mission. I have sent you there to find the ring and bring it back to the Underworld, not to indulge in your vices. In addition, as demons you won't be able to get within a mile of the ring without alerting the person wearing it. Chances are that the human who has found the ring has no idea the power that it holds— otherwise we'd have been summoned already. However, we can't afford to take risks. In hindsight, having you all down there as full-blooded demons seems unwise.

Asmodeus glanced over his shoulder at the field of black rocks as a feeling of dread crawled up his back. What did he mean... as full-blooded demons?

In order for you to get anywhere near the bearer, and to assure you stay focused, I am going to make one small adjustment for your current stay. Lucifer's voice wavered and Asmodeus could tell the son of a bitch was smiling. *It's really for your own good.*

Just as Asmodeus was about to ask what he was talking about, a burning sensation fired through his body, stealing his breath. The sudden onslaught sent him to his knees as he gasped for air and agonizing pain radiated across his chest. Asmodeus' hands hit the rocks and gravel scraped against his knees as he fought a sudden and unfamiliar wave of nausea.

Sucking in a deep breath, he pushed himself off the ground with a grunt and kneeled for a moment as he regained his bearings. He tore the sunglasses from his face, suddenly feeling the uncomfortable effects of the late afternoon sun. Up until seconds ago, the heat had not fazed him in the least. Asmodeus' palms stung and when he lifted his hands, he swore loudly when he saw speckles of blood mixed with dirt.

Demons did not bleed.

When you find the ring, you will telepath me immediately, and if necessary I will send the rest of the Brotherhood to assist. Lucifer's voice, calm, cool and detached whispered through Asmodeus' mind. *I'm sure I don't need to remind you how dire the situation is, but to sweeten the pot... whomever finds the ring and brings it back to Hell will earn a three-month vacation on earth.*

If their minds had still been connected, Asmodeus would have surely heard the others when Lucifer laid the reward before them. One of the only things that any of them looked forward to was their time on earth, and to get an extra three months would be spectacular.

However, Asmodeus was met with silence. It was an odd sensation, to be disconnected from the rest of the Brotherhood. The pulsing energy of their minds was conspicuously absent the first time in several millennia.

As you get close to the ring, Lucifer's voice floated into his mind but sounded far away, *you will feel the pulse of its power, but your abilities will be limited. Although, you'll be stronger than most humans, I'm not entirely sure what powers you'll retain. The telekinesis and ability to manipulate heat may or may not remain. It may vary from brother to brother. At least that's what's most likely.*

Likely? Asmodeus gritted his teeth as sweat trickled down his back and the pain ebbed across his chest. *You have no idea what you're doing. Do you, Lucifer?*

Ignoring him, Lucifer continued.

I have also left each of you with the ability to telepath me once it's found but not each other. Our collective mental link emanates far too much power and would definitely blow your cover... so to speak. I realize this is less than appealing but it's the only way to protect members of the Brotherhood. Lucifer's laugh rasped through Asmodeus' mind as his voice faded. *And to ensure you do what you need to do, there's nothing wrong with a little extra incentive. I can't imagine any of you want to stay on earth in this.... state.*

"You mother fucker," Asmodeus ground out as he stood up and bit back a wave of unfamiliar pain. "What did you do?"

Asmodeus held out his arms and watched as the tattoos that covered the length of his arms and ran across his back... vanished. The intricate design, seven interlocking circles with a five-pointed star at the center, was the mark of the Brotherhood and had branded his flesh for his entire existence-until now.

Lucifer made them mortal.

CHAPTER TWO

The elderly man's aura was a dull, sickly green and wavered around him in the dingy gas station like smoke but Kai kept a smile on her face. He was definitely ill, most likely cancer of the lungs based on the way he was sucking down his second cigarette in less than fifteen minutes. Kai usually saw that pea green color when someone was sick and as the old fella coughed up a hunk of phlegm, she was relatively certain her mojo was on point.

"I'm new around here," Kai said as she placed a twenty on the counter for the gas she'd just pumped. "Is there anything interesting to see in the area?"

"Yup," he rasped. His pale gray, watery eyes glanced at her briefly as he rang up her purchase on an old fashioned cash register. He adjusted his dirty baseball cap and gave her a toothy grin, which actually brightened up his weathered complexion. "This your first time in Magic Valley, I'd bet. Well, if you're like most folks you'll want to see them caves or take a ride over to Atomic City and see the first nuclear reactor."

"Caves?" Kai smiled as he rang up her purchase slower than molasses in winter, and though she tried to be patient, she was starving and had to get something to eat before she fainted. "Nuclear reactors? Sounds like a lot going on for such a... remote area."

"Yes, ma'am. Magic Valley is full of surprises." He pushed his hat back and wiped the back of his neck with a red bandana. "I'm Clive and

I'd bet my bottom dollar you're Jacob Kelly's granddaughter."

Kai stilled and the smile fell from her face as she self-consciously tucked a long lock of blond hair behind her ear. While she was used to seeing inside people, it was unnerving to have someone do it to her.

"Don't go gettin' nervous now." Clive waved one hand and sat on a stool behind the counter. "There are only two hundred and seventy five people livin' in Bliss." He shrugged and laughed through a smoker's cough. "Folks are bound to notice when someone new comes to town. Besides, Jacob told me you'd be movin' into his place after he passed and, if I didn't know that, I'd sure notice you were drivin' his old Dodge." He jutted a thumb toward the window. "That piece of crap is almost as old as me."

"Y—You knew my grandfather?"

"Course I did." Clive crushed his cigarette out in an ashtray on the counter that was overflowing with ashes and old butts. "He came here for gas for that old beater you're drivin' around."

"You were friends?"

"Ha!" Clive coughed and covered his mouth with the bandana as he laughed up a lung. "Jacob didn't have friends but I 'spose I was as close to a friend as he ever had. Ever since his wife Kristine died, man hardly spoke a word, and then when his daughter left." He let out a sigh and shrugged. "He just wasn't a people person I 'spose."

"Clearly not," Kai said under her breath. She stopped herself from going into a tirade about a man she'd never known and forced a smile. "I didn't know him. Never met him actually."

"I know." Clive nodded and gave her sad smile. "He was a cryptic old bastard. Told me that someday his granddaughter would come and take over his place. Said your grandmother, Kristine, would want that. He wanted your mama to stay but I guess Bliss just isn't for everyone."

"My grandmother." Kai smiled and slipped her wallet back into her satchel. "You knew her?"

"Sure did. Kristine was good friends with my Clara... I lost her last fall." The smile faltered and he adjusted his cap again in an almost soothing gesture as emotion filled his eyes. "Them two gals was like peas and carrots when they were young. After Kristine died,

18

my Clara tried to get Jacob to come to church and the socials but he stayed up in that house most the time. He worked around town as a groundskeeper and back in the day, well, if he wasn't workin' then he was at home with your mama. But when your mama left, well," he said on a sigh, "That was that."

"Was he a custodian by any chance?" Kai asked as she rubbed the ring with the pad of her thumb as the words from the box drifted into her mind. "Was my grandmother?"

"Nope." Clive lit another cigarette. "Your grandmother didn't work and Jacob, he took care of the grounds at the school and for the town."

"I see," she said as she pushed her hair off her face with a sigh.

"You look exhausted, young lady."

"I'm sure I do," she said with a laugh. "I've spent the past several days cleaning out my grandfather's place but there's about ten tons of junk in the attic that has to get thrown out. Not to mention all the stuff out in the old barn."

"Sounds like too much hard labor for a pretty young thing like yourself." He dug around behind the counter, pulled out a flyer and handed it to her. "This is a local guy who hauls away junk. Give him a call, he'll help you out."

"Thank you, Clive." Kai took the paper and smiled. "I may just do that. The truth is that there's a lot of junk to drag away. Not only that, but the grounds need some help."

"You know how those things go." Clive sat on the stool and gave her a big grin. "He did all that stuff for a living so when he got home, probably didn't have a mind for it. Hell, if you were a baker would you come home and bake?"

"Probably not," Kai agreed.

The sudden rumbling of a motorcycle shattered the quiet outside and made Kai jump. She laughed nervously and gave Clive a shy smile as they watched a biker roll slowly down the road and pause for a moment before pulling into the gas station. The late afternoon sun streamed in through the window and Kai squinted against the blinding light.

"Another biker," Clive murmured as he rose from the stool and hitched up his pants. "He's probably headed over to Outlaws and

19

SARA HUMPHREYS

Angels. It's a local biker joint but they make a mean burger. Folks come from all over to check out the place."

"Funny you mention that place. I'm meeting a friend there for dinner, which can't come a moment too soon. I'm starving." Kai's stomach rumbled, reminding her that she hadn't eaten in hours. It was in part because she'd been so busy and also because she was nervous about this date with Ben. "I hear their burgers are great, although it's practically the only game in town."

"That would be correct." He winked. "Our little town is made up of the post office, my gas station, a motel and two bars. Not exactly a hot spot," he laughed.

Smiling, Kai glanced back outside at the man on the motorcycle as Clive started to tell her about his favorite item on the menu. But she barely heard him because she was too busy staring at the guy climbing off the motorcycle. She knew Clive was talking but he sounded far away, as if the world around her had detached from her somehow.

Wearing mirrored aviators, the man stood and swung his leg over what had to be a Harley Davidson. Mesmerized, she watched as he gassed up his bike. He had to be at least six foot four, with a broad well-muscled back that was covered by a white t-shirt, leaving his perfectly sculpted and tanned arms in plain sight. Faded ,blue jeans skimmed over his legs and dusty, black motorcycle boots kicked up dirt as he put the gas pump back in its place.

It wasn't his strikingly handsome profile that had Kai feeling dizzy and displaced. Kai's heart raced and the ring on her finger felt hot against her skin as she squinted. She blinked because she couldn't quite believe what she was seeing—or more to the point—what she wasn't seeing.

This man, whoever he was, had no aura.

Beware the Dark Ones.

As the words whispered through her mind, the man stilled and turned around slowly until he faced the storefront. Even though he was wearing those mirrored sunglasses, Kai sensed he was looking directly at her.

Sweat broke out over her flesh and her body shook, as she watched him stalk across the parking lot toward the door of the

20

smoky shop. Maybe she was wrong and it was a trick of the light or the sun got in her eyes, blinding her and preventing her from seeing his glow.

He *had* to have an aura. There was no such thing as the Dark Ones.

As he got closer with each step, it became glaringly clear that he was without light. Kai backed up slowly and clutched the strap of the bag draped across her chest as fear and confusion swamped her. It suddenly felt as though it was a thousand degrees and as if all the air had been sucked out of the room. The long sundress she wore seemed to stick to her like a second skin as she started to sweat from head to toe.

The stranger opened the door and the tiny bell above announced his entrance. Kai backed into a rack of chips and froze as she stared at the man through wide frightened eyes.

The door swung shut behind him as he removed his sunglasses and looked at her with the most piercing, pale blue eyes she'd ever seen. Jet-black hair and dark eyebrows framed that intense gaze as he stared at Kai with something akin to awe.

"Well, I'll be a son of a bitch," he breathed. A wide smile cracked the handsome stranger's face as his eyes drifted over her. "Looks like I drew the lucky card after all."

"Kai?" Clive, his voice edged with worry, stood from his stool and leaned over the counter. "Are you okay, girl?"

Kai gaped at the stranger and fought to catch her breath. She wasn't mistaken. It wasn't the sun playing tricks on her and as the reality of the situation settled over her, everything started to spin.

"Kai?" The man's voice, deep and seductive, washed over her. "Well, then I am one lucky devil."

"Y-you're a Dark One," she murmured. The last word escaped her lips, Kai wavered on her feet and the world went black.

***

Asmodeus had been so completely taken off guard that he almost didn't catch the beautiful blonde as she fainted but, lucky for her, he snapped out of it just in time to grab her before she hit the dirty floor.

He scooped her limp body up against his chest effortlessly and the old man waved him toward the back of the store.

"Heat must've gotten to her," the old guy muttered. "Bring her here. I got a cot in the back room, you can set her down."

Asmodeus followed the man through the door and into a small room. Kai moaned softly as he set her down on the cot.

"I'll get a cool cloth for her head." He pointed at Asmodeus. "Just stay right there with Kai but don't try nothin' funny."

Asmodeus nodded, but his attention was fixed firmly on the ring on her right hand—it was the Ring of Solomon. Though it had been almost three millennia since he'd set eyes on it, there was no mistaking it.

Lucifer had been correct. Asmodeus had felt the presence of the ring before he saw it. It was a familiar pull in his gut, drawing him, almost willing him closer.

He sat on the edge of the cot next to Kai and placed her hands on her belly, careful to avoid touching the ring. Asmodeus glanced over his shoulder, looking for the old man but he was still puttering around out in the shop, looking for a cold cloth, no doubt. Asmodeus turned back and glanced at the paper in her hands. He removed it gently and saw it was a flyer advertising a local haul away service.

Kai moaned softly. There was no denying that she was a beautiful specimen of a woman. Long strands of pale, blond hair framed an oval-shaped face with high cheekbones, wide set eyes and pink, perfectly shaped lips. Her skin had the glow of summer and her body had soft looking curves in all the right places.

Kai Kelly was born to make men weak.

Lucifer may have taken most of their powers and made all of the Brotherhood mortal, but Asmodeus had seen Kai's energy field the moment he laid eyes on her. She exuded a soft white light that resembled moonlight through the mists and, once he spotted it, there was no mistaking what she was. A regular human, like the old man, didn't exude light like that—at least not one that Asmodeus could see.

Kai Kelly had blood of the Fae running through her veins.

Based on the fact that she was wearing the ring, he had to assume she didn't have any idea that she was part of a Fae bloodline.

The Fae Clans—even the ones that were comprised of human-Fae hybrids—were fully aware of the Ring of Solomon and knew all too well of the power it held. If Kai had been vested in one of the Fae clans, then she would never have put on the ring and essentially sound the alarm in Hell. No. If she were connected with other Fae, then he and the rest of the Brotherhood would be at the mercy of a flock of fairies.

Asmodeus frowned. A fairy. Shit. Of all the supernatural creatures that walked the earth, he found the Fae the most difficult to deal with. Their magic was known to be some of the most powerful, even more than the witches and warlocks. Asmodeus had only tangled with one Fae in his time and that guy had been one mean son of a bitch.

"Damn," Asmodeus said under his breath.

Kai moaned again and twitched as though she were having a bad dream. A lock of hair fell across her forehead and without thinking Asmodeus brushed the strands of gold aside. He didn't want anything to obscure his view of her gorgeous, innocent face. The pads of his fingers brushed over silken flesh and his body tightened immediately in response as a smile played at his lips.

Kai Kelly might be part fairy, he thought as he withdrew his hand, but she was *all woman*. His gaze flicked down to the ring on her delicate hand as he rose from the cot. Whatever magic she possessed was of little consequence when it came to matters of the flesh and desire. In that moment, Asmodeus knew exactly how he would get the ring. He would seduce it out from under her and be back in Hell before the week was out.

"Here's a cold cloth," the old man said, as he shuffled in through the door and pushed past Asmodeus. He sat on the edge of the cot next to Kai and placed it on her forehead. "I got a call in to the doc but he ain't answerin' his damn phone. I keep tellin' him he needs a landline but he's only got one of them cellular phones and the signals around here are for shit."

Kai groaned and her hand went to her head as she started to wake up.

"She'll be okay," Asmodeus said with his gaze fixed firmly on the ring. "Like you said, it was probably just the heat."

23

"How'd you know her name?" The old guy eyed Asmodeus warily over his shoulder. "She's only been in town 'bout a week and I ain't never seen you around here. So how do you know her, anyway?"

"I—heard you call her by her name," Asmodeus said with a shrug.

"What happened?" Kai's voice wavered as she pushed herself up onto her elbows and removed the cloth from her head. "Clive, how did—"

She stopped speaking as soon as she spotted Asmodeus. Her dark, chocolate brown eyes widened as their gazes locked and Kai's body stilled. "You," she breathed.

"This young man caught you before you hit the floor," Clive said. He scooted aside as Kai swung her legs over the edge of the cot and sat up. "Don't move too fast, now. You must have had a touch of heat stroke."

"Right," Kai said as she continued to stare at Asmodeus warily. "That must be what it was."

Her eyes, the richest shade of brown Asmodeus had ever seen, skittered over him like she was searching for something. He remained motionless as she continued her inspection, and he found himself in an unusual position. It wasn't often that Asmodeus felt as though he were the one under the microscope.

"I suppose I should thank you," Kai said to Asmodeus as she handed the washcloth to the old man. "Mister... ?"

Asmodeus paused for a moment. He couldn't give her his real name, so he settled on the name he used whenever he took his vacations on earth.

"Miles," he said with a wide grin. "Aaron Miles."

"Aaron?" Kai said through a short laugh as she rose to her feet with Clive protectively at her side. "It's nice to meet you."

"It is *very* nice to meet you," he murmured.

"Well, thank you, Mr. Miles." Kai adjusted the satchel she had slung across her body and glanced at him briefly before giving Clive a sweet smile. "Clive, I'm sorry to have caused such a ruckus. I guess I'm not used to the heat out here."

"Don't even give it a second thought," he said with a wave of a wrinkled hand. "You think our summers are tough? Wait until you live through your first winter." His smile faded and he adjusted his hat again. "I gotta tell ya, I don't feel right about you drivin' off without the doc havin' a look at ya."

"I'm fine, Clive." Kai patted him on the arm and glanced briefly at Asmodeus. "Between the heat and needing a bite to eat, I just got a little woozy." She glanced at the clock on the wall. "Oh man, I'm going to be late."

"Are you sure you're okay to drive?" Asmodeus asked, as he stuck his hands in the pockets of his jeans. "You looked like you'd seen a ghost," he said as he gazed at her intently.

"I'm fine," Kai said sharply, as she shot him a narrow-eyed look.

Asmodeus may have caught her mid-faint and kept her from falling on the floor, but he could tell that she didn't trust him. Fae, human or whatever, this woman could sense that Asmodeus was not exactly human and that put him at a disadvantage. Damn. Perhaps seducing Kai Kelly wasn't going to be as easy as he thought.

"Okay." Asmodeus threw his hands up in defeat. "Whatever you say, lady."

"I'm sorry," Kai added quickly. "I didn't mean to be so abrupt. I guess I'm just cranky from heat and lack of food."

"Right." Asmodeus nodded as he pulled the wallet out of his back pocket, complete with fake ID and money. "I'll go on record as saying this has been one of my more memorable stops." He removed some cash. "Here's twenty bucks for the gas I pumped earlier."

"Don't be silly," Clive waved him off as he coughed into his bandana. "This one's on me."

"Thank you." Asmodeus slipped the wallet into his back pocket and locked eyes with Kai. "Then I guess I'll be on my way. Ma'am," he said with a nod and turned on his heels.

"Wait," Kai said. Asmodeus paused in the doorway but didn't turn around. "The least I could do is buy you a dinner." A smile curved his lips and he turned slowly to face her. To his surprise, she had closed the distance and was standing directly behind him. "So, how about it?"

Kai clutched the strap of her leather satchel and squared her shoulders in a challenging stance. The ring briefly captured Asmodeus' gaze, before flicking back to those deep, brown eyes.

"Let me buy you a beer and a burger over at Angels and Outlaws to make up for fainting *and* for acting like an ingrate. I'm meeting a friend there for dinner in a few minutes and I insist you join us."

"Angels and Outlaws?" Asmodeus murmured. "Sounds like my kind of place,"

"Great." Kai nodded. Asmodeus stepped aside and gestured to the doorway. "After you."

As he started his motorcycle and followed Kai's car down the dusty main road of Bliss, Asmodeus couldn't help but smile. He had not only found the ring but a beautiful woman was wearing it, which would make the task of obtaining the ring far more satisfying. Asmodeus had never bedded a fairy before and there was nothing he enjoyed more than new experiences.

CHAPTER THREE

Kai sat in the booth and tried to concentrate on the laminated menu in her hands instead of on the man sitting across from her, but it was an effort in futility. She'd read the contents of the menu about a dozen times, but had not retained a thing.

She glanced at the clock. Seven fifteen and no sign of Ben yet. That was just as well because she still hadn't figured out how to gracefully explain why she had invited another man along on their date.

Kai peered at her new friend over the edge of the menu. Mr. Aaron Miles had no light. Nothing. Nada. Zip. He was a Dark One—and yet wasn't. At least he wasn't what she expected. Based on her mother's stories, she was expecting a drooling, fanged, hunched over ball of evil. Not a super-hot hunk that catches fainting women in gas stations.

Aaron caught her looking at him again and smirked. Kai's face heated with embarrassment just as the waitress came back to their table with the beers they had ordered.

"Two ice-cold Coronas with lime," she said as she slid the bottles onto the scarred, wood table. The waitress, probably in her mid-forties, gave Aaron a big smile and tapped her chin with the end of her pen as she inched closer to his side of the table. "Have you decided what you'd like to eat? A hulking fella like you would probably love our Big Devil Burger."

27

"That sounds right up my alley," he said with a wink. "Thank you, Matilda. I believe I'll take your professional advice and have that to go, if you don't mind."

"How'd you know my name?" Matilda giggled, as she jotted his order down.

"Name tag," he said in a conspiratorial whisper.

Kai watched the exchange with genuine awe. The woman was seriously ready to drop her panties, not that Kai could blame her, but the odd part was that Aaron seemed totally unfazed by it. Was he arrogant or genuinely unaware of the effect he was having on poor Matilda? He flicked his pale blue eyes to hers and winked.

Arrogant. It figures.

Kai rolled her eyes and put her menu down on the table top as she glanced past him toward the door of the bar looking for any sign of Ben.

"Oh my," Matilda said as one hand flew to her ample cleavage. "You are a charmer, aren't you? Most folks that come into this place don't bother to learn my name."

"Kai?" His voice brought her out of her thoughts. "Do you know what you want?"

The waitress huffed and gave Kai an exasperated look. She was thoroughly annoyed to have to take her attention off Aaron or have his attention taken from her.

"Oh, yes." Kai blinked and shook her head. "Sorry, I should probably wait for my friend to get here. He should be here any minute."

"Well, that's fine by me," Matilda said as she tucked the pen behind her ear. "Y'all just give me a holler when you're ready." She turned her attention to Asmodeus. "You want me to put your order in now or do you want to wait?"

"I think I'll hold off until Kai's date gets here. After all, I have to see what kind of man entices my new friend, here." He leaned back in the booth and draped one arm along the back of it as he took a sip of his beer.

"You got it, doll." Matilda sauntered off toward the bar.

Kai didn't miss the seductive sway of her hips or the fact that Aaron's gaze was fixed firmly on the waitress' ass.

"Charming," Kai sighed as she picked up her beer. "Well, I can clearly see what entices you."

"What?" He asked innocently. "I'm only looking."

"Forget it," Kai said with a laugh as she sipped her beer. "Boys will be boys. So, what do you do aside from ogle waitresses and catch fainting women in gas stations? What's your story, Mr. Miles?"

"Not much to tell," he said with the shrug of one shoulder. "I guess you could say I'm on sabbatical."

"Oh really?" Kai rubbed at the condensation on the beer bottle with her thumb. She was, in spite of her better judgment, thoroughly intrigued by the handsome enigma in front of her. "What exactly are you taking a break from?"

"Guess," he said playfully. Aaron leaned both elbows on the table and leveled a challenging look in her direction. "I dare you."

Kai's stomach fluttered as those intense, light blue eyes locked firmly with hers. Her gaze flickered over his stubble-covered chin and along his tanned, muscular arms, until she came to his large, masculine hands. Long, strong fingers were curled around the glass bottle and in a flash she pictured them curled around her arms... pulling her closer...

She cleared her throat and sat back in the booth, as her body warmed at the thought of his hands wandering over her body. Kai sipped her beer, attempting to cool the sudden and unexpected flare of desire. What in the hell was wrong with her?

Given everything her mother had told her about the Dark Ones, Kai should be running in the other direction—instead, she invited him to dinner. She was inexplicably and undeniably drawn to the stunningly, beautiful man in front of her. Mr. Aaron Miles was danger and desire all rolled into one, but above all he was unique... and forbidden.

Kai's eyes locked with his once again and met his challenge.

"Based on your build and the look of your hands, it's clear you're not afraid of hard work. You ride a motorcycle and from what I can tell, you only have one duffle bag, which means you are a man who travels light. You have a weakness for women and it would seem, based on Matilda's reaction, they have a weakness for you."

"Do you?" He asked in a low seductive tone.

29

Kai's breath caught in her throat as she held his stare. She gripped the bottle tighter as heat crawled up her back, but before she could answer him a familiar voice interrupted the moment.

"I'd like to know the answer to that question as well."

Kai blinked and looked up to see Ben standing at the end of the table wearing a perplexed look on his face as he glanced between the two of them. His aura glowed bright orange as he folded his arms over his chest. He was obviously annoyed and Kai couldn't blame him.

"Like I said, Kai," Ben began in an even tone. "You are anything but simple. You see, a simple woman wouldn't bring another man out on a date."

"Ben!" Kai scrambled out of the booth and stood next to him. She didn't miss the amused look on Aaron's face as she attempted to explain. "I know this looks really strange but I was in Clive's gas station and—and I fainted from the heat. Mr. Miles caught me and I wanted to buy him dinner to say thank you."

"I was just leaving," Asmodeus said as he started to slide out of the booth. "You know what they say, two's company and three's a crowd."

"Don't be silly," Ben said with a wave of his hand. "Please join us. After all, I should thank you, actually. I'm horribly late and if you weren't here, poor Kai would be sitting in this place all by herself." Ben turned to Kai with a contrite look. "I hope you can forgive me for being so late, Kai. I got held up on a call with a persnickety client. I promise I'll be on time for our next date."

"Who says you'll get another one?" Aaron asked with a cocky grin. "You *are* pretty late."

"I don't think we've been properly introduced. I'm Kai's *date*, Ben Flaherty."

Ben stuck his hand out, offering Aaron a handshake and the tension was thick as they stared each other down. A slow grin spread over Aaron's face as he reached over to accept. Kai was about to interrupt and say something to break the tension. However, as soon as the two men shook hands, Ben's aura sputtered and blinked, like a light about to go out. Her look of concern caught Ben's attention.

"Kai?" Ben said as he looked at Kai with concern. "Something wrong?" he asked quietly.

"No," Kai said quickly. She scooted back into the booth, making room for Ben who sat next to her. "I'm just tired from all the unpacking at the house. I'm amazed that one old man had so much crap."

Another first. The only time she'd ever seen a person's aura blink like that was when someone was dying. She'd seen it in the hospital after the car accident on the night her parents died, and it was not a sight she'd easily forget. But Ben seemed completely unaware of anything out of the ordinary. Strange. Kai hadn't felt any drain or pull on her energy when Aaron had touched her. At least she didn't think so. Of course she had been passed out at the time.

"What old man?" Aaron asked.

"My grandfather," Kai said before taking a sip of her beer. "Although, it feels odd calling him that because I never even met him. Anyway, he died and I'm his next of kin, so I inherited his place and the decades-worth of crap inside."

"Still nothing of interest?" Ben asked absently as he flagged down the waitress.

"Actually," Kai said extending her right hand, showing him the ring. "I found this in an old crate with pictures of my grandmother. It's really cool. I've never seen anything like it. Have you?"

Ben leaned forward and took her fingers in his, which were warm and soft. He had the hands of a man who'd never put in a hard day's work in his life. Kai flicked her eyes to Aaron, who was staring at the ring with an intense look on his face. He turned those ice blue eyes to her and leaned back in the booth as he took a long pull of his beer.

Kai's face heated as he blatantly stared at her while Ben looked at the ring. She'd never had anyone focus so totally and completely on her before. Oh, sure, men hit on her sometimes and when she did tarot readings, her customers tuned into her, but this was different. When Aaron looked at her, it was as though he pushed past all of her external layers, the ones the world saw, and he could see *her*.

A shiver ran up her spine and for the first time in her life, Kai felt exposed. Being able to read other people's auras was one thing but having someone look inside her that way was quite another. It was like her soul was naked and laid bare before him... his for the taking.

"Well, this is interesting."

Kai whipped her head toward Ben's voice. "What?" she asked in a panicked voice. "What is?"

"It sure is," Aaron muttered.

Kai shot him a look as Ben pulled her closer and squinted as he inspected the ring.

"What's it made of? That looks like an antique." Ben dropped her hand abruptly and waved for the waitress again. "You should have it appraised and insured. I'll have my guy in Gooding take a look at it."

"I guess." Kai shrugged and ran the pad of her fingertip over the face of the ring. "I haven't really thought about the monetary value. It obviously belonged to my grandmother, so that's all that matters to me."

"Did you know your grandmother?" Aaron's deep voice swirled over her seductively. "How can you be sure it was hers?"

"She died when my mother was a baby." Kai self-consciously dropped her hand in her lap, not wanting the ring on display for further inspection. It felt crass to be discussing the monetary value of an item that had such sentimental meaning. "Like I said, I found the ring squirreled away in an old crate in the attic which was filled with pictures of my grandmother. I just assumed it was hers."

"Well, either way," Ben said. He let out a sigh and in an oddly possessive move, draped his arm behind her along the top of the booth. "You should give that to me and let me have my guy take a look at it."

"Maybe," Kai said with a forced smile. Desperately wanting to change the subject, she turned the conversation toward the menu. "So what are you going to have for dinner?"

Matilda came over to take their orders looking pleased as punch that Kai's date had shown up. The three of them ate dinner with Ben dominating most of the evening's conversation, regaling them with various cases he'd been handling. As dinner wound to a close, she realized that Ben hadn't asked her or Aaron a single thing about themselves.

Not that it mattered because she couldn't take her mind, or her eyes, off Aaron the entire time. He barely said anything during the meal, and yet she found him far more interesting than Ben—and that probably made her nuts. Then again, that was par for the course where her taste in men was concerned.

If she was on a train platform and there were two men, you can bet your bottom dollar that she'd be insanely attracted to the bum with no job or the guy who can't keep it in his pants. That's what her last few boyfriends were like. Jobless cheaters.

So here she was, with two gorgeous men, one a successful lawyer with a blindingly bright aura and the other a drifter on a motorcycle with no light at all. A sane woman—a normal woman—would pick the hot lawyer. But Kai was anything but normal and the sanity part was still up for discussion.

Kai tried to pay for Aaron's portion of the bill, but Ben wouldn't hear of it. The three of them walked out to the parking lot and into the warm, summer evening. Kai looked up and let out a sound of awe. The Idaho sky was covered in a blanket of twinkling stars that quite literally took her breath away.

"Beautiful, isn't it?" Aaron's voice drifted over her left shoulder and the warmth from his body wafted over her bare arm in tantalizing waves. "The amount of beauty on Earth never ceases to amaze me."

Kai nodded and looked at him, expecting him to be looking at the sky but he was staring directly at her. She let out the breath she didn't realize she was holding and clutched the strap of her leather satchel closer to her breasts.

"I agree with you one hundred percent," Ben said from her other shoulder, breaking the spell. "You never get stars like this in a big city."

"Right," Kai said. She glanced between the two men and stepped forward before spinning around to face them. "Thank you both for an *interesting* evening."

"It's getting late. I should head over to the motel and check in," Aaron interjected. "Thanks for dinner and the law lessons, Ben." He turned his attention to Kai. "But most of all, thanks for letting me crash your date tonight."

"Thanks for catching me," Kai said with a short laugh.

She extended her hand to him and watched, as he seemed to be weighing his options. Filled with excitement, uncertainty and some fear, Kai held her breath wondering what would happen when their hands met. Would it hurt? Would he suck away her light? Nothing?

Finally, after what felt like forever, Aaron took her small hand into his much larger one. There was no pain and no sensation of losing energy; in fact the feel of his palm against hers was enticing. His skin was rough, calloused and hot, and had her thinking about how it would feel to have those masculine hands run over her body.

Those thoughts were swiftly set aside when she noticed a soft white light now emanated from Aaron and, for that brief instant when her hand was within his, he had an aura.

More to the point... he had *her* aura.

"Bye, Aaron," Ben said in a voice edged with irritation. Kai almost forgot he was there.

"Good night," Aaron murmured. He dropped her hand and turned to leave, but stopped abruptly. "I almost forgot." He removed a folded paper from his back pocket and handed it to her. It was the flyer that Clive had given her at the gas station. "You dropped this back at Clive's place."

"Thank you." She took the paper from him and smiled. "I've got a ton of stuff that has to get hauled away, so I'm definitely going to need this."

"I'm sure their rates are reasonable," he said with a smile. "But I bet I can do better."

"You want to haul garbage out of my attic and the old barn?" Kai asked incredulously. "Doesn't sound like a very fun sabbatical to me, Mr. Miles."

"I could stand to make a few bucks and you need the help." Aaron glanced from Kai to Ben before walking back to his bike. "I'm happy to help throw out the trash."

Kai watched as he swung his leg over and started up the bike. She didn't know what his story was or what being a Dark One really meant, all she knew was that she didn't want this man riding out of her life. Not yet. In spite of everything her mother had told her ... Kai was compelled to know more about him.

"How does $75 a day plus meals sound to you?" Kai shouted over the rumble of the Harley's engine.

"Kai?" Ben interrupted as he moved closer so only she would hear him. "This guy is a drifter. Do you really think it's a wise idea to

34

hire him to work out there with you? Alone? As an attorney and a friend, I would advise against this particular decision."

Irritation flickered up Kai's spine. She hated being told what to do or being spoken to like she was a child and currently Ben was doing both.

"Like you said, Ben," Kai murmured without taking her eyes off Aaron, "I'm anything but simple."

Kai closed the distance between herself and Aaron and although the engine of the bike was loud, she didn't miss Ben's disapproving rumblings as she walked away. She stopped next to the bike as a blast of heat washed over her, wrapping her dress around her legs.

"So?" Kai arched one eyebrow and her fingers tightened around the flyer. "What do you say?"

He revved the engine and leaned back in the seat of the bike. "I say you're on."

Kai snagged a pen from her bag and jotted the address down on the back of the flyer before handing it back to him. "I'll see you tomorrow morning. Nine o'clock sharp."

Aaron took the paper from her and tucked it into the back pocket of his jeans, all the while not taking his piercing, blue eyes off hers. He gripped the handlebars and glanced at Ben briefly before looking back at Kai.

"I guess you answered my question from earlier, Kai." Aaron revved the engine and flashed her a cocky grin. "Looks like you have a weakness for me after all."

Before Kai could tell him what an arrogant comment that was, he rode off leaving a trail of dust in his wake. Shaking with a mixture of adrenaline, lust and anger, Kai spun on her heels and toward her car.

"Are you sure that was wise?" Ben asked. He was standing by her car with a concerned look on her face. "You don't even know this guy."

"I know enough," Kai said evenly. "I appreciate your concern but I can handle myself, and besides I really do need the help clearing out the rest of the stuff. With Mr. Miles helping me it will take a lot less time than doing it alone."

"I suppose you're right," Ben said with a smile. He stepped closer, took Kai's hands in his and pulled them to his chest. She felt his heart beating beneath their linked hands and his aura burned from yellow to orange. "I feel like this date of ours didn't exactly get off to a great start."

"Well I did bring another guy along," she said with an awkward laugh. Kai smiled and looked into his eyes, paying close attention to how he made her feel. There was a comfortable, familiar feeling to Ben's spirit. When she looked into his eyes there were no butterflies, no pangs of desire. He was handsome, rich and nice and Kai wasn't the least bit attracted to him. Figures.

She glanced down at their interlocked fingers and sucked in a deep breath. "Ben, I don't think... "

"It's okay." Ben brought her hands to his lips and placed a warm kiss on her knuckles. It was sweet and almost familial in nature, bringing to mind images of a big brother or something. "You don't have to say a word, Kai. I've been an attorney a long time and if there's one thing I can do it's read people." He dropped her hands and stepped back as he reached into his pocket for his keys. "Can't blame a guy for trying."

"Thanks," Kai said. She grabbed the strap of her satchel again and let out a slow breath. "Still friends?"

"Of course." Ben winked. "But I'll keep hoping for more."

Kai watched him walk to his car and guilt tugged at her. Turning someone down was never easy and always made her feel bad, but at least Ben took it well. He was, after all, the only person she really knew out here.

"Hey, Kai," Ben called to her from the open door of his car. "Promise me one thing."

"Sure." Kai shrugged. "What?"

"Be careful with Mr. Miles." He tapped the roof of the car with his fingers. "Like I said, I'm pretty good at reading people and let's just say I couldn't get a clear read on him."

Kai shivered and crossed her arms over her chest as a warm gust of summer air whipped around her.

"It's fine, Ben. He's only going to be working for me for a couple of days," Kai insisted. Her face heated with embarrassment because Ben read her like an open book. Apparently, she didn't hide her attraction for Aaron as well as she thought she did. "I'm his temporary employer. That's all. Believe me, I don't have the time or inclination to date anyone right now."

He nodded, but didn't seem anymore convinced about the denial than she was. Who was she kidding? No one. She fiddled with the ring, seeking comfort from the family heirloom.

"I tell you what, the final copies of the documents from Jacob's estate will be ready in a day or two. How about if I bring them out to you at the house? It would make me feel better to see how you're faring. I'll even bring lunch with me, so you don't have to go to any trouble. Lunch on me." He raised his hands in surrender. "As friends."

"Sounds good," Kai laughed.

Kai waved as Ben drove off, but one name kept running through her mind. Aaron Miles. She drove her confused butt home as fast as possible and as the quiet scenery passed by, her thumb fiddled with the iron band of the ring on her right hand. A million questions swam through her head at once.

Why didn't Aaron have an aura? If he was a Dark One and they were evil, why on earth would he help her? Why did he seem to their auras with one touch without hurting either of them?

Why was she insanely attracted to him when she should be running in the other direction? What the heck was a Custodian of the Light? Did it have to do with seeing auras and why hadn't her mother told her about it?

Above the tsunami of queries, one kept rising up above all the rest. Who the hell was Aaron Miles?

CHAPTER FOUR

Asmodeus spent the night in the cheap motel and though he slept off and on, it was far from restful. His thoughts had been consumed, not only by Kai and the ring, but the unexpected arrival of Ben Flaherty.

Asmodeus swore under his breath as he pulled the Harley into the long, winding driveway of Kai's property. Sweat trickled down his back and he squirmed against the unfamiliar sensation. Being mortal was messy, but Lucifer was right to put them all down here as humans. It probably saved his life.

Ben Flaherty was Fae.

The guy was a damn fairy and, based on the strength of his light, Asmodeus would be willing to bet Ben was a pureblood or at the very least, a hybrid in full use of his powers. At first, he thought the mission was going to be over before it started, but Ben hadn't flinched. He likely saw Asmodeus' lack of an aura but if he did, Ben gave no sign of it. Not yet, at least.

When Ben suggested that Kai take off the ring and give it to him for appraisal, Asmodeus had to stop himself from jumping across the table. But Kai had showed zero interest in relinquishing the ring and zero interest in Ben for that matter. Ben, on the other hand, seemed quite interested in Kai but the real question was why? Was he after Kai or the ring? Or both?

Regardless of the answer, Ben Flaherty was going to prove to be a pain in the ass. At the very least, his presence put a wrinkle in Asmodeus' plans but it was more than that.

Asmodeus kept a close eye on Ben through the evening and was less than pleased when Ben put his arm around Kai. He didn't like it one damn bit. Not because he thought Kai was interested in Ben, she clearly wasn't but... well, he didn't have a good reason... it just bugged the shit out of him to see another man attempting to lay some kind of claim on her.

There were two options. Either Ben had no idea who Asmodeus was, or he did and the son of a bitch was biding his time. He was sure about one thing. Ben was Fae and was after that ring as much as Asmodeus was. Given the moves he was putting on Kai, Ben was probably hoping to woo it out from under her too.

Fat fucking chance.

Heat flared up Asmodeus' back and he revved the engine of the Harley, as a flock of birds swooped low and into a nearby tree. There was no way he was going to let that damned, fairy bastard get close to Kai or the ring. Given the appearance of Ben, Asmodeus knew he was going to have to pick up the pace or risk losing the ring.

If he'd been here in his non-mortal form, Ben would have spotted him immediately and that could have created a shit storm of epic proportions. A fucking fairy free for all. Instead of having dinner with Kai, he would have ended up dodging skin-searing rays of light for the evening.

The Power of the Light was a fairy's strongest weapon and, if wielded properly, it could turn man or demon to dust. Their power was fueled by innocence and rooted in purity. Some say they are an extension of the Hand of God and, based on what he'd seen, he wouldn't doubt it.

If there was any chance Asmodeus was going to have to tangle with the Fae, his powers better come back or Lucifer better give them back. Last night, at the motel, he'd tried to utilize his telekinesis and some basic heat manipulation and neither worked. He was tempted to reach out to Lucifer but given that he still didn't have the ring, he decided to hold off.

Asmodeus smirked as he pulled the bike up by the faded, red barn. Fairies in human stories were cute little sprites with wings and magic wands, but Asmodeus knew first hand that they could be as lethal as any demon.

There was nothing more dangerous than a pissed off fairy.

"You're late, Mr. Miles." Kai shouted from the porch.

Case in point.

Asmodeus chuckled as he dismounted the bike and tucked the key into the front pocket of his jeans. Kai was leaning against the porch railing and those dark eyes were peering at him over the rim of a cup of coffee. Wearing cut off jean shorts, a bright pink tank top and a pair of Converse sneakers, she looked like a homegrown, farm girl. Her long blond hair was swept back in a ponytail and as he strode closer, he saw her face was free of makeup. Kai was naturally beautiful, although she seemed completely unaware of it. But perhaps that was one of the reasons he found her so attractive.

"Morning." He stopped at the foot of the porch steps, grinning.

"You're late," she repeated with a smile.

"How do you figure?" Asmodeus asked as he removed his sunglasses and hooked them into the collar of his t-shirt. He casually surveyed the property as he climbed the steps to meet her. "It's just about nine now. Give or take. It's close anyway."

"Close only counts in horseshoes and grenades," Kai said before taking another sip of coffee.

"I see," he said moving closer so there was only a foot or so between them. Asmodeus dropped his voice low and kept his eyes on hers. "Throw a lot of grenades, do you?"

"No," Kai laughed and held his stare. "It was something my dad used to say. Sorry. It's silly." Kai rubbed her thumb along the edge of her coffee mug and he noticed the ring was still on her hand. "I don't know why I'm giving you a hard time. You're not really that late."

"Certainly not as late as your friend was last night."

"True," Kai said with a small smile as her eyes met his. "But this is business and that was—"

"Pleasure?" Asmodeus arched one eyebrow.

Kai stilled and her dark eyes remained firmly fixed with his. She was beautiful and had a purity that he'd only seen once before. In all his three thousand years only one woman had entranced him and

40

tempted him to relinquish his position in the Brotherhood.

However, when he'd told her who and what he was... Vivian had rejected him. Shunned him and cut him out of her life. Asmodeus' brow furrowed as the uncomfortable memories flooded his mind. After that fiasco, he vowed never to expose himself to that kind of ass-kicking again. Not that any of that mattered. He was here to seduce Kai and get the ring. That's it.

A cat let out a loud meow from the doorway, bringing him from his thoughts.

"Be nice," Kai said with a narrow-eyed look toward the Siamese cat. She flicked her gaze to Asmodeus and shrugged. "She's not great with—"

Before Kai could finish her sentence, the cat was rubbing up against Asmodeus' leg and purring like an engine. He leaned down and scooped up the cat, which was more than pleased by the extra attention. Scratching her behind the ears as he cradled her to his chest, Asmodeus locked eyes with Kai, who was visibly stunned.

"I can't believe it." Kai shook her head and looked from Asmodeus to the satisfied feline. "Zephyr doesn't like anyone— especially men—and she *never* lets anyone pick her up. Not even me sometimes... Looks like all kinds of women have a fondness for you, Mr. Miles. You charm waitresses and cats alike."

"Dogs tend to like me best but every now and then I meet a cat who'll warm up to me." Asmodeus glanced at the purring feline and could only imagine what his Hellhounds would have to say about this particular incident. "Zephyr, huh?" Asmodeus said. "That's derived from the name Zephyrus, the Greek God of Wind. Isn't it?"

"I guess," Kai laughed. "My dad used to read me Babar the Elephant stories when I was little and Zephyr was the name of his monkey."

Asmodeus gave her a skeptical look. "An elephant with a pet monkey?"

"Yes." Kai leaned over and scratched Zephyr. "You know about Greek gods but not Babar? What kind of childhood did you have?"

"It was almost non-existent," he murmured.

Kai smiled at him as she spoke but, quickly dropped her hand when her fingertips grazed his amid the feline's fur. Her face reddened and she looked away from him.

"We should probably get started. I'll show you the barn."

Asmodeus placed Zephyr on the ground and smiled as the cat gave him an annoyed look.

"Your father was right, by the way," Asmodeus said as he turned his eyes to hers.

"About what, Mr. Miles?"

"Being close only counts in horseshoes and grenades... but I hope you won't start throwing any at me." A smile spread across Asmodeus' face as he watched Kai's cheeks redden further. "I'll be on time tomorrow, honest." He held his hand over his heart and winked. "Ms. Kelly."

"You are too much," Kai said with a chuckle as she rolled her eyes. She pushed herself away from the railing, walked a wide path around him and trotted down the steps toward the barn. "I'm not as easy as the cat. Follow me, Rico Suave," she called over her shoulder.

The woman literally laughed in his face.

Asmodeus, too stunned to say a word, turned around and followed her toward the barn. He shook his head and ran a hand over his hair as though he might be able to soothe his wounded ego. No woman, ever in all his three thousand years, had been unaffected by his flirtations—*ever*.

It looked like seducing Kai wasn't going to be as easy as he thought. Damn. He could not remember a time when he ever had to actually *try* to seduce a woman. As the Demon of Lust... he simply did it.

He watched her as she moved ahead of him and into the barn and a smile cracked his face. Nope. Seducing Kai wasn't going to be easy, but he bet it would be a hell of a lot more fun. If there was one thing Asmodeus enjoyed, it was a challenge and Kai Kelly had just thrown down the proverbial gauntlet.

"So this place is a hot mess," Kai said on a sigh as she walked around the clutter-filled barn. "There are eight stalls and he obviously had horses here at one point or another. Too bad there aren't any here now. I used to love to ride when I was little." A wistful smile played at her lips as she tugged at an old bridle hanging on the wall. "My mom loved horses and taught me how to ride when I was barely three years old."

Asmodeus studied her carefully and noticed that every time Kai spoke of her parents, her light grew brighter. There may be no love lost for her grandfather, but the woman clearly loved her parents and missed them. Kai swiped at her eyes, emotions running just under the surface were bubbling over. She turned her back on him obviously not wanting him to see her getting upset.

"What I'd like you to do today is go through all of this and see if there's anything salvageable. Stuff that I could sell, okay? I have a Dumpster being delivered today, in fact I'm surprised it's not here yet."

"You don't want to keep the good stuff?" Asmodeus asked as he opened and closed one of the stall doors. He squatted down and had a look at the hinges, which were in surprisingly good shape. Rising to his feet, he pounded on the beams with his fist. "With a little elbow grease, this place could easily house horses again and be a functioning barn."

"I'm not sure if I'm staying here," Kai said as she picked through a pile of debris. "I'm cleaning this place out so I can sell it... if I want to."

Asmodeus sensed anger and resentment beneath the surface. Not wanting to upset her further, he simply nodded his understanding and perused the rest of the barn. A door along the left side caught his attention. "Where does this lead?" He asked pulling on the handle, only to find it wouldn't open. "It's locked."

"I have no idea," Kai muttered. "More junk, I'm sure. It's probably a storage closet."

"I don't think so." Asmodeus gestured toward the ceiling. "Did you notice that this barn has a flat ceiling and not a vaulted one? There's a second floor."

"Huh?" Kai stopped what she was doing and made a face as she stepped over a box and came over to the door. Standing next to him, she tugged on it but it still didn't open. "You're right. I have a key ring in the house with a bunch of skeleton keys. A couple of them were unmarked, so maybe one of them will work. But I wouldn't get too excited about it because, based on the rest of the stuff I've found, it's probably more junk."

Asmodeus leaned against the wall and studied her profile. High cheekbones, a small button nose and full pink lips came together to

43

form a gorgeous face. She reminded him of goddess statues from ancient Greece.

Flawlessly beautiful.

"Not everything was junk," he said quietly.

Kai turned to look at him and her eyes widened when he took her fingers in his and lifted her hand. Her skin was warm and silky soft and her slender hand fit in his with exquisite perfection. Asmodeus ran his thumb over the top of her fingers, careful to avoid touching the ring. He wasn't sure what would happen to him or how it would affect Kai if he did, and now certainly wasn't the time to find out.

"You found this," he murmured with a nod toward the ring. "It's most definitely not junk."

Kai's body quivered as he held her hand, but she didn't pull away. Her eyes searched his as he pulled her closer still. Warmth radiated from her small form and her tongue darted out, moistening her lip in a disarmingly seductive way.

"It—it may not even be worth anything," Kai said.

"It's worth something to you, so that's all that matters." He lifted her fingers to his lips and placed a gentle kiss on her knuckles. "That makes it priceless."

Silence stretched out between them with only the beat of his own heart thundering in his ears. He stared into her large brown eyes and wanted nothing more than to kiss her, to cover those plump limps with his and dive deep.

But the rumbling sound of an approaching truck quickly put a damper on their stolen moment.

"Th—that's probably the company delivering the Dumpster," Kai said as she tugged her hand from his grip. She jutted a thumb over her shoulder and started walking backward. "I should get out there and tell them how I want it—I mean where I want the Dumpster."

Asmodeus suppressed a grin as Kai stumbled over a rake briefly before regaining her balance. She huffed a strand of hair off her face and leaned the rake against the wall.

"Okay, so I'll let you get started in here." Kai stopped by the open doors of the barn and looked back at Asmodeus. She paused for a moment as though deciding on something. "Lunch is at noon. The kitchen is to the left and if you need the bathroom it's on the first floor, behind the staircase."

"Yes, ma'am." He winked.

Kai rolled her eyes but he didn't miss the smile as she walked outside. Asmodeus snagged a pair of old work gloves from one of the cluttered shelves and tugged them on. Kai's beautiful face lingered in his mind and as he started pulling apart various piles, he entertained himself with images of what she would look like spread naked beneath him.

Asmodeus, I'm assuming I don't have to tell you that you are in close proximity to the ring. Lucifer's irritated voice shot suddenly into Asmodeus' mind and set his teeth on edge. *There were several disturbances in the energy field of your location, but I am still unable to see exactly where it is. In fact, there are times when I'm having difficulty pinpointing your location as well and I suspect it's when you're closest to the ring.*

I'm not surprised. Asmodeus chucked a broken wooden wheelbarrow into the Dumpster that had been deposited in the driveway. Stalking back into the barn, he picked up another old, broken piece of gardening equipment. *I'm well aware of its location and I'd bet the reason you can't pinpoint it is because it's in the possession of a Fae.*

The Fae have the ring? Lucifer sounded almost panicked and Asmodeus didn't blame him one bit. The Fae Clans would love nothing more than to gain possession of the ring and enslave the Brotherhood.

No. Asmodeus said evenly. *Not The Fae... a fae. Kai is a fae-human hybrid, to be specific.*

While that is more than a mild annoyance, it's something of a relief. I take it she is not affiliated with any of the Fae Clans?

I don't think she is even aware of her bloodline.

Be that as it may, getting the ring could prove to be more difficult than we anticipated. Even Fae hybrids have a considerable amount of magic.

Yes. Asmodeus' mind drifted to Kai and a smile played at his lips.

SARA HUMPHREYS

If I'm not mistaken, Kai is a woman. Correct? Lucifer sounded
bored and annoyed. *I'm sure you've bedded her ten times over, so
why don't you have the ring?*

Asmodeus didn't respond but growled in frustration as he tossed
the mangled piece of metal into the Dumpster.

Well, well, well. Lucifer's gritty laughter filled his head, which
only served to enrage Asmodeus further. *Is it possible that the Demon
of Lust, the one being who rules over all lustful souls, has been
unable to seduce a half-breed fairy? Now, this is a first. Wait until the
rest of the Brotherhood hears about this. I think Mammon will take
the most joy in your difficulties.*

It's not that simple. Asmodeus snapped, as he dragged more crap
to the Dumpster. Sweat covered his skin and dripped into his eyes,
which stung like hell. He swore and swiped at them with the back of
his hand. *There's another Fae in the area and I believe he's after the
ring too.*

I suggest you get it before he does.

Really? Asmodeus' tone dripped with sarcasm. *Do you think I
want that fairy man getting ahold of the ring? Shit. Being enslaved by
the Fae is not my idea of a fun way to spend eternity. Listen, I'll get
the fucking ring. Kai doesn't have any clue about what's going on
and as far as she's concerned the ring is a family heirloom and
nothing more.*

Do you think either of them suspects who you are?

No. Asmodeus paused inside the doorway of the barn and closed
his eyes as a cool breeze blew past. *I think she can see auras because
she called me a Dark One right before she fainted. At least that's
what I suspect because, as you well know, I don't have an aura.*

A Dark One? Lucifer mused. *I haven't heard that expression
before. Fae don't typically see auras.*

Yeah, well that's what she said—Dark One. Asmodeus
confirmed. *I'm not sure what the fairy-man suspects, but since he
didn't show up at my no-tell motel last night, I'm assuming he thinks
I'm just a human. I hope so, because the last thing that I want is a
fuckin' flock of fairies swarming me.*

*I have summoned the rest of the Brotherhood back to the
Underworld but perhaps I should send them to help you instead.*

46

No. Asmodeus responded more sharply than he intended. *I can handle Kai.*

Silence filled Asmodeus' mind and for a moment. He thought the connection had been severed but a few moments later Lucifer's voice, laced with suspicion, floated back in. *Do I detect a hint of concern for the girl?*

Don't be ridiculous. Asmodeus straightened his back and fought to keep the defensive tone from his voice.

I should hope not. Lucifer made a sound of disgust. *You remember what happened last time, do you not? You were a real bastard to be around after that Vivian woman refused you.*

Enough. Asmodeus shot back in anger. He was aggravated enough without reopening old wounds. *I'm gaining Kai's trust and I'll have the ring before the week is out. I don't need any help.*

You have two days.

This is bullshit.

Two days. Lucifer bit back. *With the Fae sniffing around, we cannot risk taking any longer than that. Can you imagine what would happen to us if the Fae were to get hold of that ring?* Lucifer made a sound of disgust. *We'd be at their beck and call for eternity. Spending the rest of my existence as a slave for the Fae is not appealing in the least—especially the Fae Queen. The woman is infuriating.*

Careful, Lucifer. Asmodeus pushed back, recalling the brief, but combustible, tryst between Lucifer and Zemi the Fae Queen. It had been over two millennia since those two had their fling but Lucifer was still stewing over it. *Now you're the one who sounds like he gives a shit.*

Fuck off.

Touchy aren't we?

Well, the thought of enslavement does that to me. Lucifer continued. *If you have any sign that the Fae are closing in, I will send the Brotherhood with all of their powers fully intact. We will get the ring by any means necessary.*

Kai is an innocent, Lucifer. Asmodeus' chest tightened as he envisioned Kai being whisked away by the members of the Brotherhood to the Underworld. Picturing her there with the filthiest

47

of souls made him anxious. Asmodeus fought an unfamiliar feeling of fear and kept his response even. Feeling physical pain as a mortal was one thing, but these new and uncomfortable emotions were another. *We cannot harm her. She has to give the ring willingly.*

That's true. Lucifer's calm, bored tone sent a chill up Asmodeus' spine as he watched Kai trot down the steps with a stack of blankets. She gave him a quick smile before going back into the house, her blond ponytail swishing behind her as she disappeared through the door. In that moment, her innocence to the hidden world around her was all too clear. The overwhelming urge to protect Kai slammed into Asmodeus with brutal force as Lucifer continued.

She either gives it willingly... or... if she's dead we can take it. Asmodeus, you and I know that there are plenty of corrupted souls on earth who can do our bidding. It's one of the loopholes I'm so fond of.

Minions.

Lucifer was referring to the heartless human souls who were destined for Hell upon their death, but while on earth, they could be commanded by any member of the Brotherhood. Asmodeus imagined a series of psychotic, brutal killers coming after Kai and something inside of him snapped. Anger flashed up his back and his fists clenched at his sides at the mere idea of anyone harming her.

I'll have it in two days, Asmodeus said tightly. *If you'll recall, I'm the one who got it away from Solomon in the first place.*

Yes, but as we've discovered, someone else has found it. Lucifer let out a short laugh. *It's somehow appropriate that you are now responsible for cleaning up this mess.* All humor left his voice. *Two days or I'll take matters into my own hands.*

As the mental connection with Lucifer was severed, Asmodeus swore. He had less than forty-eight hours to get the ring before all hell broke loose in Bliss.

48

CHAPTER FIVE

The day went by in a blur with Kai making progress lugging various items out of the attic and into the Dumpster. Zephyr, of course, spent the entire time sleeping on the window seat in the living room, only moving occasionally to adjust her position. From time to time, Kai would catch a glimpse of Aaron as he made his own trips from the barn to the Dumpster and while she did her best not to stare... she failed miserably.

They'd shared lunch in the kitchen and she regaled him with stories about her parents and even told him a few about Babar the Elephant. She noticed that the man offered little information about himself and when she asked him questions, he artfully turned the conversation back to Kai and her family.

Aaron Miles had been on her mind all day or, more specifically, the way she felt when he kissed her hand that morning the barn. While the gesture may have been the same as what Ben had done the previous night, her reaction had been far different. Funny how two men could do the same exact thing and have completely opposite outcomes.

In addition to the fact that Aaron suddenly developed an aura when he touched her, there was *nothing* brotherly about the way he made her feel. Quite the contrary. In fact, it took some serious self-control to keep from jumping his bones right there in the barn. When Kai looked into those pale, blue eyes, something deep inside her stirred and fluttered to life, yawning and stretching as though suddenly awakened.

Kai peeked out the window and stole another look at him. How in the world could a man look even sexier when he was covered in dirt and sweat?

Kai had no idea but Mr. Miles sure fit that bill. The man was pure muscle, bone and sinew and his sweat soaked t-shirt clung to every sculpted curve.

She was equally sweaty and dirty but had a sinking suspicion she didn't look sexy, and she certainly didn't feel sexy. A strong breeze blew through the window and the dark, menacing clouds captured her attention. She remembered the weatherman had mentioned something about a storm coming in and, based on the blackening sky, he was right. Kai glanced at her reflection in the gilded mirror in the dining room as she headed toward the kitchen and grimaced.

"Oh my God," she groaned and attempted to wipe dirt smudges off her face. "I'm so gross right now. So *not* sexy."

Zephyr mewled her agreement and trotted past Kai into the kitchen.

"Oh excuse me," Kai muttered as she followed the cat. "Not all of us spent the day sleeping."

Kai went to the sink to wash some of the dirt and sweat from her hands. She made a sound of disgust when she saw the amount of gunk that stuck to the ring. A sense of guilt pulled at her. She should know better than to have kept the ring on while she worked today.

"Great. I have this thing for one whole day and it's already dirty." Kai pulled on the ring to remove it but it wouldn't budge past her knuckle. "That's weird," she said under her breath.

Kai looked at her hands and frowned, thinking they'd swelled from the heat, but other than being dirty, her fingers appeared normal. Squeezing liquid soap into her palm, she lathered her hands up thoroughly but still the ring would not come off.

She puffed the hair from her face and grabbed the ring again, pulling as hard as she could. Pain shot up her arm and she released her hand with a frustrated growl.

"Shit!"

"I finished up in the barn." Aaron's deep, rich voice filled the room.

Kai let out a yelp of surprise and spun around, sending soapy water flying across the kitchen. He was standing in the doorway with a grin on his dirty, beard-stubble face. His blue eyes stood out beneath inky, black eye brows and Kai wondered if it was possible for him to have gotten even better looking in the past couple of hours.

"I hope you don't mind but it looks like it's about to start pouring, so I moved my bike into the barn." He tilted his head and leaned against the doorjamb looking all kinds of sexy. Dirty sexy. "Problem?" His lips lifted at the corners.

Kai knew he was tall but somehow, framed by the kitchen doorway, he suddenly seemed like a giant. Gaping at him like a stunned sheep, it took her a moment to find her voice.

"My ring," she blurted out as she held up a soapy hand and lifted one shoulder. She tugged on it again but still the damn thing wouldn't budge. "I can't seem to get it off. My hands are probably swollen from this heat but it's weird because they look fine." Her face heated as she looked away, knowing she was a mess. "I mean aside from being dirty."

"The ring won't come off?" Aaron's brow knit with concern as he crossed the width of the kitchen and stood in front of her. "That doesn't make any sense," he murmured.

Standing this close to him, Kai got a clear idea of how tall he was. Aaron towered over her, but it wasn't just his height. He was broad and muscular, yet there was something else that she couldn't quite put her finger on. He may not have an aura but he sure as shit had energy of some kind. An energy that was unlike any she'd encountered before. She'd sensed it in the barn as well, but now it throbbed through her, like a bass beat in a nightclub.

As he took her hand in his and lifted it so he could have a better look, she felt a vibration emanating from his large frame. Kai probably should have been scared or concerned that he was going to evolve into the soul-sucking creature her mother warned her about and steal her light... but she wasn't.

In fact, Kai was more turned on than she'd ever been in her life. She swallowed hard as his strong fingers slid along hers in a deliciously sexy way. Their hands tangled together amid slippery,

51

soapy skin and it brought to mind images of the two of them in a bubble bath.

Naked and soapy. God help her. That was all she could think about.

Kai's eyes widened as she watched a subtle glow start to radiate from him as his thumb ran over hers. It was fascinating. No—scratch that. *He* was fascinating.

She studied the sharp angles of his face and watched as the muscle in his jaw flickered while he slowly and gently turned her hand, looking at the ring from different angles. His body radiated thick waves of heat and Kai's gaze flicked down his neck, over his broad shoulders and along his muscular arms. From beneath the edge of his t-shirt, a long vein bulged beneath tanned skin and ran along his bicep, which she had the insane urge to lick at like a lollipop.

Aaron's hand tightened over hers and he stilled. Only their breathing and the ticking of the cuckoo clock filled the kitchen. Cool wind from the incoming storm blew through the open windows but Kai barely felt it. All she could feel was *him*.

Kai's body quivered as she looked at their intertwined fingers. She could tell he was staring down at her through laser-sharp pools of arctic blue. In an attempt to steady herself, she sucked in a deep breath, but his rich male scent filled her head, heightening her craving for him.

Given the sweat covering the two of them, they should both stink to high heaven but all Kai smelled was sex and desire.

Kai knew that if she looked him in the eye, any self-restraint she had would vanish and, Dark One or not, she would succumb to the lust that had clawed at her since the moment she met him.

She closed her eyes, trying to think of something to say but no words came. Her mind and body were fogged by desire, heavy with need, and weak with wanting. As if reading her dirty little mind, he dragged her closer and held her hand against his chest. Jean-clad muscular thighs brushed against her and Kai felt his heartbeat pounding strong and steady beneath the surface. Calling to her, daring her to look at him.

"Kai," he whispered. His voice, compelling and rich, surrounded her like a caress. One arm snaked around her waist, like a band of iron as he held her quaking form tightly against his, which remained solid and steady. Soapy fingers tangled between them and the ring felt hot, almost burning against her skin. "Look at me."

Steeling her courage, Kai opened her eyes and lifted them to meet his. Pale, blue eyes looked down at her beneath heavy lids as his hand splayed across her lower back, pulling her closer still. She let out a sound of wonder as the glow around him brightened like a bulb, giving him an unearthly appearance.

As the light grew brighter and the winds howled, Aaron swore under his breath and covered her mouth with his.

On a groan, Kai opened to him as his tongue brushed along her lips, seeking entrance. His kiss was tentative at first, probing gently to see if she was ready but Kai was more than ready. She kissed him back, rasping her tongue along his, and in a flash any restraint he had shown was gone and it swiftly became a frenzy of lips, teeth and tongues.

Kissing her deeply, Asmodeus pulled the elastic out of her hair so that her long locks spilled down her back. He tangled his hands in her hair and tilted her head, allowing him better access, taking the kiss even deeper. One large hand ran down her back and rested on her ass, pressing her against the hard evidence of his desire.

Kai slid her soapy hands up his chest and linked her arms around his neck, pulling him closer, though she knew it would never be close enough. There was something about his energy that filled her up and she knew it would become addictive—*he* would become addictive. This man with no light was able to stir Kai's soul and ignite passion in her the way no one else ever had.

He tasted like sin, sex, and seduction and... Kai wanted more.

Aaron groaned into her mouth, and the sound of his desire and desperate need for her almost made her come apart. He slipped his hands beneath the edge of her tank top and she sighed as the rough skin of his hands rasped along her lower back. His hot flesh pressed against hers and as they stood there tangled up in each other, the cuckoo clock on the kitchen wall sounded loudly and broke through the haze of lust, bringing Kai back to reality.

What on earth was she doing? Kai was making out like some horny harlot in the middle of the kitchen with a man she didn't even know. Not really. All she knew was that he was a Dark One who kissed like he did it for a living.

Since she still didn't know what being a Dark One really meant, it would probably be a good idea to put on the brakes. Finding a tiny shred of self-control, Kai softened the kiss as her body shuddered against his with unsatisfied desire. She suckled playfully on his lip as she broke the kiss.

"Well, Mr. Miles," she said between heavy breaths.

"You should probably call me Aaron," he murmured as he placed a kiss on her forehead.

"Right, Aaron." Kai pulled back and looked him in the eyes. "That was not how I was expecting to finish your first day of work."

"I'm still getting paid, right?" he asked in a teasing tone.

"Very funny," Kai said on a laugh. He held her closer as she tossed her head back and let out a sound of frustration. "I don't even know you," she said as she stared at the tin tile ceiling.

"This is us getting to know each other," Aaron murmured as he trailed hot, wet, butterfly kisses down her throat.

"Mm-hmm."

Kai's eyelids fluttered closed and she sank into the seductive sensations as the sound of rain falling on the roof added to the richness of the moment. She unlinked her fingers from behind his head and splayed her hands over the back of his neck and as the ring grazed his skin... Kai's entire world shifted on its axis.

Aaron cried out in pain, grabbed the back of his neck and shoved her away from him abruptly. Kai stumbled backward, holding the edge of the counter to keep from falling over, and gaped at Aaron in horror.

The glow he'd had when holding her was gone, but that was the least of her problems. It was his eyes. They glowed bright red and shone at her beneath jet-black brows. When he saw the way she was looking at him, Aaron dropped his arms to his sides and squared his shoulders. For a moment, she thought he actually looked apologetic but standing in front of the open window, with the stormy sky behind him, he looked more dangerous than ever before.

Kai's hands covered her mouth and she watched in horrified

fascination as a massive tattoo appeared out of nowhere, covering both of his arms. It was fuzzy at first, like static on a television, but within seconds a bold, intricate tattoo, black as coal, was emblazoned up those muscular arms, disappearing beneath the t-shirt. Kai shuddered because only moments ago those arms had been wrapped around her.

"What are you?" she said in a trembling voice. Kai backed up slowly, moving around the table, needing to put something more than distance between them. "My mother was right. Stay away from me."

"Kai, wait." Aaron's voice was even deeper than before and his eyes glowed brightly. "I do not want to hurt you. Please, you have to listen to me. The ring you're wearing is not simply some family heirloom. It's the Ring of Solomon and carries more power than you can possibly imagine."

"You're a Dark One," she whispered through quivering lips. Tears stung the back of her eyes as fear threatened to consume her. "You have no light. No aura. B-but your eyes—"

"I know you're frightened but you have to listen to me. As long as you wear the Ring of Solomon you are in grave jeopardy. There are parties who are willing to stop at nothing to retrieve it." His expression was grave but tenderness laced his voice. "I don't want to see you get hurt, Kai. Please, give me the ring."

Nausea swamped Kai and everything started to spin as lust was swiftly replaced by primal fear. She had to get out of here. *Now.* Without thinking, she spun on her heels and ran out of the house as fast as she could. Her heart pounding in her chest, she pushed open the front door and ran down the porch steps into the driving rain.

With rain stinging her face, she slipped in the muddy driveway and fell to her knees, barely feeling the tiny rocks as they cut into her flesh. She scrambled to her feet and stumbled toward the car when she realized she didn't have the keys. They were in the house in her bag. Kai let out a strangled sob, glancing over her shoulder toward the house, but Aaron was nowhere in sight.

She swiped strands of hair from her eyes and squinted against the sheets of rain. Lightning streaked across the sky, lighting up the property and bringing the barn into focus. Weak with fear and shaking with adrenaline, Kai ran into the barn, yanked the door closed and with all her might, pulled the lock down tightly.

Kai spun around and leaned against the barn door. She squeezed her eyes shut and as sobs wracked her fatigued body, a familiar voice floated through the barn.

"He's a demon, you know."

Kai's eyes flew open at the unexpected sound of Ben's voice. She looked frantically around the now spotless barn in search of him. Movement to the left caught her eye and as another crack of thunder and lightning erupted outside... she saw him. Dressed in his impeccable suit, with not a hair out of place, he stepped out of the shadows and moved toward her slowly.

"Ben?" Kai barely recognized the sound of her own voice. It was small, scared and shook with all the fear she was feeling. She looked him up and down and noticed he was dry as a bone. It was pouring outside and he didn't have a drop of rain on him. Her face twisted with confusion as the ring began to burn against her skin. "Wh—what are you doing here?"

"Did you hear what I said?" Ben's voice, calm and even, filled the barn. He continued to move toward her. "His name is not Aaron Miles. It's Asmodeus and he is a demon. I knew there was something different about him when I met him last night because, as I'm sure you noticed, he has no aura. But I wasn't entirely certain of who he was until you touched him with the ring."

"The ring?" Kai said absently. She blinked as the room started to spin and for a moment she worried she'd faint. Digging her fingernails into her palm, Kai struggled to keep herself together.

"Yes." Ben spoke softly as he inched closer. "The ring removed whatever spell he was using to hide his true nature. He was sent here to kill you and take the ring back to the Underworld but you mustn't let him have it, Kai."

"Kai!" Aaron's voice boomed loudly from the other side of the door as he pounded on it. "Let me in," he shouted. "Please, let me explain."

"What are you talking about?" she whispered. "This is crazy."

"You need to come with me." Ben extended his manicured hand as an insincere smile bloomed. Quicker than a snake, he grabbed her by the wrists and yanked her to him. "Or you could just give me the ring and be done with this whole mess."

Ben's mouth hovered dangerously close to hers and though Kai struggled to get away it was no use, his grip was iron clad. He breathed deeply along her neck and made a low growling sound.

"Let me go," she ground out.

"Give me the ring," he seethed as his fingers encircled her wrists to the point of pain.

"No!" Kai shouted as she struggled against him. "Ben, please stop. I can't give it to you or anyone. It won't come off."

As bolts of pain whipped up her arms, somewhere in the back of her mind she remembered a self-defense class and the acronym S.I.N.G. that stood for solar plexus, instep, nose and groin. These were the sensitive places on the body to attack when being attacked.

Ben grabbed her hand and tried to pull the ring off. Pain shot up her arm and she screamed in agony, as it felt like her skin was being be torn from the bone. Then, with every survival instinct she had and her last bit of strength, Kai stomped on his instep. He grunted in surprise and leaned forward, just in time to have his balls come in contact with her knee.

As he released her, Kai stumbled backward and a thundering fireball exploded as the door of the barn shattered into splinters of burning wood and smoke. Struggling to catch her breath and with her hand feeling like it had been put through a shredder, Kai looked over to see Aaron, or Asmodeus or whoever he was, standing in the doorway.

He was quite literally wrath incarnate.

"You will not lay one hand on her, you fucking fairy." Eyes glowing, muscles straining and with the storm raging behind him, Asmodeus stepped into the barn with his burning gaze fixed on Ben. Kai probably should have been terrified, but to her great surprise she felt nothing but relief. Without taking his eyes off Ben, Asmodeus extended his hand. "Come with me."

"I don't think so, demon," Ben seethed. He raised both hands, uttered a language Kai had never heard and she watched in horror as his aura flashed and a shock wave of yellow light rippled across the room and slammed into Asmodeus.

Kai screamed and watched as Asmodeus was thrown back outside like a ragdoll. Ben ran toward Kai and grabbed her arms. Kai screamed and kicked at him as rage, confusion and outright fury filled her.

Struggling against him, she placed both hands on his chest and let out a primal scream as a gargantuan surge of power shot through her body and into Ben. The force sent him flying across the barn and slammed Ben into the wall, dropping him to the ground in a limp heap.

Shaking and crying, the ring cooling against her skin, Kai leaned against the wall for support as her body tingled with newfound power. She let out a startled cry as Asmodeus appeared suddenly next to her. Before she could say a word, he pulled her into his arms and held her against his chest as she sobbed with terror and confusion.

"I killed him." She kept repeating the muffled words over and over against his chest. "What's happening? Oh my God. I killed Ben."

"He's unconscious, Kai, he's not dead. But we will be if we don't get out of here now." Asmodeus took her head in both hands and kissed her forehead, his lips hot against her skin. He pulled back to look her in the eye. "Come with me and I promise I'll explain everything."

"What happened?" she sputtered. "He—he had fucking laser beams shoot out of his hands. And me—I—"

"Ben is Fae... and so are you." He lifted one shoulder. "Well, half."

"Fae? I'm a fucking fairy?" she said with no humor in her voice. Her brow furrowed as she recalled the words written on the crate. She flicked her eyes to his, her voice was edged with urgency. "The box—the box that I found the ring in. It said Custodians of the Light."

"I've never heard that expression before," he said as a deep line formed between his eyebrows and his voice dropped low. "But I promise we'll find out what it means."

Kai stilled and her eyes wandered over the strange tattoos that now covered his arms. "Is it true?" she whispered in a quivering voice as she raised her eyes back to meet his. "Are- are you what he said you are?"

"Yes." His mouth set in a tight line and the muscle in his jaw flinched with tension. "But I am not here to harm you and I won't allow anyone else to hurt you either."

Shivering and wet, with his strong, warm arms encircling her, Kai searched his eyes, which were once again the cool, pools of blue and all she saw was concern. She glanced at Ben, still passed out in the corner, and then back to Asmodeus. He may be a demon, or a Dark One, but in the short time she'd known him, he'd done nothing but be kind.

Ben moaned and stirred.

"We have to go." Asmodeus' grip on her tightened and his eyes once again glowed red, as he leveled his burning gaze in Ben's direction. "When he wakes up he's going to summon others."

Kai said nothing but nodded and swiped at her teary eyes. What could she say? Her life had just gone from a little bit odd to completely insane in less than an hour.

"Of course he will." A slightly hysterical laugh bubbled up and she shrugged. Tears stung at her eyes and she wished now, more than ever, that she could speak to her mother. The old familiar ache in her chest, the hole that was there since her parents died, opened and threatened to swallow her up.

She stepped back as Asmodeus got on the Harley. He started the bike and revved the engine, waving for her to join him. She walked over, almost in a trance, wondering if perhaps this was merely a dream and she'd wake up any minute, laughing at her subconscious but as the heat of the engine blew over her wet, bare legs she knew it was all too real. Feeling exhausted, frightened and with few options, Kai swung her leg over and settled in behind him.

"Hold on tight," he said as he pulled out of the barn. "But do me a favor and try not to singe me with the ring. It hurts like hell."

"Aren't you from there?" Kai said with more than a little sarcasm.

Asmodeus smirked at her over his shoulder but said nothing as Kai wrapped her arms around his waist, careful to avoid touching his flesh with the ring. Squeezing her eyes shut, she pressed her cheek against the broad, muscular expanse of his back and held on for dear life as they rode down the dark, Idaho highway and into an uncertain future.

CHAPTER SIX

Kai had never been so mentally or physically exhausted in her life. Soaked to the bone from the driving rain and dog-tired, she fought to keep her heavy eyelids from closing. The only reason she hadn't fallen asleep was because, if she did, she'd fall right off the back of Asmodeus' motorcycle.

Clinging to his warm, firm body also helped keep her grounded in reality. She pressed her face against his back and smothered a hysterical giggle. Reality? Demons, fairies and a magic ring all added up to a big bag of crazy.

She watched the scenery fly by in a blur. It was still dark and though she didn't know how long they'd been riding, it felt like hours. With the damp air breezing over them and only the sound of the engine filling her head, Kai took stock of their surroundings and realized that, at some point, the terrain had transitioned to a total desert-like environment.

Kai had zero idea where he was taking her and there was a part of her that didn't care, because all she wanted to do was wake up from the nightmare her life had become. Until a few hours ago, Kai thought seeing people's auras was the weirdest thing about her.

Apparently not.

Nope. She was some kind of fairy half-breed, her grandfather's attorney and would-be suitor was a fairy, and the gorgeous hunk of man she was plastered to, on the back of a Harley Davidson, was a demon.

Right. Seeing auras seemed downright pedestrian at the moment.

With her arms wrapped around him and their bodies pressed tightly together, Asmodeus glowed like he had in the kitchen. Even though the façade of being human had vanished, Asmodeus still absorbed Kai's aura when they touched. As odd as it was, it actually gave her comfort because it was one thing about him that had remained the same.

The heat and vibrations from the motorcycle hummed through her weary body, making her feel as though she had become part of the machine. Kai sucked in a shuddering breath and tightened her grip around Asmodeus' waist, careful to keep the ring from touching him.

She recalled what had happened back at the house when the ring grazed his neck. The man's eyes had glowed red, like two hot coals, and tattoos as black as midnight appeared out of nowhere, up those thick, muscular arms. But it wasn't only his physical appearance that changed. It was the hard, unfeeling look on his face that hit her like a punch in the gut.

She sighed and rested her cheek against his back. Asmodeus' muscles tensed in response and he placed one large hand on her arm.

"We're almost there," he shouted over his shoulder above the roar of the bike. "Just hang on."

"Almost where?" Kai asked as she tightened her hold on his waist and adjusted her butt on the seat. His stomach muscles rippled beneath her arms and she fleetingly wondered if the man had a single ounce of body fat. She probably should've been freezing but his body heat kept her warm in spite of how wet she was and how cool the air felt. "Where are you taking me?"

"Someplace safe." He revved the engine and shouted over his shoulder. "Hang on. The turnoff for Isadora's place is up ahead but the roads from here on out aren't paved which will make for a bumpy ride."

"Really?" Kai shouted with more than a little annoyance. "I just found out that you're a freaking demon and for some inexplicable reason I got on a motorcycle with you in a rainstorm. I'd say that I'm capable of handling bumpy roads—literal or otherwise."

"Fair enough," he said with a short laugh.

After what felt like an eternity of teeth clattering bumps, Kai finally spotted a glimmer of light ahead in the seemingly endless darkness and for a minute she wondered if it was a mirage. Like a castaway adrift in the ocean for days who was finally seeing land, pure relief swamped her as she saw the faint outline of a house.

Sitting up in the seat, Kai looked past Asmodeus and squinted into the dark night, praying that this Isadora person wasn't going to try and rip the ring off her hand too. Who was this woman, anyway? Could she be a former lover of Asmodeus?

A sudden and unexpected feeling of jealousy washed over Kai as she imagined him in the arms of another woman.

She rolled her eyes at her foolishness. Why on earth was she getting jealous? He was a demon and, according to the fairy-man, Ben, Asmodeus was only here to get the ring. Her heart squeezed in her chest as she thought about how gently Asmodeus held her hand, the seductive feel of his lips on hers. Was it all an act and part of his attempt to get the ring, or did he truly feel something for her?

Reaching their destination, he pulled the bike to a halt. Kai looked to the right and standing in front of a ridge of mountainous rock, was a tiny, ramshackle cottage. Kai almost wept with relief. It was a crooked little place that looked like it might be glued together and she had a fleeting memory of the tongue depressor houses she built once with her father.

This little house had a similar feel and in a funny way, it gave her a sense of comfort. Two lanterns hanging from wooden posts at the end of the gravel walkway swung in the dark, calling to Kai, welcoming her as if waving at her to come inside.

As Asmodeus shut off the bike and kicked the stand down, Kai removed her arms from around his waist, but flinched as her stiff muscles cried out in protest. She arched her back and stretched her arms over her head, working out the kinks from the longest motorcycle ride of her life and even though the engine was off, her body still hummed.

She let out a sound of relief as she stretched, and it took her a moment to realize that Asmodeus hadn't moved. He was sitting stone still on the bike, his fingers wrapped tightly around the handlebars and staring straight ahead.

As Kai dropped her arms and rested her hands on her thighs, her breasts brushed his back and he flinched, almost imperceptibly. If she hadn't been straddling him from behind, with her hips pressed tightly against his, she wouldn't have noticed.

"Get off the bike," he said tightly, without turning around. His voice, low and deep, was barely audible. "Now."

"I thought you'd never ask," Kai said with a heavy sigh.

Kai slipped off the bike quickly and watched as the glow of her aura dimmed, flickered over his form and then vanished when their bodies no longer met, leaving him lightless once again. Her eyes narrowed as she watched him dismount the bike. Asmodeus' entire demeanor had changed. He was cold, distant and detached and, as far as she could tell, he was doing his best not to look at her.

Asmodeus stuck the key in his jeans pocket before turning around to finally face her. He couldn't exactly avoid her at the moment but he sure as hell seemed like he was trying.

"Go inside," Asmodeus said, jutting his chin toward the house without looking at her. "Now."

"What's your problem?" Kai asked with more than a little annoyance. Hands on her hips, she puffed stray hair from her face and stood in front of him in the most challenging stance she could muster. "You're acting like *I'm* the one who lied to you. You were the one who pretended to be something you're not. Talk about telling the biggest fib *ever.*"

"I never actually said I was human," he said in an irritatingly calm tone.

"I'd say that's what most people would consider semantics."

"I call it a necessary evil." His sharp, blue eyes flicked to hers briefly before glancing over his shoulder at the empty desert. "Now that you know what I am and why I'm here, it will make things much easier and we can cut to the chase."

"I barely know what *I am.*"

"Yes, you do." He continued scanning the surroundings. "You're a fairy hybrid. It's not that complicated."

"You're insufferable."

Anger, frustration, and the sting of rejection burned in Kai's chest. This man was quite literally the only person—human-demon-whatever—that she had and he was giving her the brush-off. A few short hours ago, they'd been making out hot and heavy but now he was acting like it never happened.

She wasn't looking for him to proclaim his love to her but he could at least act like they weren't complete strangers. Her mouth set in a tight line and the ring burned against her flesh as her emotions began to get the better of her.

"Look at me," Kai said as she shoved at his shoulder, mindful not to use the hand with the ring. He didn't flinch and she may as well have been shoving at a wall of steel. "Damn it. I said, look at me."

She shoved at him again but her hand slipped, sending her face-first into his chest.

Quicker than lightning, Asmodeus grabbed her wrists and dragged her body against his. Soft met hard in one swift motion as her breasts crushed against him and all the breath rushed from her lungs. His fingers encircled her arms like handcuffs and his skin burned against hers as he began to glow with her aura in a now familiar way.

"Do not test me, woman," he growled.

Asmodeus' mouth hovered inches from hers and his musky scent filled her head, making her dizzy with need. She wanted to feel something other than fear and confusion, to lose herself in the taste of him. Those icy, blue eyes stared down at her beneath a dark, furrowed brow and his body hardened against hers as the aura around them now gleamed red with desire.

"Don't shut me out," Kai whispered as she leaned further into him. Pressing a kiss against his throat, she murmured, "I can't do this by myself."

Kai leaned back to look him in the eye, his hands still linked around her wrists, she found herself staring into bright, red orbs. This time, instead of being frightened, when confronted with part of his true nature, she was intrigued. He was exotic, dangerous and... unexpected.

Her lips parted and she sucked in a shuddering breath just as his mouth covered hers. When Asmodeus groaned, the sound alone almost made her come apart. He tugged her closer as their tongues tangled, both of them clamoring for more.

This is what she needed, what they both needed, to feel something other than fear or confusion. Kai tilted her head as he deepened the kiss, drinking from her desperately. On a growl and without breaking the kiss, Asmodeus grabbed her bottom, picked her up and spun around before depositing her on the motorcycle.

Kai wrapped her arms around his neck and leaned back as he straddled the bike and swiftly pulled her into his lap. She sighed against his lips as the heat of his erection pressed against her most sensitive spot, sending electric zings of carnal pleasure through her body.

He rained kisses down her neck as one hand slipped up her shirt, flicked her bra aside and captured her breast. Kai moaned and held his head to her throat, as she linked her legs around his waist and ground against him. Streaks of need shot through her as his experienced hands and talented tongue feasted on her. She arched against him and reveled in the erotic sensation of the heat of his body mixed with the brisk breezes of cool evening air.

Kai flicked her eyes open as she writhed in his arms but when she caught a glimpse of the house out of the corner of her eye, it brought her careening right back to reality. They were making out on a Harley in front of some woman's house and her shirt was almost over her head.

Asmodeus grabbed the handlebar with one hand and held her around the waist with the other as he suckled her breast. Kai gripped his shoulder and struggled to find her way out of the lust-induced frenzy. As his flesh pressed against hers, heat fired through her and everything began to spin. Kai squeezed her eyes shut in an effort to stop the sudden wave of dizziness.

"We have to stop," Kai whispered. She grabbed him by the hair and kissed him, wanting to taste him one more time. She suckled his lower lip and held it between her teeth briefly before releasing it and resting her forehead against his. "I can't do this," she said between heavy breaths as her fingertips stroked his scalp. The dizziness ebbed back as she fought to catch her breath. "Not here."

"I've made love in almost every place imaginable but not on a motorcycle." Asmodeus' body stilled and he pulled back, looking her in the eye. "We'll have to remedy that."

His gaze was once again a cool blue, but her aura still engulfed them both and Kai couldn't help but smile.

"That's amazing," she said with wonder as her gaze skittered over him.

"I have to admit, it's not the first time I've been told that," he teased. Asmodeus kissed the corner of her mouth and gently put her shirt back in place and settled his large hands over her hips.

"Not that." Kai rolled her eyes and trailed her fingers down his muscular, tattooed arms. Her hands rested on his muscular thighs which were taut and solid beneath her eager hands. "You have a light when I touch you—an aura."

Asmodeus' expression hardened and he leaned back slowly as though he hadn't quite heard what she said. "What did you say?"

"When we touch skin to skin you absorb my light and you actually have an aura." She trailed her fingers over his. "See?"

Asmodeus' watched intently but said nothing.

"It freaked me out at first too because when we shook hands, you started to glow but as soon as you dropped my hand, you were a Dark One again. Then when you shook hands with Ben, it made his aura sputter, like a bulb about to go out. I thought maybe it would hurt or something, but believe me... touching you doesn't hurt. Makes me dizzy with desire, but doesn't hurt." She smiled and reached out to wrap her arms around him again but he grabbed her wrists, stopping her. Kai's brow furrowed. "What's wrong?"

He frowned and the cold detached look in his eye was back with a vengeance.

"We don't have time for this." Asmodeus' jaw clenched as he held her away from him. Without another word, he dismounted the bike and dropped Kai's arms like a couple of hot potatoes. "If this were one of my usual vacations on earth, fucking would be at the top of my priority list but we have other matters to attend to." Walking around the bike, he avoided her gaze and gestured toward the house. "Let's go."

Kai gaped at him as she tried to understand what the hell was going on. "Are you for real?"

"We have to get the ring off your finger and see if Isadora knows anything about the Custodians of the Light."

The sting of rejection mixed with flat-out anger burned in Kai's chest and though tears stung the back of her eyes she refused to let them fall. She hopped off the bike and turned her back on him as she put her clothing back in place. A million questions raced through her mind but before she could ask a single one, a raspy, feminine voice floated through the air.

"Well, look what the cat dragged in." Startled, Kai spun around toward the voice. Standing on the covered porch was one of the oldest, smallest women Kai had ever laid eyes on. Kai's face heated with embarrassment as she wondered if she had witnessed any portion of their make-out session.

The lights from the open door behind her gave her an almost ethereal glow and for a second Kai wasn't even sure if the woman was real. However, a pale pink aura fluttered around her gently, reassuring Kai that she was indeed real.

Hunched over and leaning heavily on the cane in her right hand, she had a gray blanket with Native American designs draped over her shoulders and a thin, white cotton nightgown fluttered around her legs. Her white hair hung in two long braids framing a wizened face.

Asmodeus had moved in next to Kai in his typical stealthy manner. Thick waves of heat emanated from his body and washed over her shivering form. She crossed her arms over her breasts in an effort to stop shaking but it was no use.

Even though her body still clamored for his, and she wanted to snuggle against him, she resisted. Being rejected, yet again, wasn't at the top of her priority list. She wasn't entirely sure she could trust him but, at the moment, he was all she had.

"Is this your mother or something?" Kai asked as quietly as possible. She glanced at Asmodeus who gave her a doubtful look and shook his head.

"His mother?" The woman asked with genuine humor. She let out a sharp laugh and banged her cane on the boards of the porch a couple of times. "No, child. Although I can understand why you'd think that given my current state of affairs," she said with a gesture toward her body.

"Hello, Isadora." Asmodeus' voice rumbled around Kai, shattering the quiet of the desert. "It's been a long time."

"That's putting it mildly," Isadora said with a raspy laugh. "And you haven't changed a bit. Still as handsome as could be but as you can see, time has not been as kind to me. I suppose some might say you made a deal with the devil himself."

Kai glanced from the old woman to Asmodeus. Isadora must know Asmodeus' true nature and it sounded like she knew him when she was a young woman. Had they been lovers or only friends? Before she could ask any questions, Isadora started in with queries of her own.

"What have we here?" Isadora's intent gaze landed on Kai.

"I'm Kai Kelly," Kai said in a surprisingly strong voice.

"Isadora, I…", Asmodeus began.

"Hush." Isadora held up her hand. "I wasn't asking you, mister."

Kai pressed her lips together to keep from laughing out loud at the way this little old woman put big, bad Asmodeus in his place. Kai stole a glance at him. His tattooed arms were folded over his chest, his eyes glowed red and the look on his face said it all. He was not amused but he must have a good deal of respect for Isadora to hold his tongue. Kai didn't know a lot about Asmodeus but she suspected he wasn't the kind of man who was used to being shushed.

The old woman made her way down the steps with surprising ease as Kai watched her intently. Moving slowly but surely, Isadora closed the distance between them and stopped directly in front of Kai. She was tiny and couldn't have been five feet tall.

Isadora cocked her head to one side and looked Kai up and down. Kai did her best not to squirm under the scrutiny of her bright green stare. Isadora's eyes were the color of emeralds and though they were set in a tanned, wrinkled face, they had the boldness of someone much younger.

"She's Fae," Isadora said bluntly. Leaning back, she pressed her lips together and kept her inspecting gaze on Kai. "Yes, sir."

"How did—" Kai began.

"Yes, indeed." Isadora pointed a crooked finger at Kai. "And she's got witch in her too."

"What?" All the air rushed from Kai's lungs and she shook her head as she rubbed her arms vigorously. "Witch? What are you talking about?"

"Takes one to know one," Asmodeus murmured.

"Hush up," Isadora snapped as she swatted him on the leg with her cane without taking her eyes off Kai. "This poor child is exhausted, confused and doesn't know which end is up. So, why don't we take this inside because I'd be willing to bet she's got about a million questions. Don't you, girl?"

"Y—yes." Kai nodded and fought the tears. Her shoulders shook as she tried to keep from sobbing out loud. "I feel like I'm going crazy."

"I bet you do." Isadora shook her head and made a sound of disgust as she shot Asmodeus a look. "Park that damn thing around back. I'm taking Kai in the house so she can have a hot shower and we're gonna get some food into the girl before she wastes away." She winked at Kai. "Then we'll get some of your questions answered."

"Thank you," Kai said with a shuddering breath.

Kai swiped at her eyes with the back of her hand and held herself together. She glanced at Asmodeus who was staring at her with that cold look. Emotionless and detached. Those were the two words that came to mind as he leveled those pale, blue eyes in her direction.

A split second later, Isadora grabbed Kai's hand and was staring at the ring with wide eyes. Her hands were rough and warm but in spite of her age, Isadora's grip was like iron and her aura now glowed bright fuchsia. Kai stood still as the old woman looked at the ring.

"It—it won't come off," Kai blurted out. "It's stuck... or something."

"It's the Ring of Solomon," Asmodeus said tightly.

"I'll be damned," Isadora said, with awe.

"I'd give just about anything to know what on earth that means." Kai bit her lip against her fear, but the sight and sound of this little old lady, swearing like a sailor, was a welcome bit of silliness amid a symphony of chaos.

"Like I said," Isadora murmured as she turned her attention to Asmodeus. "Lots of questions to be answered." Putting her glittering green eyes back on Kai, Isadora squeezed her hand reassuringly before releasing it. "You're going to be alright, child."

"Thank you," Kai whispered.

"Don't thank me yet. Something tells me you've got a long, winding road ahead of you." Isadora waved her cane at Asmodeus and wrapped her other arm around Kai's waist as she started walking with her toward the house. "Do as I said, Asmodeus. I may not be the sweet young thing you remember, but I can still cast a spell that will shrivel your demon dick. So get moving."

Kai slapped her hand over her mouth to stifle a giggle and glanced over her shoulder at Asmodeus who looked less than amused, but did as Isadora asked. She looked down at the diminutive woman at her side and smiled as she said, "I can't imagine he's used to being spoken to that way."

"I don't suppose he is." Isadora winked at her and laughed as they climbed the steps together. When they reached the landing she paused and leaned heavily on her cane as she caught her breath. "Have you laid with him yet?"

Kai's face heated with embarrassment as she glanced back to see if Asmodeus was within earshot but, thankfully, he wasn't. She tucked her windblown hair behind her ear and shrugged as she shook her head. They hadn't... yet.

"No?" Isadora made a *tsking* sound as she started into the house. "Now that's a damn shame. That man was the best lay I ever had and even though it was decades ago... I remember it like yesterday."

"You and Asmodeus... "

"You bet your ass we did." Isadora let out a hearty laugh. "It was many years ago but, girl, he ain't the Demon of Lust for nothin'."

"Demon of Lust?" Kai asked, not quite sure she'd heard Isadora correctly.

"He didn't tell you who he was?"

"No." Kai frowned. "Until a few hours ago, I thought he was human."

"Not surprised." She shook her head. "He's a member of the Brotherhood—the Seven Princes of Hell—each of them represents one of the seven deadly sins. Asmodeus is the embodiment of lust and damn if he doesn't live up to the name." She pursed her lips together

70

and made a sour face. "Just be glad that Satan didn't find you and the ring first. He's the Demon of Wrath and a pain in the ass—always finding a reason to stir up trouble. Oh he's handsome too, they all are, but I'll take lust over wrath any day of the week," she said with a wink.

"No wonder women were falling at his feet," Kai said. She smiled. "Even my cat—Oh my God!" Her hands flew to her mouth as she realized she ran off and left her poor cat alone at the house. She stared at Isadora. "Oh shit. I don't even know if she was inside. What if the coyotes get her?"

"Cat?" Isadora let out a hearty laugh and tapped her cane on the floorboards again. Smiling, she took Kai's hand in hers and squeezed, the warm metal of the ring pressed against her skin. "What's her name?"

"Zephyr," Kai said.

"Well, Zephyr will be just fine. First of all, cats domesticated themselves. They only hang around with us because it suits them. Now a dog, on the other hand, they're dependent on us but not cats. It's one of the reasons so many witches like having them as companions. They're independent creatures and can take care of themselves. Trust me, she'll be there waiting for you when you return. Won't be too pleased with you, but she'll be there." Isadora tapped Kai on the leg with her cane. "Come on, let's get you a shower and something clean to wear."

Kai followed her and as she turned to close the door, she saw Asmodeus stalking up the walkway toward the house. Kai's breath caught in her throat as his intelligent, icy blue gaze captured hers. As big as he was, he moved with almost feline fluidity and unnatural quiet. Without a word, he took the steps in two strides and stopped just a few inches from her.

"We'll be safe here for a while. She's got a cloaking spell on this place, so we should be hidden from the Fae," he said as thick waves of heat undulated from his towering form. She realized that the heat she'd felt on the motorcycle was from him more than it was from the bike. Kai wondered if his unusually warm body temperature was part of his being a demon. The beginnings of a beard covered his square jaw and the muscle beneath the skin flickered as he glowered at her.

"We can trust her."

"Really?" Kai kept her voice low. "I'm still wondering if I can trust *you*. For a demon you sure do run cold in the blink of an eye. One minute you're acting like you can't get enough of me and the next you can't stand touching me."

Silence hung heavily and his brow furrowed. His lack of response was more infuriating than anything else and it made Kai want to scream.

"Will we be staying with all of your former lovers while we're on the lam? Because if that's the case, then perhaps we should shack up with some of my exes," Kai prodded. "Ya know... just to even the playing field."

His expression hardened and his eyes flashed red, but Kai didn't retreat. Asmodeus placed both hands on the doorway on either side of her, leaned close, his face just inches from hers. His masculine scent filled her head and, in spite of the situation, her body responded. Desire washed through her and it took some serious self-control to keep from jumping his bones right there on the porch, but she held her ground.

"If you want to stay alive, then you will do *exactly* as I say and you will *go* wherever I tell you to. You *will not* leave my sight for one second until we get that ring off your finger and give it to the Brotherhood." Asmodeus leaned closer, his lips just a breath from hers and his voice dropped to a whisper. "And just to be clear, the last place on earth we will be going, is anywhere near *any* man who has touched you."

"Careful, Asmodeus," Kai murmured. "Your demon is showing." Before he could respond, Kai stepped back and slammed the door in his face.

CHAPTER SEVEN

Asmodeus stared out the front window of Isadora's cabin, watching for any sign of the Fae—or the Brotherhood for that matter. But, so far, the only movement had been a few vultures circling high above the desert. It was shades of beige and brown as far as the eye could see and the clear blue sky had barely a cloud in it. He glanced over his right shoulder toward the closed bedroom door for the tenth time in as many minutes. Kai was taking a shower and it seemed like she had been in there forever.

He glanced at Isadora and smiled as he watched her stir whatever she was cooking up in the two enormous iron pots. Knowing her, it was some kind of potion, or part of a spell. She'd been a real beauty in her day and though they'd been lovers, she was one of the only women he'd actually remained friends with.

Isadora was a witch and spent most of her years traveling with a circus as a fortuneteller but this little place had been in her family for generations and he knew this was where she'd settled down.

Asmodeus was certain if anyone could help them, it would be her. Isadora was one of the most talented witches he'd ever encountered. She could have been one of the High Priestesses on the Witches Council but never pursued it, although he wasn't sure why.

The main room of the cabin was sparsely furnished with a table and chairs at the center and a soft armchair by the stone fireplace. A woven rug covered much of the worn, wood floorboards and the

73

walls were decorated with various masks and charms. Bundles of dried herbs and several ceramic jars lined the thick, wooden mantle, which was scarred from years of use.

Normally, her Book of Spells was perched at the center of the mantle but Isadora had it open on the table. She'd been scouring it since they'd arrived and found two spells that might work to remove the ring. As soon as Kai emerged from the bedroom, Isadora was going to give them a try.

"Looks like I'm not the only one who's changed," Isadora chuckled as she stirred her potions on the stove. She tapped the wooden spoon on the edge of one of the cast iron pots and laughed out loud. "You are not the man or demon I knew all those years ago."

"I'm not sure what you're getting at," Asmodeus responded without looking at her. He moved to the other window and pushed the lace curtain aside as he continued to keep watch.

"Yes, you do." Isadora crossed to the small wooden table and sat in a well- worn chair with a sound of relief. "It's the girl or, to be more specific, it's your feelings for her."

"The only feelings I have are about the ring and making sure it gets back to Hell, where it belongs." Asmodeus folded his arms over his chest and focused on keeping his tone even but to no avail. He sounded as irritated as he felt and it pissed him off that Isadora saw right through him. "I'm here to retrieve the ring and that's all."

"Bullshit," Isadora said.

"Careful, Isadora." Asmodeus turned slowly and leveled a stern gaze at her. "Regardless of the changes you think you see, I still don't like being spoken to that way."

"Oh, hush up and sit your big ass down." She waved her cane toward a chair on the other side of the table. "This isn't Hell and I'm not one of the tortured souls you get to command for eternity. This is my house. I'm a tired old witch, and you and I both know that girl in there doesn't have time for bullshit." She pointed a crooked finger to the other chair. "Sit down."

"You, however, have remained the same in many ways. Still bossy." Asmodeus let out a beleaguered sigh and did as she asked. Leaning back in the chair, he looked at her with raised eyebrows. "Yes?"

"Since you arrived, you haven't said a word to me about *why* you brought her *here* and *not* to the Brotherhood. For Goddess' sake, she practically fell asleep the second she came into the house and it wouldn't surprise me if the poor child passed out in the shower. Your little Fae-witch is wearing the Ring of Solomon, which I always thought was just some made up story to keep you and the rest of the Brotherhood in line."

"Yes," Asmodeus said evenly. "Thank you for the recap. What's your point?"

"Why are you here and not in the Underworld?" Isadora's green eyes stared at him intently.

"As you know, the ring won't come off." He folded his hands in his lap, hoping to seem unconcerned. "You are the most powerful witch I know, who I can also trust. I thought you might have a spell that would get the ring off her finger—and hopefully you do."

"Mm-hmm." She narrowed her eyes. "That's fine and dandy and we're going to try it when she comes out. But why didn't you bring the ring back to the Underworld with her still attached to it? I know you haven't been starin' out my windows because you like the scenery. " Her white eyebrows raised. "You're hiding from the Brotherhood, aren't you? You're hiding *her*."

"How could I possibly hide from them?" He asked innocently. "You know we are connected by a collective consciousness."

"Do I look stupid?" Isadora cast a doubtful look in his direction. "You and I both know that you can disconnect from the Brotherhood and cut them off when it suits you." A smile curved her weathered lips. "If memory serves, when you and I took a tumble in the hay all those years ago, you were here on an unsanctioned visit. You told me then that you cut off Lucifer and the others so you could come up to earth to help your brother, Mammon."

Asmodeus' jaw clenched. Isadora was one of the most perceptive women he'd ever known and, despite her age, she had a memory like an elephant. Her green eyes twinkled and the array of lines around her mouth deepened as her smile grew.

"I'm doing what's necessary," he said, evenly.

"I call bullshit on that too."

"Fine." He lifted one shoulder. "Call it what you want."

"You haven't slept with her."

"Contrary to what people think, I don't have sex with every woman I encounter while I'm on earth."

"Ha! I'm sure it wasn't for lack of trying." Isadora placed one gnarled hand on the table and pushed herself up from her chair before shuffling over to the stove again. "She didn't fall victim to your charms right away, did she?"

Silence hung between them as he refused to confirm or deny her statement. Asmodeus watched her small, hunched form, but when she turned around, those sharp, green eyes reflected her witty, intelligent spirit.

Isadora was right on the money. He should have brought Kai back to the Underworld with him when he realized the Fae were after the ring. Asmodeus had no doubt that the other members of the Brotherhood would have done exactly that if they were in his position.

Taking the ring to the Underworld was the only way to ensure the Fae didn't get it, but it also would mean subjecting Kai to the worst souls in existence. There was no way he would expose her to that kind of darkness. She was too good for that.

"I'm not bringing her back to the Underworld because I can accomplish this task on my own without the rest of the Brotherhood." Asmodeus kept his voice matter of fact, hoping Isadora would believe his lie. "Can you imagine the indignities I would suffer if I had to request their assistance? Mammon is still catching shit for requiring my help the last time he was here. Lucifer is an insufferable ass as it is, so I'd rather not spend the next millennium listening to his crap. I've been keeping watch for any sign of the Fae—not the Brotherhood. I'm sure that your cloaking spell around the property is brilliant, but the Fae are notoriously crafty."

Another lie.

He was worried about the Brotherhood far more than the Fae. He only had a day left before Lucifer would send the others, along with their minions, to collect Kai and the ring.

"I have to get the ring off her finger and send it back to Hell." He held her stare. "End of story."

"I see," Isadora gripped the knob of cane. She nodded and gave him a doubtful look. "Why haven't you slept with her?"

"Why are you obsessed with my sex life?" He smirked. "Is it due to your lack of one?"

"I have plenty of sex." Isadora winked and settled in her chair again. "I'm old. Not dead. Now, answer my question. You are, after all, the Demon of Lust and, if memory serves, the only thing you like more than sex is the chase." Tapping her fingers on the tabletop she eyed him intently. "It's more than that, though isn't it?"

"It's business."

"No." Isadora shook her head. "You really do feel something for her and instead of admitting it, you're hiding behind duty and obligation. I'd say you're being a stubborn ass. Still feeling the pain from when that Vivian woman told you to piss off?"

"Hardly," Asmodeus said with as much boredom as he could muster. Yet, the truth of her words cut deep. Vivian had rejected him and cut him out of her life and the life of their son, who he'd only recently reconnected with.

"Well, Vivian was human and wasn't exactly wrapped right. But as we know, Kai is not human, at least not entirely, and the girl seems to have her shit together. Seems to me you're fucking up an opportunity to end up with a woman who can handle you and all the baggage that comes with you."

"You always were direct, Isadora. I used to think it was one of your best qualities." Asmodeus shook his head and laughed, but his smile faded as Kai's sweet face drifted into his mind. He wanted her. He wanted Kai more than any woman he'd encountered—even more than Vivian. Perhaps it was because she didn't fall at his feet and hop right in bed with him. But whatever the reason, he knew now that he could never have her.

His plan to seduce Kai in order to get the ring had vanished the instant he saw the horrified look on her face in the kitchen—when she saw who he truly was and it repulsed her. His brows knitted at the memory of the sheer terror in her eyes and the way she scrambled out of the house to escape him.

She only came here with him because she was scared and confused and had no other options. Being with him was a last resort and basic survival instinct. She'd leave him as soon as she had another option—

just like Vivian had—and he wouldn't blame her. Kai was the embodiment of innocence and light and he... well... he wasn't.

His resolve had weakened briefly when Kai pressed that beautiful body against him. He'd almost taken her right then and there on the Harley, but her latest revelation had stopped him cold.

Asmodeus was taking Kai's light—her soul. Every time he touched her, she was losing a little bit of her soul to him, but the most terrifying thing was that he wasn't trying to do it.

All members of the Brotherhood had no aura—no soul. Demons were empty vessels waiting to fill up on the souls of the damned. They did it every day when a new batch of tormented sinners arrived in the Underworld and it was where they got their power. Yet, when the new day dawned the demons were empty once again. Soulless and dark. They could also absorb the souls of their minions but it was *always* done with intent.

Asmodeus didn't know why he was unintentionally sucking her light from her but he knew it had to stop. Kai Kelly was too good for him. She was an innocent with an exquisite, enlightened soul and he was a soulless demon who could bring her nothing but death and darkness.

Kai was not his to take. It was that simple.

"I don't need to sleep with her anymore." He squared his shoulders and met Isadora's questioning gaze. "I had planned to seduce the ring out from under her but after everything that's happened, it's not necessary. Fucking her would only be a distraction from my mission."

"Thanks for the clarification." Kai's overly sweet tone, with an edge of go- fuck-yourself, filled the small cabin and Asmodeus' gut clenched. "At least I can take sexual harassment off my list of worries."

Kai had heard everything he said. Shit.

Unmoving, he sat in the chair as the sound of her bare feet padding along the floorboards whispered through the air. Adorned in one of Isadora's nightgowns, she made her way around to the other side of the table.

She was beautiful. Her blond hair, combed off her face, was still wet from her shower and though the thin cotton nightie covered her, it did little to hide the tempting curves of her breasts and hips. Without sparing him a single glance, Kai sat in the chair opposite him and kept her attention on Isadora, who was in the process of pouring her a cup of tea.

"Glad to see you're back in the land of the living," Isadora said as she pushed the ceramic teacup across the table. "Drink this. It'll give you a little more pep."

"Isadora has found two spells she can try that might get the ring off." Asmodeus rose from his seat and went back to the window. Not because he was really worried about anyone being out there at the moment, but because of the look on Kai's face. She looked at him like she hated him and given the circumstances it was just as well. He held her challenging stare and kept his voice even. "We need to do this as quickly as possible."

"No." Kai's voice, clear and calm, filled the small cabin.

"What?" He turned slowly and glared at her. Anger flickered up his back and the tattoos on his arms burned. "No to what?"

"No to all of it." Kai sipped her tea and those big brown eyes stared boldly back at him over the edge of her teacup. "Even if I could take it off, I'm not giving the ring to you or anyone else."

"Kai, you must give me the ring." Asmodeus' hands balled into fists at his side. "You have no idea the kind of power it has."

"So why don't you tell me?" Kai placed her teacup on the saucer and pulled her feet under her on the chair, making herself comfortable. "So far, all I know is that the Brotherhood and the Fae want the ring, but I still don't know why."

"The less you know about it, the better it will be for you." Asmodeus turned his back on her. Hands on his hips and staring out the window, he wrestled with just how much he should tell her. "All you need to know is that as long as you wear it, your life is in danger."

"You may be a demon but you're also a macho dickhead."

"Maybe." He spun around and met her defiant glare. "But I'm the only thing standing between you and a very unpleasant ending with the Fae and the rest of the Brotherhood. Dickhead or not. I'm all you've got, sweetheart."

79

"I can take care of myself. I was on my own for quite a while before you came storming into my life and, if memory serves, *I'm* the one who knocked Ben unconscious. Not you." Her dark eyes flashed and the lines in her forehead deepened. "I may not know how to use whatever power I've got but I'm a quick study. I'm not some stupid little girl you can simply command and, in case you forgot, this ring is the only thing I have left from my grandmother."

"Your grandmother?" Isadora interrupted. Her eyes narrowed as she leaned both hands on the end of her cane and glanced from Asmodeus to Kai. "Asmodeus failed to mention that to me... "

"I found the ring in a crate in the attic of my grandparents' house."

"All by itself?" Isadora asked skeptically. "Just rollin' around in there?"

"Well, no. It was with some pictures of my grandmother with my mother when she was a baby."

"There's more," Asmodeus interrupted. "On the outside of the crate it said, *Custodians of the Light.*"

"Son of a bitch. I didn't think they were real." Isadora's eyes widened and she leaned back in her chair as she continued to stare at Kai. She shot Asmodeus a look that could kill. "You could have saved us a whole lot of damn time if you'd told me this when you got here."

"I'd never heard the term before," he said evenly.

"Yes," Isadora said with a weary sigh. "Well, I have." Isadora muttered under her breath and waved one hand over the Book of Spells, which promptly closed with a loud clap. Seconds later it flew through the air onto the mantle and back in its usual spot. Asmodeus noted that Kai observed the entire thing with obvious fascination but no fear.

"Your aura burned orange when you used your magic," Kai said quietly.

"Not surprised you see auras or that the ring won't come off, and all of that is just the tip of the iceberg for you, young lady." Isadora looked at Kai with a serious expression. "*You* are a Custodian."

"What?" Kai laughed out loud and rolled her eyes. "I don't even know what that means."

"According to the stories I've heard, Custodians of the Light are exactly what the name says. They guard the light from the darkness." Isadora jutted her chin toward Asmodeus but kept her attention on Kai. "More specifically, Custodians are on earth to be sure the demons don't submerge the world into chaos. Then again, it could also have something to do with the Power of Light that the Fae have. Not sure about the witch connection. Hell. I'm not sure about any of it." Isadora let out a sigh. "Except that you are quite a unique, young woman."

"But—"

"Could your mother see auras?"

"Yes."

"What about your grandmother?"

"I—well, I don't know. She died when my mother was very little and she could barely remember her. My mom hadn't spoken to my grandfather since she married my dad."

"Not surprised." Isadora nodded. "So your mother could see auras and spoke with you about it?"

"Yes." Kai nodded. "But she didn't want anyone else to know about it and discouraged me from telling people. My mom flipped her lid when I opened up my tarot shop."

"Well, if she'd never really been taught about the gift, then her wariness of it makes sense. Sometimes a small amount of information is worse than none at all." Isadora glanced at Asmodeus. "You say the pictures you found were of your grandmother. Was she wearing the ring in the pictures?"

"No." Kai shook her head and looked at the ring before turning her attention back to Isadora. "I—I don't think so. But on the back of one of the photos, it said, *my sweet Katherine the next Custodian.* Katherine was my mother."

"Mm-hmm." Isadora's aged hands gripped the top of her cane tightly. "Your grandmother must have been taught by another Custodian, probably her own mother, but died before she could pass it on."

"Kai's grandmother couldn't have been wearing the ring," Asmodeus interrupted. "The Brotherhood would have felt it, the way

81

we did when Kai put it on. We wouldn't even have known the ring had been found if it stayed in that box."

"Mm-hmm." Isadora pursed her lips. "Anyone else ever wear this ring?"

"Once." Asmodeus ran a hand over his face and let out a weary breath. "After it was relinquished, I tossed it into the sea and thought that was the end of it."

"Clearly not," Kai said as she held up her right hand.

"Your grandmother must have been taught by someone who told her that she shouldn't wear the ring." Isadora twirled her cane between her hands as a thoughtful look consumed her. "Was there any kind of altar in your grandparents' house?" Isadora jutted a thumb toward the mantle. "Something like this? A place she might have used for worship or to practice her magic?"

"No." Kai shook her head. "Nothing like that. To be honest there was barely any evidence my grandmother existed, except for the crate I found in the attic. I obviously shouldn't have put the ring on but I didn't know."

"Obviously." Asmodeus smirked but his expression hardened quickly. "I should have brought the ring to the Underworld when I took it from Solomon but I won't make the same mistake twice. You will give it to me and I'll take it back where it belongs."

Kai shook her head. "No."

"It has to be given willingly, doesn't it?" Isadora murmured with a far off look in her eye. "And it obviously didn't get stuck on old Solomon's finger."

"No, it didn't and yes, it has to be given willingly." Asmodeus flicked his attention to Kai. She was staring at the ring and running the tip of her finger over the face of it. The sad look in her eyes made him want to smash all the furniture in the room. He cleared his throat and turned his gaze back to Isadora. "Or the bearer has to be dead."

"Dead?" Kai's head whipped up and her frightened eyes met his.

"She's an innocent," Isadora snapped as she pushed herself up from the chair. "The Brotherhood can't harm her."

"I'm not that innocent," Kai said with a laugh as she avoided Asmodeus' gaze. "I'm not a virgin."

Asmodeus' eyes burned as he wrestled with the gut instinct to punch something at the mere mention of Kai having lovers. It was stupid and he knew it, but it didn't make it less true. He loathed feeling jealous over such a ridiculous idea and yet, he couldn't help himself. What a revolting development.

"That's not the kind of innocence we're talking about," Isadora said. "The point is that your soul is pure. You aren't corrupted by evil so the Brotherhood can't harm you."

"No, we're not supposed to be able to," Asmodeus said quietly without taking his eyes off Kai. "But the minions can get to her and so can the Fae."

"What the fuck is a minion?" Kai asked in a barely audible whisper.

"Humans who can be forced to do a demon's dirty work," Isadora said. She made a sound of derision and shuffled toward the stove. "Worst of the worst."

"And we now have only twenty-four hours left before Lucifer sends the rest of the Brotherhood, with the help of their minions, to retrieve the ring. I talked him into giving me some time to get it on my own, but he's notoriously impatient and the son of a bitch may not even wait. The only thing that might buy us more time is that the power of the ring is somehow masking our location. Lucifer was complaining about it yesterday but if I know my brothers, they'll find us eventually." He strode to the table, leaned both hands on the scarred wood surface and brought his face even with Kai's. Her sweet scent, a mixture of lilacs and soap, filled his head and threatened his composure. "Both the Brotherhood and the Fae will take this ring with or without your cooperation. Dead or alive. Now do you understand?"

"You never answered my question." Kai kept her eyes on him, meeting his challenge. "*Why* are the Fae and the Brotherhood so interested in the ring?"

Asmodeus' jaw clenched as he wrestled with how much to tell her. What would she do if she knew the true power it held? Would she use it against him and the rest of the Brotherhood? Before he could make the choice, Isadora made it for him.

"According to legend, the Ring of Solomon has the power to control the Underworld," Isadora said in a quiet, almost reverent tone. "Isn't that right, Asmodeus? Or, more to the point, that ring has the power to control the entire Brotherhood. Combine that with the fact that you are more than likely a Custodian... Kai Kelly, you can quite literally, command Hell."

Kai's complexion paled as her dark eyes filled with fear and something in Asmodeus' chest squeezed as he watched her wrestle with all that was being thrown at her. He pushed himself away from the table, needing to put some distance between them.

"That's why Ben wanted it?" Kai's voice wavered as she looked away and wrapped her hands around the teacup. "He wants it so he can control all of you and command Hell?"

"Yes. The Fae would love nothing more than to have the Brotherhood as their slaves."

Kai sat up in her chair as she looked between the two of them. "Why haven't Ben and the other Fae come after us?"

"The ring may be masking your presence from them as well as from the Brotherhood, and Isadora's cloaking spell is also hiding us. Limiting the use of my powers will also help keep us off the radar, so to speak."

"The girl's right," Isadora murmured. "Fae can find others of their kind easily. Especially one like Kai, one that isn't trained to control her power or contain it. You may be hidden here in my home but it's surprising the Fae didn't find you before you arrived."

"Control Hell?" Kai said in a rush as she stared at the ring. "I can't control anything. Until I put on this damned ring and Asmodeus came riding into my life, I never shot freaking light beams out of my hands. Control? This is the most out of control I've felt in my life and that's saying something." She sucked in a deep breath. "I wish my mother was here."

"So do I." Isadora patted Kai's hand reassuringly. "It's a damn shame your grandmother died before she could teach your mama."

"My mother knew about the ones with no light." Kai wiped her tears away. Her chin tilted and her voice was edged with an icy chill. "She warned me about the Dark Ones like Asmodeus. No aura. She said they would take my powers and leave me a shell of myself."

"That's interesting," Isadora said quietly. "I wonder how she would know about them if no one taught her?"

"She was right." Asmodeus swore and turned his back on her,

unable and unwilling to subject himself to that accusing look in her eye. "I have no soul and if you stay with me much longer, neither will you. We will find a way to get that ring off your finger, I will take it back to the Underworld and both of us will go back to our lives."

"Hold your horses, mister." Isadora's exasperated tone drifted over his shoulder. "This ring is more connected to Kai than it has been to anyone else. It has to be. Think about it for a minute. Asmodeus, you said that Solomon had no trouble removing the ring and handing it over. Right?"

"Correct," Asmodeus replied.

"That's not the case for Kai, is it? The ring seems to have bonded with her— as though it's a part of who she is."

Asmodeus nodded but kept his back to them.

"You're not going to get that damned thing off her hand until you find out more about her kin and the Custodians of the Light. We have to find out who trained your grandmother."

"My family is all dead and gone, Isadora." Kai's voice, weary and edged with sadness tugged at Asmodeus, making him feel like an even bigger shithead than he already did. "All I have is that big old house in Idaho."

"Yes, I know." Isadora nodded as she shuffled toward her bedroom. "Be right back."

The door shut with a soft click leaving Kai and Asmodeus alone. Absolute quiet filled the room but he could feel Kai's eyes on him, studying him. He glanced over his shoulder and to his surprise Kai was standing behind him.

"I'm not giving up the ring, Asmodeus. Not yet."

He turned so that they were facing one another. His initial instinct was to tell her again what a bad decision that was but he refrained. It might have been because of the determined look on her face or the intelligent glint in her eyes, but he found himself unable or unwilling to argue with her. When he said nothing, she continued.

"I have a proposition for you." Kai inched closer, the thin fabric of the white nightie doing little to conceal her womanly curves. She was just inches from him but her warm energy wafted over him in subtle, erotic pulses. "If you're interested?"

"I'm listening." Asmodeus kept his hands at his sides, his fingers twitched, eager to grab the nightgown and strip her body bare but he resisted. He fleetingly realized that while he wanted Kai more than any woman he'd met, she was the first woman he refrained from sleeping with. Talk about a fucking ironic turn of events.

"Help me find out who my family really was. Who *I* am." Her large dark eyes were locked with his as she inched closer, just a breath away. "I thought I was alone. This ring could be the key to finding out who I am—or who I'm supposed to be— please don't rob me of that."

Surprise filled him as Kai's soft, warm fingers grasped his and her thumb ran over his knuckles in gentle, reassuring strokes. A touch he suspected was meant to reassure but all it did was inflame his desire for her. Between the pleading tone of her voice and the achingly tender brush of her flesh against his, he was lost.

"I have no desire to control you or the Underworld." Kai's gentle tone tugged at him. "Please. Help me get some answers. Maybe once I have more information and know about this whole Custodian thing, the ring will come off."

The feel of her soft fingers in his nourished and enticed him, but with each second Asmodeus knew he was doing her more harm than good. He looked down at their joined hands, her delicate fingers tangled with his much larger ones, and saw that she was right—her aura flickered over his skin. The tattoos on his arms tingled with energy—*her energy*—and even though he wanted to pull her into his arms and breathe her in, he yanked his hand from hers.

With each touch, he was taking a little bit more from her. How long before it started to harm her? How many times could he touch her before he took it all?

"Fine." Asmodeus nodded his agreement but didn't miss the wounded look on her face when he recoiled from her touch. He folded his arms over his chest and stepped back, increasing the distance between them, even though he wanted nothing more than to cradle her in his arms. "We've got twenty-four hours to get you your answers. Then I get the ring and take it back to the Underworld."

She opened her mouth to respond but the bedroom door opened, causing Kai to jump. Asmodeus spun around, instinctively shielding Kai's body with his and though several ideas of who or what would be standing there flickered through his mind, the sight before him wasn't one of them.

"Holy shit," Kai breathed. "Isadora?"

"In the flesh, child." Isadora was no longer old or wrinkled but the young beautiful witch Asmodeus had bedded so many years ago. Long waves of raven hair fell to her waist and her hourglass figure was swathed in a black dress reminiscent of days gone by. The only feature that remained the same was those glittering green eyes.

"How did—what the heck?" Kai stepped out from behind Asmodeus and stared with amazement. A huge smile covered her face. "You're gorgeous... and *young*."

"Yes, but it's only temporary. I typically use this spell when I'm feeling frisky. As you can imagine, it's far easier to get laid when I look like this." Isadora winked and moved to the stove. She grabbed two bottles from the shelf and made quick work of filling them with potion from one of the pots. "If you think I'm going to take the two of you to the Witches Council looking like an old hag, well you've got another thing coming."

"What are you talking about?" Asmodeus' patience was running thin. The only race who disliked demons almost as much as the Fae were the witches. The Brotherhood had Satan to thank for that one. "Why the Witches Council?"

"Here take this." Isadora handed Kai one of the bottles but slipped the other in the pocket of her dress. "This is one of those just-in-case potions. When you drink it, you simply picture where you want to go and there you'll be. Always good to have an emergency transporter potion in times like this—it's also untraceable for about six hours. So whoever or whatever is after you won't know where you've gone and it'll give you a head start."

"I thought you were working on potions to remove the ring?" Asmodeus asked with mild irritation. "Shouldn't we try that before resorting to a visit to the Witches Council?"

"One of 'em was for the ring but based on the Custodian factor, it won't do a lick of good. I made the transporter potion too. You two are on the run, after all. Aren't you?"

Isadora pushed Kai toward the bedroom. "I left you some

clothes on the bed. Go change and then we'll get going."

Kai didn't move but kept staring at Isadora, fascinated by the dramatic transformation.

"Answer me, Isadora," Asmodeus pressed. "Why do you insist on taking her to the Witches?"

"Kai's got witch's blood in her along with the Fae. Since going to the Fae for help would probably end badly, it makes sense that we start with my people. If anyone is going to know more about the Custodians, it's the Witches Council. Those bitches are even older than me. We'll start there and, as long as you behave yourself, I'm sure the High Priestesses will keep their spells to themselves."

"What the hell?" Kai said with a shrug as she headed to the bedroom. She cast one last glance at Asmodeus. "I've got nothing else to lose."

As the door closed behind her, he couldn't stop thinking about how wrong she was.

CHAPTER EIGHT

Standing in Isadora's kitchen, wearing an outfit that could only be described as gypsy attire, Kai fiddled with the potion bottle in the folds of her skirt. The white, off the shoulder, peasant blouse had a delicate embroidered design along the edges and tied perfectly at the waist. The navy skirt with silver charms stitched around the hips fell almost to the floor and jingled when Kai walked.

She hoped that she wouldn't have to sneak up on anyone because it would be impossible in this get-up. Even the sandals she wore had silver charms around the ankle.

While it wasn't an ensemble Kai normally wore, Asmodeus must have liked it because he had barely taken his eyes off her since she came out of the bedroom.

Asmodeus didn't look so bad himself.

Isadora had given him a fresh pair of jeans and a black t-shirt that fit his well-sculpted torso like a second skin. The tattoos snaked over the thick muscles of his arms and disappeared beneath the edge of the sleeve seductively. She couldn't help but wonder where the rest of it went. Kai had to force herself not to stare at him like the sex-starved woman she was.

She'd never thought about sex this much in her entire life and chalked it up to the fact that he was the Demon of Lust. Too bad he was doing his best to avoid touching her or looking at her. Nothing will kill a girl's ego like rejection, and to be turned down by the

Demon of Lust had to be some kind of landmark moment. Wonderful.

"Take my hands," Isadora said as she stepped between them. "Close your eyes and keep your breathing even. No matter what happens don't let go of me until I tell you to."

Asmodeus flicked his gaze to Kai as she closed her eyes. With Isadora's smooth hand in hers, Kai fought to keep herself calm. As silence filled the room, she started to wonder if anything was going to happen... and then Isadora began to chant.

> *Goddesses of Wind, hear my call.*
> *Take the faithful to the Witches Hall.*
> *Fly us to the sacred spot beneath.*
> *Where no children cry and no women weep.*
> *Along the secret path no mortal can trace.*
> *An oasis hidden under the mountain's face.*

Isadora's voice, low and soft, whisked around them like a summer breeze and as she spoke, the ring burned against Kai's flesh. Isadora repeated the chant three times and as she completed the third cycle, a snap of electricity flickered over Kai's skin and in a flash the world was spinning as the floor vanished beneath her feet.

Kai felt like she was flying in a cool tunnel of darkness but the journey ended as quickly as it began. With a teeth-rattling jolt, the floor was solid beneath her again and a cool, damp wind blew her skirt around her legs. Shuddering and sweating, feeling like she'd just been tossed around in a tornado, Kai kept her eyes squeezed shut and for a moment she thought she might be dead.

Seconds later, she felt someone grab her by the shoulders and shake her, calling her name but the voice sounded so far away. A large hand cradled her face as hot flesh seared against her cheek and her body burned from the inside out. Everything felt heavy, as though she was being sucked into quicksand. Kai wanted to dig her way out, to fight the thick, suffocating air but her arms seemed as though they were made of lead.

A man kept calling her name. Asmodeus?

She wanted to shout back to him, to tell him that she was right here, but it was an effort in futility. As his voice drifted further and further away, Kai tried to scream but no sound came as she tumbled into the abyss.

***

Kai felt like she was floating on a cloud. She smiled as she snuggled deeper into the ridiculously soft blankets and pillows. The soothing scent of lavender filled her head and she let out a satisfied sigh as memories of her childhood home in Vermont flickered through her mind. She was home. This bed felt just like home. Kai hugged the body pillow and kicked off the covers so she could wrap her leg around the pile of blankets.

The sudden sound of a deep, baritone voice ripped Kai out of her reverie and back to her twisted reality.

"I'm not going anywhere and if you know what's good for you, you'll back off."

"Are you threatening me, demon?" Replied an unfamiliar female voice.

"I certainly hope so."

"Asmodeus?" Kai murmured.

Her eyes flew open as she shot up in the bed and looked wildly around the unfamiliar bedroom. The cavernous space looked like the set for a historical drama. Kai was sitting in a massive four-poster bed with a white, gauzy canopy overhead. The bedding was sage green and white silk and there were enough goose down pillows to suffocate a small army.

Tall, ornate windows framed with panels of velvet were to the right. The windows lined gray stonewalls and directly across from the bed was a floor to ceiling fireplace with a roaring fire. Kai got the distinct impression she was in a castle.

Asmodeus was standing in front of the flickering flames, eyes glowing and arms folded over his chest, looking every bit the demon he was. All he was missing was a set of horns. Isadora and two women Kai had never seen before were standing in front of him looking less than pleased. They all turned to look at Kai when she spoke up but Asmodeus remained where he was.

"She's finally awake," said the tall blond woman. She was rail thin and probably close to six feet tall. Wearing a Renaissance era gown made of red velvet trimmed in gold roping, she stared at Kai with cold, blue eyes. "You've seen that she's fine. Now be on your way, demon. Isadora should know better than to bring one of *your kind* here. Willow will be less than amused and you might find yourself at the wrong end of one of her spells."

"The name is Asmodeus," he said with a growl. "And Willow can complain all she wants but I'm not going anywhere without Kai." He locked eyes with Kai and quickly added, "And the ring."

Kai's heart squeezed in her chest as he swiftly corrected himself. *Just the ring.* That's all he wanted. Once he got the ring, he'd be gone and she'd be alone. Again.

"Don't be such a bitch, Rosalyn, and Asmodeus, keep your boxers on. Rosalyn is full of as much piss and wind as you are." Isadora, still looking young and beautiful, pushed past the two women and came to Kai's side. "How are you feeling, Kai?"

"I—what happened?" Kai held the covers to her chest, even though she was still fully dressed, she felt insecure and exposed. "Where are we, anyway?"

"Larrun Mountain in France." A small woman with short red hair stepped forward and gave Kai a warm smile. Her emerald green dress was similar in style to the blonde's, but made of satin. It covered her petite frame perfectly and matched the green in her wide-set eyes. Her voice was edged with an Irish brogue. "Technically we're deep within the mountain. I'm Alisha, by the way. Rosalyn and I are secretaries to the Witches Council."

"What?" Kai looked at the windows and pointed. "If we're inside the mountain, how can I possibly see the sunshine or the sky?"

"It's a spell." Asmodeus crossed around to the other side of Kai's bed but kept his burning gaze on the three witches. "Like their appearances, what you see isn't what you get." His tone softened and his eyes flickered back to blue when he turned his attention to Kai. "You fainted as soon as we arrived and have been passed out for half an hour."

"What's the last thing you remember?" Isadora asked.

"I—I'm not sure." Kai's eyebrows knit together as she tried to recall the jumbled memories. "We were in Isadora's house and then it felt like we were flying but then the floor was under my feet again. Asmodeus, I remember feeling your hands on my face... "

"It doesn't matter," Asmodeus interrupted, his tone both urgent and impatient. "What's done is done. How long until they will see us?"

"It matters to me." Kai shot him an irritated look.

"Not surprised you fainted," Isadora said with a reassuring pat on Kai's leg. "The first time you travel that way can be a doozy. I puked after my first trip and Rosalyn almost wet her pants."

"Enough," Rosalyn snapped. Hands clasped behind her back, she stood at the end of the bed looking at Kai like she was a bug that needed to be squashed. "You aren't a full-blooded witch and that's probably why your reaction was so extreme. Could be the Fae blood causing the trouble or her human blood. What a mess."

"Rosalyn," Alisha said in a reprimanding tone. "She's our guest and a friend of Isadora's."

"Yes. A *friend* who is wearing the Ring of Solomon." Rosalyn's eyes flared with anger and sent a chill up Kai's spine. "She doesn't even know what to do with it. All that power and little knowledge will add up to nothing but trouble."

"I have no interest in controlling Hell," Kai shot back. She hated being bullied and that's exactly what this witch was trying to do. Kai sat up and pushed the covers aside while glancing briefly at Asmodeus. "I am, however, interested in learning how to control whatever powers I have, finding out what it means to be a Custodian of the Light, and figure out why this damn ring won't come off my hand."

An odd tingling sensation flickered over Kai's flesh as all the tiny hairs on her body stood on end. Anger and frustration clawed at her and a funny buzzing sound filled her head as she broke out in a sweat.

"Kai?" Asmodeus' tone was quiet. "Take a deep breath and calm down."

"Why?" Kai's hands balled into fists as heat crawled up her back and the ring burned against her skin. She slipped off the edge of the bed as all three of the witches took a step back but Asmodeus moved closer, his body heat pulsing over her in thick waves. "I want answers but I keep fainting like some old lady," she said with a nod in Rosalyn's direction. "And this broad's attitude isn't helping."

"She needs to learn some control before she hurts someone." Rosalyn's face paled and she inched closer to Alisha as she glanced between Kai and Asmodeus. "Do something about her, Isadora."

"Why are you acting like you're afraid of me if I'm just some Fae-witch mutt?" Tingling heat throbbed in Kai's chest as her impatience grew. "Aren't you the ancient powerful witches?"

"It's not you," Isadora said in a calm, even voice. She nodded toward Kai's hands. "It's the ring. We have no idea what you can do with it or what it can do with you."

"I've seen what she can do," Asmodeus murmured as he continued to inch closer. "And so has she. That fairy man is probably still passed out in the barn."

"Oh shit," Kai whispered.

Her heart pounded in her chest like a jackhammer as stomach-churning power pumped through her veins. Kai glanced down at her hands and saw that her aura glowed bright red and the ring was engulfed in a blinding layer of white light that was slowly spreading over her fingers. She swallowed hard and fought the fear that crept in and, just when she thought she was going to lose it, Asmodeus loomed largely in front of her.

"Look at me, Kai," he said firmly. Red eyes gleaming beneath a dark furrowed brow, his huge frame towered over her. Most anyone else would probably have been frightened of this larger than life man but seeing him there, with his calm, commanding presence, Kai was actually relieved. "Steady your breathing and focus all of your energy on me."

"What is he doing?" Rosalyn hissed.

"What he has to do," Isadora murmured.

The women were saying something else Kai could barely hear them. Their voices faded away, as though she and Asmodeus were the only ones left in the room. Keeping all of her attention on him, staring into his resolute expression, Kai knew he was an immovable force. Strong. Steady. Unrelenting. Somehow, looking into that ruggedly handsome face, she knew everything would be okay.

Unable to speak, afraid that weird light might come flying out of her mouth and incinerate everyone, Kai nodded. Asmodeus raised his hands, with his palms facing her and encouraged her to do the same. Shaking with an energy that was barely contained, Kai lifted her quivering hands and while saying a silent prayer, laid her palms flat against his.

The instant their flesh touched, a streak of lightning whizzed beneath her skin and the buzzing in her head grew louder. She watched with fascination as her bright red aura flickered up his arms and engulfed him with astonishing speed. The white light on the ring crept over the red and began to soften the glow.

Kai focused on slowing her breathing down and tuned into the thundering beat of her own heart. Bit by bit, and with every pump of blood, her body cooled and the glow around them fluttered to a pale yellow. The buzzing in her head subsided and the hint of a smile played at Asmodeus' lips as his eyes flickered back to blue.

"Better?" He asked as he dropped his hands, breaking their connection.

"Yes," Kai murmured, looking him up and down. She stepped back to get a good look at him, unsure if she what she was seeing was real. "Whoa."

"What is it?" Asmodeus peered at her warily.

"Even though I'm not touching you... Asmodeus you still have an aura." Kai pointed at him and a smile spread over her face. "It's faint but it's there. You have a—"

Just as the words escaped her lips, the soft yellow light around him flickered and went out. It was as if someone came along and blew out a flame.

"I can't have an aura if you're not touching me," he said quickly. "It's not possible."

"Damn it," Kai growled in frustration. She cocked her head and squinted but still nothing. "It's gone."

"It was probably just some residue from helping you channel the energy of the ring," Asmodeus bit out. He turned his back on Kai and faced the three witches, who Kai had practically forgotten were there. "How soon until Willow and the rest of the Council will see us?"

The three women were staring at Kai and Asmodeus as if they'd just sprouted horns. Rosalyn and Alisha looked frightened, but Isadora was obviously intrigued.

"I will have to see them first," Isadora said. She tossed her long raven hair over her shoulder and winked at Kai. "Nothing those three bitches love more than a little ass-kissing. You two stay here and I'll come get you when it's your turn to pucker up. Give me about an hour."

Rosalyn opened the massive mahogany door and held it as Alisha and Isadora whisked out into the hallway. She started to leave but stopped just before closing it. Rosalyn's long, bony fingers lingered on the brass knob as she leveled a wicked gaze at Kai.

"In case you were thinking of wandering off, we've bewitched the room. You can't leave until we come retrieve you. It's for your own safety." Rosalyn slammed the door and Kai heard a lock slip into place with a sickening thump. She ran to the door but just as she reached it the entire door vanished, and Kai found herself pounding on the rough, cold stones of a wall.

CHAPTER NINE

"Damn it," Kai hissed. She spun around and leaned against the cool stones as she locked eyes with Asmodeus. Her stomach flip-flopped as those blue eyes studied her intently. "Looks like we're not going anywhere right now."

"No." The muscles in his chest flexed and his hands curled into fists. "Not yet. But believe me, if I wanted to get us out of here I could."

"So why don't you?" Kai folded her arms over her breasts, the charms on her skirt jingling as she moved. "I'm not so sure I trust anyone other than Isadora."

"We're not going anywhere until we see the High Priestesses and find out what they know."

"You mean, *if* they know."

"They know something." Asmodeus looked away from her and went to the fireplace. Staring into the flames and leaning both hands on the enormous mantle, his body was taut and tense. "Did you see the way Rosalyn and Alisha reacted to the fact that you're wearing the ring? Believe me, they're privy to information we need but I'm running short on patience and we're running short on time."

The amber light of the fire flickered over his long, powerful body making him look as though he himself were on fire. Silence settled between them as she thought about the way he absorbed her aura and wondered why he didn't have one to begin with.

97

"Asmodeus?" Kai pushed herself away from the wall and the charms on her skirt jingled. Slowly, she closed the distance between them until she was only a few inches away. "Why don't you have an aura?"

He didn't look at her but his entire body stiffened and the ropy muscles of his arms bulged as he gripped the mantle tighter. The log in the fire crackled and snapped as the flames ate away at it and it reminded Kai of how it felt when the power of the ring surged through her.

"I have no soul," he murmured. "You asked me once, what kind of childhood I had. Well, I didn't. The Brotherhood—all seven of us—we were created specifically to deal with the souls of the damned."

Kai stared at him in stunned silence. How could this man believe he had no soul? He'd shown her nothing but kindness and protected her. It made no sense.

"I don't believe it," Kai said firmly. She stepped closer, the heat of his body mixed with the fire and washed over her enticingly. Breathing in his masculine scent, she moved her body so the fabric of her skirt brushed against his legs. "Not a chance."

"What you *believe* is irrelevant," he ground out through clenched teeth.

"You saved me, Asmodeus." Kai trailed one finger along his forearm and the moment her flesh met his, his body flinched. She smiled as the yellow light of her aura flickered over his arm and engulfed him even faster than before. Kai paused for a moment but when he didn't pull away she continued. "How can you think you don't have a soul?" Kai murmured as the pad of her finger whispered against the crook of his elbow and followed the path of the tattoo, the hair on his arms rasping temptingly beneath her skin. She inched closer, her nipples poking through the thin fabric as they brushed against him. "You could have dragged me back to the Underworld or called on some minions to kill me and take the ring... but you didn't. You've protected me, shown me kindness and patience. You may be a demon, Asmodeus but you aren't soulless."

"Yes, I am." Asmodeus pushed himself away from the mantle and spun to face her. He loomed over her, muscles straining, hands clenched, looking feral and dangerous but Kai held her ground.

"Demons—the Brotherhood—we feed on the souls of the damned. Every day, when a new flock of pathetic, cursed creatures come through the gates of Hell, we are there to greet them. I fill up on their energy like a spiritual leech and when a new day dawns, I'm empty again, waiting to feed on the next batch."

"Then why do you get an aura when I touch you?" Hands on her hips, her chin tilted at him defiantly, she got right in his face. "And why does it scare the shit out of you? What's the matter?" Kai poked him in the chest but he didn't budge. "Afraid I'll take your demon juju away and rule your world with this stupid ring?"

"No, you impossible woman," Asmodeus growled. He leaned close, almost touching her. His mouth hovered a breath away from hers as his deep, gravelly voice surrounded her. "It's not me I'm worried about. It's you. Every time I touch you, I'm stealing a little bit of your soul. Don't you understand? I'm feeding on you—on your soul. You should be running in the other direction and remember the warning your mother gave you about the Dark Ones."

"I'm not afraid of you, Asmodeus." Kai barely recognized the husky, needy sound of her voice. She leaned in and gasped as her sensitized nipples brushed against him and heat pooled between her legs. Her entire body throbbed with desire and unsatisfied lust. "And the last thing I want to do is stay away from you. In fact, all I can think about is touching you. Maybe it's because you're the Demon of Lust or maybe it's because you're the single most attractive man I've met. But whatever the reason... I want you, Asmodeus."

Kai slid her hands up his arms and draped one leg around his, the charms on her skirt tinkling in the air like angelic music. She pulled her body tighter against him and the growing evidence of his desire, but his arms remained at his side. His body tensed beneath her touch and the ring burned against her flesh as the flames of desire consumed her.

"I know you wouldn't hurt me," Kai whispered against his cheek, the stubble on his chin creating delicious friction against her lips. "Touch me. Please, Asmodeus. I want to feel your hands on me."

"I don't want to hurt you," he growled.

"Then don't deny me the one thing I'm asking for."

Arms still at his side, Asmodeus leaned back and looked her in the eye. His square jaw was set and two red slashes glowed at her beneath a dark brow. His erection throbbed against her stomach and Kai felt as though every single nerve ending in her body was primed and ready to explode. She held her breath and for a split second, she thought he was going to shove her away as he had before.

Not this time.

In a blur, his mouth crashed to hers and Kai let out a sigh of pure pleasure as their tongues met. He tasted like sin, sex, lust, and all that goes with it. Kai moaned as his strong hands slipped beneath the edge of her blouse. His hot flesh seared against her as his long fingers splayed against the small of her back and branded her as his with every stroke.

It was a frenzy of lips, tongues, and teeth, as they tasted one another with all the pent up frustration from the past twenty-four hours. Kai held his head in both hands, angling so she could delve deep. His tongue teased along hers, demanding and taking everything she had to give.

Without breaking the kiss, Asmodeus scooped her up in his arms and carried her to the bed. Paying thorough attention to her mouth, he laid her down and settled his much larger body over hers. Kai moaned contentedly as the hot, hard length of him settled between her legs in just the right spot.

He suckled her lip and kissed the corner of her mouth before placing both hands on either side of her head, as he held himself above her.

"You are beautiful, Kai Kelly." The deep and seductive tone of his voice, combined with the lustful look in his eyes, made her shiver. A wicked grin cracked his handsome face as he ground himself against her with just enough pressure to make her gasp. "There's only one way you could be even more exquisite than you are now."

"Oh really?" Kai breathed as she arched against him, itching for more. More of his touch. His taste. More of *him*. She wanted to lick and nibble every sinful inch of him. Kai smiled as she ran her hands up his arms and along the tattoo before slipping her fingertips beneath the edge of the t-shirt sleeves. "How?"

"When I make you scream," he whispered between kisses along her throat. Kai shivered in anticipation, her body taut and ready, she

100

turned her head giving him access to the sensitive skin. "I want to make you come, Kai. So tell me what you like."

Kai wanted to answer him but she couldn't form a coherent thought, let alone a sentence. She couldn't think. All she could do was *feel.* Her body hummed with energy, with life... power. With every kiss, stroke, and whisper of flesh against flesh, Kai was more alive than ever before.

As he trailed kisses along her collarbone and his hands encircled her waist, she knew Asmodeus wasn't taking her soul. If anything, he was nourishing it.

Rising to his knees, he straddled her on the soft, billowy bed as he removed her peasant blouse. A low growl rumbled in his chest when he set eyes on her bare breasts and the sound of it made Kai shiver.

He needed this as much as she did.

"You're perfect," he whispered as he trailed his fingers over her breasts and rasped the pad of his thumb across her erect nipples. "Soft, curvy and womanly."

"And yours for the taking," Kai murmured.

She sat up and kissed him again, pleasure whisking over her as her breasts crushed against his chest and the cotton of his t-shirt rasped over her sensitized nipples. His hands cradled her head with breathtaking tenderness as she slid her fingers beneath the edge of his t-shirt. Kai moaned against his mouth as the muscles of his back rippled beneath her hands. Impatient, wanting to feel his flesh against hers, Kai shoved his shirt up and sighed as their bodies met.

Asmodeus tossed his shirt aside and flipped onto his back, pulling Kai on top of him. She sat on the hard, pulsing evidence of desire and writhed against him as their tongues tangled, but it wasn't enough.

She needed—no *had* to have more.

Reaching between them, Kai undid the button of his jeans but he grabbed her wrists and pulled her hands away before she could claim him. He arched one eyebrow and slowly shook his head as he gave her that wicked grin.

"You first," he whispered.

Asmodeus sat up and captured her lips with his before she could protest. Wrapping one strong arm around her waist, he held her against him as he moved to the edge of the bed. Kai locked her legs around his waist and her arms linked around his neck as she kissed him. Her fingers threaded through his dark hair as she teased the edge of his tongue with hers. Kai nipped his lower lip as one large hand found her breast and squeezed.

With Kai wrapped around him, Asmodeus stood from the bed and carried her over to the long bank of windows. He set her down on the wide stone ledge before stepping back and leaving her panting.

"What are you doing?" Kai asked as she trailed her index finger over the hard planes of his defined abs. She grabbed the waistband of his jeans with both hands and pulled him back to her but Asmodeus ensnared her wrists, again shaking his head.

"It seems you can't behave yourself, Ms. Kelly." Standing in front of her, he positioned himself in between her open legs. The skirt was hiked up to her waist, but fabric spilled over and covered the top half of her thighs. "I'm going to have to make sure you keep your hands to yourself."

Kai gave him a puzzled look and gasped when he urged her backward and the skin of her back met the cool glass of the window. He held her arms out to the side so they were pressed against the drapes that framed the window. Asmodeus slipped each of Kai's hands beneath the silk, tasseled ropes that tied back the curtains, clearly wanting to use them to his advantage.

Her entire body hummed with anticipation. Asmodeus held her gaze, while he took his time securing her wrists and tightening the ropes. Kai shivered as she watched and took in every wicked inch of him. If sex could become a person—it would be definitely look like him.

His broad, muscular chest was covered in a dusting of dark hair that tapered down and disappeared beneath the unfastened button of his jeans. Every single bit of his body was built to satisfy a woman—and he'd been with countless women. For some bizarre reason that fact didn't bother Kai because somewhere deep in her gut, she knew this unusual man was made to be hers.

Asmodeus placed a tender kiss at the corner of her mouth and whispered, "They're not too tight are they?"

Kai, her breath coming in short, quick gasps, said nothing but shook her head as she wiggled impatiently. She hooked her legs around him and grinned as she pulled him toward her but once again he shook his head. With surprising tenderness, his hands rested on her thighs as he pushed them apart gently. He stared at her as his talented fingers found their way beneath the folds of the skirt and whispered up her legs.

He captured her lips as he brushed his thumbs along the tender flesh of her inner thigh and kept moving upward until her reached her hot, wet center. Kai let out a gasp as his thumbs flicked over her clit and he grinned against her mouth.

"That's the spot," he murmured.

"Yes," Kai breathed. "That's it."

"There?" He asked wickedly as he ran one finger along the center of her damp panties. He applied more pressure to the tiny nub as he flicked her nipple with his tongue and scored it gently with his teeth before moving to her other breast. "Or there?"

With her hands tied out to the side, the cool glass against her back and his hot, wet mouth on her bare skin, Kai's body was on fire, burning from the inside out. She'd never been more turned on or in a more erotic situation in her life and she never wanted it to end.

Asmodeus dropped to his knees and pulled her backside to the edge of the stone windowsill and the movement pushed her skirt up, baring her pink panties to the cool air. Panting and squirming with need, Kai watched as hooked his hands over her legs and trailed kisses up the inside of her left thigh. She spread her legs more, wanting to give him better access to what he surely desired.

Her aura glowed over both of them with an even brighter intensity than normal and she had no doubt it was fueled by her desire for him.

Pulling her panties aside with one finger, he blew tantalizingly on the swollen, sensitized flesh and looked up at her with glowing eyes. Hands still tied, Kai wiggled her bottom toward him, her hands flexed and her fingers curled as she begged to touch him and just when she thought she'd scream with frustration... he dove deep.

His hot mouth covered her and Kai screamed as his tongue flicked back and forth over her clit. His arms, hooked over her thighs,

103

held her down as he mercilessly continued his assault, tasting her and teasing her to the edge. With each lick and suckle he'd bring her closer but ease off just before she hit the peak.

Shuddering with wave after wave of white-hot pleasure, Kai screamed his name, begging for more. Asmodeus plunged his tongue into her over and over and suckled her clit until the toe-curling orgasm ripped through her.

Limp and completely satisfied, Kai rested her head against the glass and fought to catch her breath. Body quivering, she kept her eyes closed for a moment to try and regain her bearings. Her eyelids finally fluttered open as Asmodeus untied her wrists and she let out a short laugh as he placed her hands into her lap in an almost business-like manner.

"I'd say you've earned the title Demon of Lust," Kai said through heavy breaths as she sat up and pulled her skirt down to cover her legs. He walked to the bed and retrieved their shirts, which would have been fine if it felt like he hadn't been avoiding looking at her. "Asmodeus? What's wrong?"

"You should put this back on," Asmodeus said flatly as he handed her the peasant blouse without sparing her a glance. Her aura light still lingered over his body. "Right now."

He stalked over to the fireplace and she finally got a glimpse of the rest of his tattoo. The chain of circles went up both arms, across his shoulders and there was a bigger circle at the center with some kind of design in it. But he pulled on his t-shirt before she could get a good look at it.

"Asmodeus?" Kai hopped off the ledge, her legs still felt rubbery so she leaned against it as she put her shirt back on and tied it at the waist. "Look at me."

"They're coming back," he said without turning around. "I can hear them down the hallway so put yourself together. We'll be going before the High Priestesses any minute."

"Okay, fine." Kai looked at the wall where the door used to be and then back to him as dread clawed at her. "Why won't you look at me?"

Silence stretched out between them as he refused to answer her. Kai stormed over to him and grabbed his arm as she spun him to face her. Her heart sank when she saw the cold, detached look on his face.

"What is it, Kai?" Asmodeus folded his arms over his chest and leveled a questioning gaze at her. A bored tone edged his voice. "I gave you what you wanted, didn't I?"

Kai flinched and she stepped back as though he'd struck her and he may as well have. The words and his suddenly cold demeanor hurt as much as any punch in the gut would have—maybe more. An empty, aching feeling radiated through her chest as she gaped at him. As she struggled to make sense of his behavior, the light around Asmodeus flickered and went out—leaving him dark once again.

"Why are you acting like this?" Her voice was barely audible. She wrapped her arms around her chest in an effort to keep from shaking, but it was no use. "I don't understand. Two minutes ago we were—"

"We were doing something I've done with countless women over several millennia." His voice, flat and unfeeling, cut through her like a knife. His brow furrowed and something that looked a lot like regret flickered briefly over his features. "It was just sex. That's all."

She searched his eyes for answers. Why was he doing this? Why would he be loving, tender and passionate one minute and then cold and cruel the next? Given everything they'd gone through together, the least he could do was be kind. But what did she expect? Kai scolded herself and hugged her arms tighter. Did she think this man—this demon—was going to run off and spend his life with her?

How could she be such a fool? Kai had never been the type of woman who could separate her libido from her heart, and she hadn't realized until just this moment that Asmodeus had a hold over both.

Anger, hurt and confusion filled Kai and without thinking about it, she hauled off and smacked Asmodeus across the face with her right hand. *Hard.* The force of the blow shimmied up her arm and rattled her hand. She grimaced as the iron band of the ring practically broke her finger but Asmodeus didn't move, didn't flinch. Nothing. Kai stilled and looked from her hand to his face. The ring hadn't burned him.

"Asmodeus," Kai murmured in an almost reverent tone as she turned her wide eyes to his. "The ring didn't burn you."

The crease between his brows deepened as he flicked his attention to the ring and then to Kai. He ran his fingers over his cheek as he held her surprised stare. "Come to think of it, it didn't hurt you when we were... " Kai trailed off and blushed as she took a step backward, needing to put some space between them before finishing the thought. "... when we were fooling around."

The two of them stood there staring at one another and though they were only a few feet apart, it felt like much further. Everything was changing faster than Kai could keep up with, and the one thing that had been keeping her sane was thinking she had Asmodeus in her corner.

Until now.

"That doesn't make sense," he murmured. Asmodeus reached out to take Kai's hand but she tucked it in her pocket. His brow furrowed and the muscles in his jaw clenched when she avoided his touch. "I don't understand what's happening."

"No." Kai shrugged. "Doesn't feel very good does it? Feeling confused and not knowing which end is up—it sucks. I have no idea why this stupid ring doesn't burn you anymore. I also don't know why you've suddenly turned into Mr. Freeze. But there's one thing I do know."

"What's that?" He asked quietly.

"You may not be human," she said through trembling lips, "But you sure can be hurtful like one. I guess I shouldn't be surprised, though, should I? My mother said the Dark Ones would hurt me ... didn't she? I guess she was right after all."

He opened his mouth to say something just as a crackling noise erupted behind Kai. She spun around to see the door once again materialize in the wall and a moment later, Isadora opened it with a big smile on her face but it vanished as soon as she set eyes on the two of them.

"Shit," Isadora sighed and looked the two of them up and down. Shaking her head, she held the door open and gestured for them to come with her. "Leave you two alone for a little while and all hell breaks loose. Not sure if you've been fucking or fighting—or both— but you better put your bullshit aside. The High Priestesses are ready to see you."

"Let's go." Kai nodded and swiped at her eyes with the back of her hand as she swept to the door without giving Asmodeus a second glance. She stuck her right hand in the pocket of her skirt and fiddled with the ring as she gave Isadora a strained smile. The cool bottle of the travel potion clinked against the ring and gave Kai a modicum of relief. If things got really bad, she could use it to disappear, at least for a while, and she knew exactly where she'd go.

"You okay?" Isadora asked softly as she wrapped her arm around Kai's shoulders and gave her a reassuring squeeze.

"I'm fine." Kai straightened her back and flicked her eyes briefly to Asmodeus who was watching her intently. "I've changed my mind about something, though."

"What's that?"

"As soon as we figure out how to get the ring off my finger, I'm giving it to Asmodeus. He can take it and go straight to Hell."

CHAPTER TEN

As they approached the massive altar Asmodeus had every one of his senses on high alert. Directly in front of the gleaming, black stone altar, the three High Priestesses were seated upon their thrones, which were made of branches. He'd refrained from using his abilities since he'd gone into hiding with Kai but he was more than prepared to use them here—if necessary.

The Witches Council had a long, tumultuous history with the Brotherhood mostly due to Satan's on-again off-again affair with Willow, the oldest and highest ranking priestess. For the past millennium, Willow and Satan had been in the off- again phase and, at the moment Willow was staring at Asmodeus as if he was guilty by association.

He subtly took stock of the cavernous Council chamber and noted the only way in or out was the door that they had entered through and, like the door in the bed chamber, this one vanished the moment it closed. The stone walls were covered in thick blankets of ivy and a gurgling stream ran along either side of the flagstone path that led to the altar steps which were made of a series of fallen tree logs.

There were no windows to speak of but at the peak of the vaulted ceiling, there was a bright spinning light that strongly resembled the afternoon sun. However, he knew the environment was enchanted to create this appearance. The sound of birds chirping and frogs croaking floated around him and the entire space made him feel as though they

108

were in a forest instead of deep inside Larrun Mountain.

Kai walked alongside him to his right and hadn't said a word to him, or spared him a glance, since they left the bedchamber. Not that he could blame her. The smack she'd given him still stung but it wasn't his face that hurt. The look on her face when he'd rejected her was worse than any punch she could throw, but he knew it was for her own good.

He acted the way he did because it was the right thing to do. He should never have succumbed to his desires and feasted on her body and soul. It was a deplorable lack of self-control and judgment but in that moment, with her beautiful, nubile body brushing against him... he simply could not stop himself.

Carnal lust and his basest desires had taken over. He was lost in the fresh lavender scent of her skin, the silken whisper of her lips and the sweet, honeyed taste of her pleasure as she came apart in his arms.

Yet, after it was over and he saw the weak glow of her aura flickering over her limp form like a bulb about to go out, Asmodeus was horrified by what he had done. He had absorbed an appalling amount of her light and they hadn't even fully made love. He knew then that he could never have her again—not at all. He had to cut her off and the best way to do that was to make her hate him.

Isadora stopped at the foot of the altar, her head bowed in deference to her leaders, but Asmodeus knew she didn't really give a shit. It was all for show and to quell their overblown egos, but damn if his old friend wasn't a good actress.

"My mistresses," Isadora said in a strong voice. "These are the individuals who are seeking your guidance and knowledge."

Stepping aside, Isadora motioned for them to approach the altar steps but Kai didn't move. Asmodeus glanced at her and the frightened look on her face made his chest ache.

"Step forward," Luna bellowed. The smallest of the three, with pale blond hair that flowed to her waist, she sat on the edge of her throne with an irritated look on her face. "Girl. Come here."

"My name is Kai." Kai squared her shoulders and tilted her chin as she walked toward the steps but stopped at the base. "I--I am a Custodian of the Light."

"We shall see," Willow said softly.

Asmodeus moved in behind Kai, but kept his eyes on Willow. Her bright red hair was tied back in a long braid and her sharp dark eyes were fixed on him.

"No one told you to approach, demon," Willow bit out.

"You have no control over me, Willow." Asmodeus kept his tone even and calm but inched closer to Kai. "I am here to get the ring and return it to the Underworld where it belongs."

"Ha!" Raven clapped her hands and pulled her feet up on the chair. She linked her arms around her knees and played with the fabric of her purple skirt. Long black hair flowed over her shoulders in thick waves and her coffee colored skin glowed with the illusion of youth. "What makes you think the Ring of Solomon belongs in the Underworld, Asmodeus?"

"Raven, you know the power it possesses." Asmodeus smirked.

"True." Raven giggled and her lavender eyes twinkled with mischief. "It will be no fun at all if you get to take it back there. I was kind of hoping the Fae would get their hands on it, but Willow is still so pissed at Satan, that she'd probably give almost anything to—"

"Enough chatter," Willow, said impatiently. "Kai, Isadora has told us about your unique... *situation*. I explained to her that I had to see the ring for myself before we could go any further. I have to be sure that you are entitled to the information you seek." She crooked one long finger at Kai. "Come here."

"Do as she says," Luna added tersely.

Kai glanced over her shoulder at Asmodeus but before he could follow her, Luna waved one hand in the air and chanted something under her breath but Asmodeus saw it and countered. The witch wanted to play dirty but he was in no mood.

Asmodeus called on the power deep inside him, heat flashed over his body as he raised both palms. A fireball shot toward Luna and exploded in mid-air as it met her spell. Kai yelped and stepped back, away from the steps but Asmodeus didn't miss the fact that she was holding her right hand to her chest and it had begun to glow.

Luna swore and rose from her seat but Willow, who hadn't taken her eyes off Asmodeus, placed one hand on Luna's arm and urged her to sit. Raven giggled and rested her chin on her knees as she looked between them.

"I suggest you keep your spells to yourself, Luna." Asmodeus' voice boomed through the room. "I have no time to screw around and very little patience."

"Funny," Willow simpered with a quick look to Kai. "That's not what I heard."

"Do you want to see the ring or not?" Kai asked boldly.

Willow waved Kai forward. Taking the steps slowly, Kai's skirt jingled as she bravely approached the three witches. Asmodeus, his body tense and ready to respond in a blink, watched the scene intently. If any of them attempted to do anything to Kai—he would kill them. Consequences be damned.

The three priestesses rose from their thrones and gathered at the center of the altar platform. Kai stopped in front of them, sucked in a deep breath and held out her right hand, showing them the Ring of Solomon.

All three witches leaned closely but they didn't speak. Luna, Willow and Raven nodded and, though they weren't speaking out loud, Asmodeus knew they were communicating telepathically. He looked to Isadora for answers but she shrugged and rolled her eyes as she mouthed the word *drama queens*.

Finally, after what felt like an eternity of silence, they stepped back and clasped hands. Luna and Raven were on either side of Willow and they stared at Kai in silence.

Kai put her hands on her hips before turning around and giving Isadora and Asmodeus a look that screamed *what the hell?*

"Well?" Kai asked in exasperation. "You've seen the ring. Now what can you tell me?"

Luna and Raven reached out toward Kai with their free hands but remained silent.

"They want to connect with your spirit, Kai," Isadora said.

"They'll be able to get a better read on you that way."

"Why didn't they just tell her that themselves?" Asmodeus seethed. Anxiety flickered up his spine and he inched closer to the steps.

"The three of them are connected by a collective consciousness and if they speak it will break their concentration." Isadora nodded and waved. "Go on, Kai. It's okay."

111

Kai licked her lower lip and nodded, but Asmodeus could tell that even though she was putting on a brave front, she was terrified. Her delicate hands reached out tentatively and then he saw her suck in a deep breath as she placed her fingers in theirs.

A bright light flashed from Kai and quickly engulfed the four women. A loud humming sound pulsed through the room as the light grew brighter still and became so blinding, that Asmodeus could no longer see Kai but only the outline of her body.

Panic consumed him as he watched her small form get swallowed up. A deep, sonic, bass pulsed around the room like an invisible snake. Whipping around them with incredible speed, the sound became deafening.

Asmodeus took the steps in one leap and dove into the light with little thought about what it would do to him or to Kai. All he knew was that he had to get her out of there.

Heat fired over him and as his hands penetrated the light, they connected with Kai's shoulders. Blind and deaf from the powerful force, his fingers curled over her and with every ounce of strength he had, pulled her toward him.

He flew back and landed on the flagstone path with Kai's lifeless body splayed over his. Facedown, her blond hair covered his chest and unadulterated fear filled him when he realized she wasn't moving. Asmodeus gently laid her on the ground and brushed the hair from her face, holding her hand in his he whispered her name.

"She is a Custodian." Luna's voice floated down from the altar. "But she must find her grandmother's Book of Spells. That is where she will find the answers she seeks."

"What have you done to her?" Asmodeus whipped his head to face them and he knew his eyes glowed red.

"We awoke the parts of her that were dormant," Willow answered.

"How do we get this ring off her finger?" he asked urgently, although deep in his gut he already knew the answer.

"You won't," Luna said firmly. "Kai will wear that ring for as long as she possesses the light."

Asmodeus swallowed hard and glanced at Isadora, who looked

as bothered by this whole thing as he felt. Kai possesses a light because she's alive, so if what they're saying is true... the ring will only come off when she dies.

"Given her Fae and witch bloodlines, this girl will be around for a very long time. My, my, my," Willow simpered. "I can't imagine the rest of the Brotherhood will be very happy about that. Can't have a Fae-witch hybrid running around with the Ring of Solomon on her pretty little hand. What on earth will they do?"

"Don't you mean what will *he* do, sister?" Raven giggled. "You know first- hand that the demons never choose a woman over the Brotherhood."

"Shut up," Willow spat.

Raven giggled and covered her mouth as she peered at Asmodeus. He glowered at them because he knew exactly what they were talking about.

The Brotherhood came first. No woman had ever come between them. Willow and Zemi, the Fae Queen, knew that first-hand, didn't they? Satan and Lucifer gave up the women they loved for the duties of the Brotherhood. If only Asmodeus' choice were that simple.

He looked into Kai's beautiful face and the dull ache in his chest grew. She moaned softly as she started to wake up and Asmodeus kissed her forehead as he knelt beside her and held her hand in his.

Walking away from her was one thing and he'd been prepared to do that but that wasn't even an option anymore.

Asmodeus only had two choices left.

Let the Brotherhood kill Kai to get the ring or fight his own brothers and die to protect her.

CHAPTER ELEVEN

Ever since Kai woke up in the Witches Council chamber, her body throbbed with what could only be described as an undercurrent of energy. It felt like a ripple of electricity ran beneath the surface of her skin and she half expected to see little flickers of it coming off her head like one of those lightning lamps they always had at science fairs.

Asmodeus had tried to help her to her feet, but Kai was still pissed and she pulled her arm away, not wanting him to touch her. To her surprise, and everyone else's, a streak of yellow light ripped across the room, making the ivy burst into flames.

Awkward.

Willow, Luna and Raven insisted that Isadora show Kai how to channel her energy so that she didn't set the entire facility on fire. In fact, the High Priestesses sent them outside to ensure their secret compound was left unscathed by Kai's attempts to use her newfound powers. So for the past several hours, Kai had been working on getting the hang of channeling the now ever present energy and so far she felt like a great big dummy.

Asmodeus, the one person she thought she could count on, had turned into a giant, silent, glowering jerk. He'd barely said two words to her since their exchange in the bedchamber, which was ironic. *He* was pissed at *her*? That was rich. Wasn't he the one who went from hot to cold in a New York minute? What right did he possibly have to be upset with her?

Kai glanced over her shoulder at him but he looked away and folded his arms over his chest as though he was keeping a look out for Ben or the Brotherhood. But Kai knew he was doing his best to avoid any contact with her.

Tears stung her eyes as she spun back around and glared at the one, singed pile of hay and the two others that remained totally untouched. So far she stunk at the magic thing—at least when she tried to use it on purpose.

Standing in the middle of a wide, green field that sat between two snow-capped mountains, Kai squinted as she shielded her eyes from the sun. Self-doubt and frustration simmered cruelly as she kicked at the grass, making the charms on her skirt jingle.

"I feel like an idiot," Kai muttered under her breath. Arms extended, palms facing out, she focused on the haystacks on the other side of the field. "Where are we anyway, Isadora? Aren't you worried that someone will wander by and see me shooting light out of my hands?"

"This whole area is enchanted," Isadora said with more than a little exasperation. Lying on the grass, she stretched her arms over her head and images of Kai's cat Zephyr came to mind. Eyes closed she waved her hands absently. "No one will see you unless I want them to. Think of it as being in an invisible, soundproof chamber in the midst of the great outdoors. However, if you see any sudden or unusual looking rays of light, do let me know."

"Rays of light?" Kai asked as she continued to try to get her powers to work. "You mean like sunlight?"

"Any light," Isadora said as he propped herself up on her elbows. "The Fae use beams of light to travel between dimensions."

"What do you mean between dimensions?" Kai dropped her hands to her side and gave Isadora a quizzical look. "The Fae aren't in this dimension and what do you mean they use beams of light?"

"Well they hang out here from time to time but the Fae world is in a different dimension. I'll tell you more later but you've got work to do right now." Isadora jutted her chin toward Kai. "Focus, Kai. Close your eyes and picture that light inside you. That is where the core of your power lies."

"It's your soul," Asmodeus said quietly.

115

"Well that's a little dramatic," Isadora scoffed. "But kind of."

"Fine," Kai sighed. She closed her eyes as Isadora instructed and picture her own aura in her mind. "Tell me more about the light and how the Fae use it to travel."

"Concentrate, Kai." Asmodeus' bossy tone drifted over Kai's shoulder with irritating clarity. "We don't have time for silly questions and nonsense about the Fae."

"Oh, really?" Kai turned around slowly and glared at him. Hands on her hips she strode toward him. "I'm *so sorry* if I'm taking too long to learn how to use magic, you big jerk. Unlike you, I am not accustomed to having balls of light flying out of my skin, so excuse the hell out of me for all of my *silly questions*," she said making air quotes. Heat fired over her flesh as her frustration grew. "And the information about the Fae isn't nonsense, thank you very much, it happens to be a part of who I am and up until yesterday, I didn't even know that. So give me a break. Okay?"

"Kai," Asmodeus' voice was even but firm and he dropped his arms to his sides as she approached. "Be careful."

"Why?" Kai shouted. Anger crawled up her back as the little hairs on her arms stood on end. Static electricity flickered around her in the air and heat spread through her chest. "Why should—"

As sweat broke out over her flesh, Kai answered her own question. Shaking, she held up her hands and saw the bright, white light of her own aura as it merged with a red glow that emanated from the ring. Her heart rate increased and the air around her suddenly felt thick, as though she was suffocating.

"What's ha-happening?" Kai asked in a shuddering breath.

"It looks like the High Priestesses did indeed help you tap into your power but you better learn some control. Those bitches cracked the seal but your emotions are triggering the natural defenses of your Fae side," Isadora said calmly. No longer lying on the grass, she'd moved in to Kai's left and spoke in soothing tones. "The Fae are known for being highly emotional and witches are deeply connected to nature. It's obvious that Asmodeus over here is capable of triggering some intense feelings in you but being out here in this natural setting, also seems to be amplifying your powers."

"I'm afraid to move," Kai whispered as she held Asmodeus'

now glowing red gaze. "I don't want to hurt anyone. Asmodeus, can you stop it like you did in the bed chamber?"

Asmodeus raised his hands, but Isadora grabbed his arm and tugged it down, preventing him from interceding.

"No," Isadora snapped. "Kai, you have to learn how to control it on your own. Close your eyes," she said quietly. Kai did as she was asked. "Good. Now tell me what you're feeling. Talk us through it."

"It's as though there's a rope of electricity running just under my skin," Kai said in a shaky breath. She held her hands in front of her, palms facing her belly. "It feels like it's looking for a way out."

"Good, child," Isadora's voice drifted over her like a comforting blanket. "I want you to imagine that you're running your hands along the rope, feel it, rushing beneath your fingers. Can you see it?"

"Yes." Kai's brow furrowed and sweat beaded on her upper lip as she strained to get control. "But why?"

"Your mind is your most powerful tool and controls all of your magic." Isadora's voice was gentle, but firm. "Now...do as I said."

Kai said nothing but nodded as she did as Isadora instructed. She pictured a beige, rough rope whipping beneath her hands so fast that the palms of her hands actually burned.

"Good. Feel it rasping beneath your fingers and when I tell you to, I want you to grab it," Isadora commanded. "Now!"

With the image firmly in her mind's eye, Kai curled her hands into fists and as she did, her body jolted with a surge of power. She gasped as every cell of her body lit up with energy. A humming filled her head and the vibration of power she'd felt since waking up grew stronger but for the first time, it didn't feel out of control.

"You have it, girl?"

Kai nodded. Body rigid and fists clenched, she grit her teeth as the otherworldly power vibrated through her.

"Good. Turn to your right. Remember those short pine trees?" Isadora asked as Kai nodded wordlessly and shifted her body in that direction. "Good. Now throw it," Isadora shouted.

Kai threw a prayer to the universe as she tossed the massive surge of energy toward the cluster of pine trees. Heat bloomed in her chest as the prickling rush of power gathered before radiating down her arms and rushing to the target. Kai screamed in triumph as brilliant streams of light shot from her hands and slammed into the trees. A split second later the branches erupted into flames.

Shaking with triumphant, adrenaline and with the ring on her hand throbbing with residual energy, Kai turned to Asmodeus and found herself staring into his glowing red gaze. His broad, muscular body loomed largely in front of her and at first glance, she thought he looked angry but it was something far more surprising---pride.

"What's the matter?" Kai said breathlessly, as the now familiar energy hummed through her body in an oddly comfortable way. It was as if the energy, at first a separate force, had now merged with Kai and two became one. "Never seen a girl throw ropes of firelight before?"

Asmodeus' eyes gleamed red as Kai inched closer but before he could answer her question, thunder rumbled and the blackest clouds she had ever seen blew in over the mountain behind him. Asmodeus growled and spun around, instinctively shielding Kai's body with his.

Black as coal, thick and billowy the odd cloud formation moved at an unnatural speed and as she watched with wonder, the ring burned against her skin like a warning.

Something or someone was coming and they were coming for her.

"What the hell is that?" Kai whispered with a mixture of fear and awe.

"The Brotherhood," Asmodeus murmured. "They found us."

A massive clap of thunder boomed through the tiny valley as the dark mass of clouds blotted out the sun and jagged streaks of lightning ripped across the sky. One bright, white bolt after another punctured the ground, scorching it, as though blindly searching for a target. Kai shrieked as the tree in front of them was struck and burst into flames.

"You must have some damn strong magic, Kai, if they found you through my cloaking spell," Isadora said. "Looks like that ring isn't masking your presence as much either."

"You mean they're in that cloud?" Kai cried with disbelief.

"No." Asmodeus watched the lighting streaks as they continued to rip across the landscape. Holding Kai behind him and remaining stone still, he linked his large hands around her wrists gently. "The cloud is probe of sorts. Lucifer is using it to pinpoint your exact location. Isadora, we have to get her out of here now. If I use my power, they'll find her through my energy waves."

"The transporter potion," Kai added quickly. "Won't that give us a few hours?" She turned to Isadora who, to Kai's shock, had turned back into the old woman she'd first encountered. "Isadora? Are you alright?"

"Go! I'm using everything I've got to reinforce this shield," Isadora shouted. "I'll hold them off as long as I can. Drink the potion and as you do, think of wherever it is that you want to go. But hold onto Asmodeus or you'll leave him behind."

Standing next to Kai, with her hands extended toward the sky, Isadora was chanting something with her eyes closed. Her long white hair whipped violently around her and her aura glowed a brilliant shade of amber. The winds howled around them as leaves and twigs flew through the air like shrapnel while tentacles of lightning continued to strike the ground in search of them.

Kai pulled her arm from Asmodeus' grasp and reached into her pocket, hidden in the folds of her skirt, searching for the precious elixir. She stumbled as a large gust of wind threatened to sweep her into the sky and she probably would have been whisked away if it weren't for Asmodeus. Eyes glowing, he linked one arm around her waist, steadying her and Kai breathed a sigh of relief as her fingers curled around the smooth glass bottle.

"I guess you're coming with me?" Kai asked, pulling the cork out of the bottle with shaking fingers. His hand splayed across her lower back as he held her close, but he said nothing. Kai lifted it to her lips. "Bottoms up."

The cool liquid coated her tongue and she grimaced from the bitter taste. As Kai drank it all down, one thought filled her head.

Take me to my grandmother's Book of Spells.

Thunder ripped through the sky and as a bolt of lightning zipped toward them, Kai dropped the bottle before grabbing Asmodeus' biceps with both hands. Her breath rushed from her lungs as the mountains vanished from sight and blue light whirled around them like a tornado in slow motion. Even though she was frightened, Kai remained resolute as Asmodeus' glowing gaze locked on hers.

119

Worried she might throw up or faint, Kai clung to Asmodeus and focused on his unwavering stare. In her peripheral vision she spotted flowing bands of energy in varying shades of blue. A glimmering light of turquoise, cobalt, and navy wrapped around them as the funnel of light swallowed them up and everything fell silent.

A split second later, the lights vanished and a wood floor materialized suddenly beneath their feet. Kai's hands remained firmly locked on Asmodeus' biceps as he held her adrenaline-fueled body against his rock hard form. His eyes flickered back to blue but he didn't loosen his hold on her.

"Looks like the potion worked," Asmodeus murmured, flicking a glance at Kai's mouth. His fingers pressed deeper into the small of her back. "You're safe for the moment."

Kai nodded as he stared down at her and her cheeks heated when her body immediately responded to his. However, as memories of his rejection came rushing back to the forefront, her lust cooled. Safe was a relative term lately. She might have been momentarily free from bodily harm but her heart was still in danger of getting another lashing from Asmodeus.

Safe? Yeah, right.

"No thanks to your brothers." Looking away, Kai broke the spell and extricated herself from his embrace. As she stepped away from him, she took in their surroundings in search of the one item she'd wanted to find. "It has to be here."

"Would you mind telling me where exactly *here* is?" Asmodeus asked as he squared his shoulders.

"I'm not exactly sure," Kai said quietly, glancing around the unfamiliar space. "If there was some light, maybe I could actually see it."

The words were barely out of her mouth when four lanterns flickered to life around the room, casting a dim glow. Kai let out a sound of awe and laughed nervously while looking from one lantern to the next.

"Cool," Kai whispered. "Ask and ye shall receive."

"So it seems," Asmodeus murmured.

"Sacks full of money," Kai shouted playfully to no one in particular. She looked around expectantly but when nothing happened she pursed her lips and elbowed him playfully. "Oh well, it was worth a try."

They stood at the center of a dusty room that immediately brought to mind the attic of the old farmhouse but this place was far more interesting. It looked like a small studio apartment, minus the kitchen.

"Not to sound like an ingrate but what do you mean, that you aren't entirely sure where we are?" He asked. "You were the one who brought us here. Are you telling me you didn't know where you were taking us?"

"I had something specific in mind." She shrugged. "What's the big deal? We got out of there, didn't we?"

To the far left of the room, there was a railing and what looked like an opening to a flight of stairs that led God knows where. On the opposite side sat a queen size bed adorned with bright, colorful pillows and a patchwork quilt. Years of dust and cobwebs loomed above the intricately carved headboard of the bed and there was a tiny nightstand with a pile of books.

To the right there was a sitting area, complete with a couch, armchair and coffee table. There were no windows and the ceiling was angled, giving the distinct impression of an attic. But when Kai saw what was behind Asmodeus, she let out a sound of awe.

"Look. It did work. " Wide eyed, Kai tapped Asmodeus on the shoulder and pointed behind him as a smile cracked her face. "When I drank the transporter potion I said I wanted to be taken to my grandmother's Book of Spells."

CHAPTER TWELVE

Asmodeus had never experienced real fear before finding Kai and it was not a feeling he wanted to become better acquainted with. His chest was tight with anxiety and tension settled in his back as he looked at the impossibly infuriating woman who, in only two short days, had managed to turn his entire universe on its ear.

He watched intently as Kai surveyed the space and his hands curled into fists at his side and fought the urge to touch her again. The warmth of her body was noticeably absent and he didn't like it one damn bit.

His jaw set as he realized what a fucking mess he was in. Asmodeus was royally screwed because for the first time in his existence he cared more about someone other than himself. The weight of that realization was unsettling, off-putting, and more than a little aggravating. His existence was far simpler when he only had to worry about ushering the damned to Hell.

When Lucifer's lightning cloud appeared, nothing mattered to Asmodeus other than making sure Kai was safe. Not his brothers. Not what they'd think of him for sheltering her. Nothing. All that mattered to Asmodeus was assuring Kai's safety. In that moment, with lightning striking all around them, he knew he would do anything to protect her---even go to war with the Brotherhood.

Wrapped up in his own thoughts, he didn't register what Kai had said until she brushed past him. He turned to find her standing in front of what looked like an altar. It was a table of polished mahogany wood, which had a scrolled design carved into the edges, and the surface was littered with similar objects to the ones Isadora had.

Bundles of herbs, feathers and bottles of various potions ran along the back edge from end to end. Taller than a regular table, it was more like the height of a bar and sitting at the center of it, perched on an easel, was an enormous, well-worn book with a familiar symbol on the cover. It was about four inches thick and had an iron lock, which seemed to be firmly set in place.

Asmodeus recognized the symbol immediately but it was not what he was expecting to see. He thought that Kai's grandmother's spell book would be the same as Isadora's but it wasn't. This book was embossed with the same exact symbol that was on the Ring of Solomon and tattooed on the back of every member of the Brotherhood.

However, there was one difference. Written in gold letters around the symbol were the words...*Custodians of the Light.*

Kai ran her fingers gently over the worn brown leather cover and brushed the lock with her fingertip. However, instead of picking the book up like he expected her to, Kai settled her hands on the surface of the table and rubbed absently at the film of dust. Asmodeus stilled but kept his sights on Kai because while he had many questions, he was certain that she had more.

"The symbols are the same," Kai said quietly.

"Yes. The symbols on the ring and the spell book match." Asmodeus wanted to touch her, to pull her into his arms and comfort her but he refrained because he didn't think he could stop himself from taking it further. "Don't you want to open it and see what's inside? This is what we've been looking for. All of the answers are in there, Kai."

"No." Kai shook her head and looked up at him, her brown eyes edged with sadness. She titled her head, her blonde hair falling across her forehead, as she whispered, "Not all of them. Turn around."

Asmodeus' brow furrowed as Kai's delicate hands settled on his arms urging him to turn and even though his gut instinct was to resist—he didn't. His muscles stiffened as Kai stood behind him and slipped her hands beneath the edge of this shirt. He grit his teeth against the seductive feel of her fingertips as they skimmed up his ribcage, pushing the fabric up and exposing his back.

Knowing what she wanted to see, Asmodeus reached behind his head, tugged his shirt off and tossed it carelessly to the ground. Hands at his side, he fought the surge of desire that fired through him as her soft flesh brushed over his. He closed his eyes as Kai traced the design of his tattoo with her fingertips, the heat of her body wafting over him seductively. Asmodeus once again found himself wrestling for control.

He wanted Kai but not just for her body. Asmodeus wanted to possess her, touch her, and claim her in every way possible. The all-consuming need to devour her body and soul was scraping at him from the inside out and threatening his weakening resolve. There was no stopping it because he knew that even now, with the few gentle strokes of her fingers he was taking her light. He didn't have to see it to know it was happening and quite frankly, he didn't want to.

It would only remind him of the monster he truly was—A Dark One stealing the light of an innocent.

"Stop," Asmodeus said, without turning around. "Kai…"

"Your tattoo," she murmured. Kai inched closer, the fabric of her blouse brushed against his back. His eyes burned red as need and carnal lust fired through him. "I thought it was similar but the one on the ring is so small, it was hard to tell….but it is. It's the same symbol as what's on the ring and on the book."

"It makes sense, doesn't it?" Asmodeus bit out. "The Custodians of the Light have the power to control the Brotherhood."

"I suppose," Kai whispered, her voice drifting over him seductively. He stilled when her hands fluttered up his arms and traced the interlocking circles of the tattoo. "This design, the one that leads up your arms to the larger one at the center of your back, it's a chain. There are seven links. Do these represent the seven of you in the Brotherhood?"

Asmodeus nodded curtly but said nothing. Need fired through him and every inch of him hardened while Kai continued her exploration. No woman had ever inspected him this way, or taken an interest in him beyond the immediate pleasures of the flesh. It was intensely intimate and erotic to have Kai looking at him this closely, to surrender himself and allow her the freedom to discover all that he was.

She was examining the design emblazoned over his back but it was more than that. She was revealing him, exposing him, peeling back the layers of his responsibility. The woman was cracking open the shell that he had dwelled in since time began.

Asmodeus flinched, almost imperceptibly, as Kai's delicate fingertips trailed around the larger circle between his shoulder blades, the one that matched the ring and the spell book.

"Is that all you believe that you are?" Kai asked quietly. "Just a link in the chain and bound to your duty. With no end and no beginning."

"It is what it is, Kai." Asmodeus turned slowly, her hands falling away from his back. "I am bound, for all eternity, to the Brotherhood, and the damned souls that dwell in the Underworld. It's why I was created. That is my purpose and nothing more." Without taking his gaze from hers he nodded toward the book. "Speaking of which, you should be getting back to yours."

The expression on Kai's face went from sweet and gentle to cold and detached in a split second. Her mouth set in a tight line and she stepped back, increasing the distance between them.

"Fine." Kai spun toward around and picked up the spell book before slicing an annoyed glance his way. "You can put your shirt back on. I saw everything that I needed to see."

"Agreed." Asmodeus tilted his head in deference as she took the book over to the small sitting area. Avoiding his gaze, Kai sat on the couch and inspected the lock. He picked up his shirt and dragged it back on. "It looks like you'll need a key."

"I think I've already got it," Kai said quietly as she squinted and inspected the circular indentation on the square lock face. "The ring is the key."

Asmodeus moved closer and braced himself for whatever came next. For all he knew, the minute she opened that book he could be toast.

"Here goes nothing." Kai glanced at him and then at the ring as she curled her right hand into a fist. "Maybe you should stand back or something?"

"Concerned for my safety?" He arched an eyebrow at her. "How touching."

"Do you try to be a jerk or does it just come naturally?"

"Well, I *am* a demon, you know," he said playfully.

"Whatever." Kai tried to suppress a smile but the glimmer of one lingered. "Don't say I didn't warn you." She let out a slow breath and whispered, "Here we go."

Kai held the thick binding of the book with her left hand and as her face twisted into a mask of concentration, making a fist, she pressed the ring into the lock and turned it to the right. The distinct sound of a lock opening echoed through the dark space, and a smile cracked Kai's face as the square iron panel fell open.

"Holy shit," Kai breathed. "It worked."

With great care, Kai lifted the cover of the book and a crackling sound filled the room as the binding of the book groaned in protest. Asmodeus, fairly certain he wasn't going to erupt into flames, moved closer as curiosity got the better of him.

"May I?" Asmodeus asked, gesturing toward the book.

"Sure." Kai shrugged and dropped her hands into her lap. "Go ahead."

Asmodeus sat next to Kai on the couch. He moved to pick up the book but as his fingers grazed the binding, the cover snapped shut and the lock clicked firmly back into place.

"Ha!" Kai sat up and pointed at him. "Looks like you're not allowed to touch it." She unlocked it again, flipped to the first page and held it open with both hands. "Let's see what this dusty old book can tell us."

"I would love nothing more than to find my existence is tied to you instead of the souls of the damned," he murmured and at first didn't realize that he'd said those words out loud. But as Kai's smiling brown eyes latched onto his, it was clear he had. "Kai...what does it say?"

"Right," Kai sighed looked back at the book. "But don't go anywhere and leave me here alone, okay?"

"Never," he whispered.

She nodded and turned her attention back to the book. He resisted the urge to brush her hair over her ear and slide his fingers along the nape of her neck. Keeping his hands to himself, Asmodeus realized that dwelling in the Underworld was a walk in the park compared to this torment.

"It's hard to make out," Kai said. "It's so faded and the pages are so old, I'm afraid it might fall apart."

She ran one finger over the first page and squinted as she leaned closer, trying to decipher what was written. He leaned in, wanting to feel the weight of her body against his, even if it was only for a moment.

Seven Custodians will complete the circle.

She who wears the ring holds the light for the dark.

"That's weird." She nibbled on her lower lip and inched closer to the book. "It says *for* the dark not *from* the dark."

Keeping her voice even, she continued reading.

When the circles of seven are dark no more, the prophecy will be fulfilled and keepers of the damned will roam the earth.

Kai let out a sound of frustration.

"So, let me get this straight. I'm a Custodian of the Light, right? But it says *she who wears the ring* and my grandmother never wore the ring but she was a Custodian too, wasn't she? But according to this prophecy, if you guys get light from the Custodians, then you're free to walk earth. So would that mean there would be Hell on Earth?"

"It would seem so," Asmodeus said quietly. "When you put on the ring, it must have set this prophecy in motion."

"Awesome." Kai let out a sharp laugh. "So I'm all that's standing between Hell and Earth? Well, not just me. It says there are seven custodians but who knows where the other six are." Her brow furrowed. "But wait a minute. Why is it a big deal for you to walk the Earth? You're here now and you've been to Earth before."

"Yes, but with limited abilities and for a finite amount of time and not all seven of us at once." Asmodeus' mind raced as he tried to calculate what all of it meant. "The Brotherhood has always been tied to Hell and to the souls of the damned. Our visits to Earth are brief and we must always return to the Underworld. I've never heard of any prophecy that would allow us to come here freely.

"What if you don't return to the Underworld?" Kai looked at

127

him with curiosity. "You said that you get three month passes here once every hundred years, so what if you stayed longer than that?"

"I would cease to exist."

"So, what? You'd just vanish?"

"Yes."

"That sucks. Then if all seven of you get filled up with light from the Custodians, then the Brotherhood could roam the Earth with no restrictions?" Kai asked. "Does that mean that the damned would come with you?"

"Possibly. But none of this happens without taking your light," Asmodeus murmured. The fearful way she looked at him filled him a looming sense of dread. He looked at his arm as it brushed along hers and noted the faint glow that crept over his flesh. "Even now, I'm taking your light from you."

"I'm fine," she insisted.

"But if I take it all, you won't be." His voice dropped to barely audible tones as the weight of the truth settled over them both. "If I take all of your light then you will die."

Asmodeus went to stand up, to increase the distance between them, but Kai grabbed him and pulled him back down next to her.

"Just hang on a second. I feel fine so I must have a lot of light or whatever." Kai slowly let go of his arm. "You're not hurting me when you touch me and I think we established how much you weren't hurting me when we were back in that bedchamber." The smile faded from her eyes. "Well, not with your touch. Your words, however, they hurt like hell."

"It is for the best." He straightened his back and kept his voice cold. He didn't miss the pained expression that flickered over her face as he abruptly changed the subject. "Let's see what else it says, but be quick. We have less than six hours until that spell wears off and we can be detected again."

Kai's mouth set in a tight line and she nodded as she turned back to the book. He knew she was upset and hurt by his rejection, but he kept telling himself it was what had to be done. Careful not to allow his body to brush hers any further, he looked back at the book. Asmodeus' attention was immediately captured by a list of names at the bottom. All seven members of the Brotherhood were listed and next to each of their names was a number.

Asmodeus was number one.

"There has to be a spell in here that can take off the ring so I can give it to you." Kai said as she ran her finger down the page. "I mean..." She stopped abruptly and her finger halted at his name. "Asmodeus. Lucifer. Satan. Mammon...this is the Brotherhood. Wait. There are numbers next to the names. Maybe it's like an index or something, or a chapter listing."

A knot formed in Asmodeus' stomach as Kai flipped to the next page and he saw his name emblazoned across the top in jagged lettering and beneath it was the Roman numeral one.

"It's a bunch of spells." Kai flipped quickly through the next several pages. "But these ingredients aren't exactly going to be easy to find. Something tells me that Wal-Mart doesn't carry mudbugs or any of this other stuff." She leaned closer. "Although, I do recognize some of the herbs and flowers. So maybe I'm not a total loss as a witch or whatever I am."

There were spells for everything that someone might need to control a demon, or more specifically, control Asmodeus. He flinched when he saw one that clearly had to do with his ability to get a hard-on. He paled, hoping Kai wouldn't see it, but she did.

"This particular spell could come in handy if you get out of line." She gave him a sidelong glance and winked. "But since I don't know how to get the tears of a warlock, you're safe for now."

"I see you haven't lost your sense of humor," Asmodeus replied as he tried not to look horrified at the notion of being rendered impotent. "But I suppose I will have to be on my best behavior."

"This isn't a spell book, it's more like a hundred and one ways to control a demon." Kai nudged his knee with hers and lifted one shoulder as she turned the pages. "There's a section of spells in here for each of you guys. It's kind of funny actually."

"How so?" Asmodeus rose from the couch. He was feeling frustrated and confused, which was exacerbated by being so close to Kai. "You are in danger of being taken to the Underworld by my brothers or being abducted by the Fae. This blasted book was supposed to provide you with more information and all it has managed to do is generate more questions. Tell me, Kai. How is any of this humorous?"

"Maybe funny isn't the right word. It's...ironic. I wouldn't have found this book without you, Asmodeus. If you hadn't taken me to see Isadora, I never would have discovered any of this." Kai closed the book and locked it before rising from the couch. Her voice was steady and her serious brown eyes met his as she moved around the table toward him. "I think it's interesting that in order to find the spells that could help me kick your demon ass, I needed *you* to do it." She closed the distance between them and stood just inches from him, her skirt brushing over his legs. "Why do you suppose that is?"

"I wish I knew." Asmodeus kept his hands curled into fists at his side, fighting the waves of desire that rippled through him ferociously.

"Because I was made to be yours," Kai said seductively. Brown eyes peeked at him beneath a row of dark lashes as her hands settled on his waist. "My whole life I've been searching for true love, for honesty and passion, for that one person who would fit with me perfectly and seamlessly. I'd search for it in every aura I read, every light I saw. All this time, Asmodeus, I thought the answers would lie in the light but instead, I found them in the dark."

Asmodeus remained still as her fingers slipped beneath the edge of his shirt and her thumbs brushed the muscles of his belly. His cock twitched and throbbed when her fingernails rasped along the skin of his waist in enticing strokes. Urgent need fired through him and he growled as he snatched her wrists, tugging her against him. "Stop that. I don't want to hurt you."

"Then stop torturing me," she whispered. Kai brushed her lips over his knuckles as he held her hands against his chest. "I don't want to be afraid anymore, Asmodeus."

"You should be," he rasped. Pushing her away he released her arms and stepped back but the wounded expression on her face just about did him in. "We don't have much time left before the Brotherhood, not to mention the Fae, discover where we are. I suggest you use that time to find a spell in that book that you can use to protect yourself or better yet, get that blasted ring off your finger."

"Fine," Kai seethed. She spun around and snatched the book off the table before storming past him to the bed on the other side of the room. "I don't even know exactly where *here* is but sure," she said sarcastically. "I'll do my fucking witch-fairy homework."

"Good." Asmodeus folded his arms over his chest as she flounced onto the bed.. "But you can relax because I *do* know where we are."

"Oh, really Mr. Smarty Pants?" Kai said without looking at him, as she flipped through the first few pages of the book. "Where are we?"

He crossed to the railing along the left side of the room and positioned himself by the opening that led down to a flight of stairs.

"We are on the second floor of your grandfather's barn."

CHAPTER THIRTEEN

"What?" Kai hopped off the bed with the heavy spell book in her hands and ran over to where Asmdoeus was standing. Grabbing the railing, she peered down the dark staircase. "Are you sure?"

"Quite." He smirked at her with the annoyingly arrogant look that made her want to alternately smack him or kiss him. "I wasn't certain at first but I've picked up on a familiar energy. It seems your cat is waiting for you downstairs."

"Zephyr?" A grin bloomed over Kai's face. When she tried to go downstairs Asmodeus' massive frame blocked her path. Kai glared up at him. "What's your problem?"

"At the moment, it's you and your ridiculous habit of running off without taking a moment to think about the consequences."

"We are under a cloaking spell, aren't we?" Kai clutched the cumbersome book to her chest and cocked one eyebrow at Asmodeus. "And if you managed to pick up on the fact that my cat is down there, then I imagine if there was anyone or anything else lurking on the property, you would have gotten wind of it. Correct?"

"Well, yes," he said slowly.

"Then what's your damage?" Kai let out an exasperated sigh. "Is there anyone else down there other than my cat?"

"Not that I can detect, but—"

"Good." Kai waved one hand, urging him to step aside. "Then move it."

Asmodeus didn't move but continued staring at her with his arms folded over his chest. Kai took a deep breath, struggling for patience. She knew that getting pissed at him would not help because it only seemed to make him dig his heels in more. So she decided on going for the pity card.

"Listen. I know you're a demon and I may have some witch and fairy blood but really, I'm just a simple human girl at heart. Aside from the fact that my life has been turned upside down, I'm exhausted, I'm starving, and I could use a snuggle,or two, from my cat, especially since snuggling with you isn't an option. So unless you want me to faint from hunger and accidentally zap your demon ass with white light, I suggest you let me go down there."

Asmodeus seemed to mull over his options. Finally, after what felt like forever he turned and headed down the steps without a word. Kai followed him down the dark, narrow staircase with the book held tightly against her chest. She heard the lock give way with a dull clicking sound and as Asmodeus pushed the creaking door open slowly, she couldn't help but hover right behind him.

He stopped in the open doorway and peered at her over his left shoulder with that cocky, lopsided grin. Kai rolled her eyes and nudged him ahead and even though she could tell he wanted to tease her for acting like a fraidy-cat, he had the good sense not to.

They moved quietly through the darkness of the barn but the smell of burnt wood and smoke filled Kai's nostrils.

They stepped through the jagged, charred hole that used to be the barn door but Asmodeus swung his left arm out, stopping her from going any further. He held one fingers to his lips and Kai, without even realizing what she was doing, curled her hand around his forearm and snuggled closer. A soft glow emanated from both of them as he shared her light, but the night remained quiet, with only the chirping sounds of insects littering the dark.

Asmodeus kept saying that stealing her light was a bad thing, but Kai's gut instinct told her that it wasn't. Seeing the shared glow between them actually gave Kai comfort and made her feel like she wasn't alone. Given the increasing weirdness in her life, being a part of something, or someone, was reassuring. Even if that *someone* was a six foot, three inch hunk of otherworldly hotness.

133

Kai was just about to ask Asmodeus if it was okay to move ahead, when the lone mewling of a cat ricocheted across the property from the direction of the house. Looking past the Dumpster that was still sitting by the barn, Kai scanned the moonlit property. It took only a moment to find the source and a smile cracked Kai's face as she spotted a pair of familiar, luminous eyes staring back at them from the steps of the house.

"Zephyr," Kai whispered in a strangled voice. Tears stung her eyes as the weight of the past twenty-four hours settled over her. "She's okay."

"Go on," Asmodeus murmured. "But we shouldn't stay here too long."

"Thank you." Kai popped up on her toes and brushed his unshaven cheek with a kiss before running across the yard.

Zephyr met Kai at the bottom of the steps and she immediately began purring like a freight train. Kai placed the book on the stairs before scooping the cat up and raining kisses all over her sweet, furry face. The affectionate moment didn't last long as the petulant Siamese soon clamored to get down and back to her busy schedule of licking herself.

"Gee, thanks," Kai laughed as Zephyr hopped from her arms and flounced into the house with her tail in the air. "Nice to see that you didn't change while I was away."

"We should go inside," Asmodeus said. He surveyed the property with the same serious intensity she'd seen at Isadora's house. "And no magic."

"Right." Kai let out a snort of derision as she hoisted the book off the steps and trotted up to the still open front door. "I don't think you have to worry about that. I don't have any eye of newt handy."

Kai made a face as she looked at the leaves and other debris that had blown in the house while she was away. "Although I have to admit finding a spell to clean the house would be great."

She placed the spell book on the dining room table and glanced at the grandfather clock in the corner. It was almost four in the morning, but truth be told, she had no idea what day it was and exhaustion flooded her as she ran her finger over the cover of the

134

book.

"There are enchantment spells in there as well." Asmodeus closed the front door and joined her in the dining room. "Enchantment spells and charms are driven by the spoken word and don't require potions. I would suggest you familiarize yourself with some of them, as I don't doubt that they will come in handy for you."

Kai felt his presence next to her and as the heat from his body drifted over her, she resisted the urge to snuggle against his chest. That's all she wanted to do. Pathetic, she thought. How pathetic was it to still be drawn to someone who's made it heartbreakingly clear that he's not interested.

She recalled what he'd said after they'd fooled around. *I gave you what you wanted.* The hollow ache of humiliation filled her chest at the memory of it. He'd only been with her out of pity or obligation and to throw herself at him now would only result in more embarrassment. When the Demon of Lust turns you down for sex, the level of mortification is off the charts.

"Kai?" His voice was gentle, tender almost. "Are you alright?"

"No, Asmodeus. I'm not alright and I doubt I ever will be again." Kai held up her hand to keep him from responding and couldn't even bring herself to look at him. She was terrified she'd see pity in his eyes and that would probably push her right over the proverbial edge. "You don't have to say anything and in fact, I'd really appreciate it if you didn't. I'm going to grab something to eat and you are welcome to help yourself to anything you want in the kitchen. Then I'm going to take a shower and change out of this gypsy get-up, so I can at least pretend to feel normal. By my count we have just over five hours until our presence can be detected."

Without waiting for a response, Kai went into the kitchen with Zephyr at her heels while Asmodeus remained in the dining room. She snagged a half full bottle of white wine from the fridge, a hunk of cheese and a box of probably stale crackers from the cabinet. He watched her silently and said nothing as she brushed past him before stopping briefly to grab the spell book.

Her arms full, she stopped at the bottom of the staircase and looked at Asmodeus, who stood in the archway of the dining room. Bathed in moonlight from the windows, he looked more desirable and

135

mysterious than ever. His serious gaze peered at her with their trademark intensity while he studied her. Arms at his sides, the muscles of his biceps twitched almost imperceptibly as he bowed his head in deference.

"I'll figure out how to get this ring off my hand and then you and I can go our separate ways." A smile played at her lips. His body was tense, poised and ready to strike at whatever enemy might come calling, but the smile faltered as she realized who it was he would likely have to fight. Her voice dropped to just above a whisper. "I'm sure the last battle you want to have is with your own brothers. Asmodeus, I'm sorry for any trouble that I've caused you and it's glaringly obvious that I never should have put on this ring. It's turned both of our lives upside-down but I'm going to try and make it right. Then you can go back to the Underworld and I can take a stab at a normal life. Who knows? Maybe I can find a nice fairy man to settle down with? Someone who won't mind if light beams shoot out of my hands." She let out a curt laugh. "I wonder if there's a dating site for freaks like me."

Without waiting for him to respond she trotted up the creaking staircase and ran down the hall to her bedroom. Kai shut the door behind her with her foot but not before Zephyr slipped into the room and hopped onto the queen size bed. Kai placed everything on the quilt next to the cat before scratching her ears.

"What the hell am I going to do?" Kai murmured. Zephyr peered at her through bright blue eyes and meowed loudly. "That sounded a lot like, *you're-screwed*. Well, a glass of wine and a hot bath may not get the ring off my finger but it might help clear my head."

Kai peeled off her clothing and tossed it on the rocking chair in the corner before grabbing the bottle of wine and going into the adjacent bathroom and running the bath. The massive claw foot bathtub filled quickly and she let the water get hot enough so that it was almost unbearable.

She snagged a glass off the bathroom sink and poured most of the wine into it. Kai took a sip and sprinkled in some foaming bath salts she'd brought with her from home before sinking into the water on a sigh.

She breathed in the heavenly lavender scent as it filled the steamy room. Kai closed her eyes and draped one arm over the edge of the tub, as she allowed her weary body to be enveloped by the scented water. She sipped the rest of the wine as she replayed the events of the past day over and over in her head but questions about the Fae kept coming to mind.

It didn't make sense to Kai that the Fae would harm her. Wasn't she one of them? In that moment Kai decided that if she couldn't find a spell that would remove the ring, then she would convince Asmodeus to ask the Fae Queen for help.

It was true that Ben had tried to take the ring but he'd been *alone*.

Kai drained the rest of the wine and placed the empty glass on the little wicker table by the tub. She squished bubbles between her fingers as she ran over everything in her mind, as if focusing on a mundane motion like that would help clear her head.

What if Ben *was* acting entirely alone? All this time they were operating under the assumption that the entire fairy world was after the ring but if that was the case then why hadn't any others come after them?

The more Kai thought about it, the more sense it made that Ben was acting on his own. What if Ben wanted the ring so he could control the demons and then use them to overthrow the Fae Queen?

"That's it!" Kai sat up quickly, sending water sloshing over the sides of the tub. "I have to find out if that's true. We are running out of options and time, so Asmodeus is going to have to put his bullshit with the fairies aside."

She hoisted herself out of the tub and stepped out on to the plush bathmat. Soapy water dripped over her naked body and she shivered as the cold air drifted in through the open door from the bedroom. Kai yanked a towel off the rack but when she reached over to close the door, she found herself staring into a pair of familiar blue eyes. And they didn't belong to the cat.

Asmodeus stood in the bedroom and was staring at Kai in all her soapy, naked glory. She probably should have shrieked at him in outrage and covered herself up.

But she didn't.

Holding his stare, Kai slowly straightened her back as his heated gaze lazily slid over her nude form from head to toe and back again. The towel slipped from Kai's hands and as it fell silently to the floor, the only sound she heard was the thundering beat of her heart as it hammered in her chest. She tried to control her breathing, so she wouldn't sound as turned on as she felt, but that was an effort in futility.

No man had ever seen her this naked or exposed. In every other intimate relationship she had, Kai would insist the lights be off during sex. She'd try to cover her nakedness whenever possible, always making the mad dash for the towel.

But not with Asmodeus.

Kai wanted him to see her. She wanted to show him every single part of herself and share herself with him in every way a woman could know a man. Even though the reality of doing that terrified her, it empowered her as well.

"Is there something I can do for you?" Kai asked in a husky and almost foreign sounding voice. Her body shivered but not from the cold. It was the hungry look in Asmodeus' eyes that had her blood humming. "Asmodeus?"

"Yes," he murmured in a deep, barely audible tone. "You should cover yourself."

"Why? You could leave. Couldn't you?" Kai shrugged casually, even though she was freaking out on the inside. "You already rejected me twice and have made it crystal clear that you don't want me, so what does it matter if you see me naked?"

"You think I don't want you?" Asmodeus strode toward her as he spoke, slowly and deliberately making his approach. Kai's heart beat faster with each step he took and the ring burned against her flesh as desire flared hard and fast. He stepped through the doorway of the bathroom moving closer until he stood just inches from Kai. His massive frame crowded her in the small space but Kai held her ground. "You cannot possibly fathom the torment I feel when you're near me."

"Oh I think I do." Kai tilted her chin defiantly and gritted her teeth against the surge of lust that fired through her, as her nipples brushed along the rough fabric his shirt. "Given the fact that you have repeatedly pushed me away, I'd say that I'm an annoying pain in the ass who frustrates you and the faster we can get you this stupid ring, the better off we'll be both be. Then I'll be free to go find a guy who won't find me so…frustrating."

"You do frustrate me but not for the reasons you're thinking." His voice, low and seductive, curled around her. It mixed with the lavender scent and Kai grew dizzy with need. He trailed one finger along the soapy flesh of her arm as he spoke, and Kai gasped when his other hand slipped along her waist and down the curve of her hip. "How could you possibly think that I don't want you? What I feel for you goes far beyond *wanting*. It is my own personal Hell to be near you and not touch you, and even though I know I could be hurting you, I can't seem to stop myself. It's selfish… and it's wrong."

Asmodeus brushed his lips across her forehead as one strong hand curled around the back of her neck. Kai's eyes fluttered closed, his gentle, but insistent touch making her weak with wanting.

"And if you mention the mere notion of being with another man," Asmodeus pulled back, his heavy lidded gaze locking with hers as his fingers pressed against the flesh along the nape of her neck, "I can't be held responsible for what I would do to any fool who would make the egregious error of trying to touch you."

"Oh really?" Kai cocked one eyebrow as her hands found their way to the edge of his t-shirt. "That's a pretty bold statement, not too mention chauvinistic and possessive. What on earth makes you think you have the right to feel that way?"

"I don't," he rasped. Asmodeus' left hand cupped Kai's ass before sliding along the slick flesh of her thigh and hoisting her leg over his hip. He tugged her against the steely evidence of his desire and growled, "But you were right, Kai…you were made to be mine and only mine."

In a blur, his mouth crashed onto hers and any ounce of self-control either of them had evaporated like steam on the mirror. His tongue, hot and demanding, tangled with hers as Kai lifted his shirt, exposing the defined muscles of his chest. He broke the kiss briefly as he took it off and tossed the offending garment aside.

Kai let out a shuddering breath, her breasts crushing against the firm planes of Asmodeus' chest. Capturing his lips with hers, Kai reached between them and fumbled with the button of his jeans before unzipping his fly and releasing him. Kai moaned as he licked and suckled her lips while the hot, heavy weight of his engorged cock settled into her eager hand.

Asmodeus let out a growl as Kai worked the smooth, heated flesh in the palm of her hand. He kicked off his boots, stepped out of his jeans before making a sound of pure pleasure. Wrapping his arms around Kai, he held her naked body against his like he would never let her go.

It was tempting and forbidden to finally succumb to the lust that burned between them ever since the moment they set eyes on one another. But in that instant it wasn't just about sex. It was about reveling in the exquisite pleasure of skin rushing against skin and one soul touching another. Kai didn't care what Asmodeus said. He had a soul and she saw it every time she looked in his eyes.

"This can't be wrong," Kai whispered as she trailed kisses down his throat and tightened her grip on his steely shaft. Asmodeus threw his head back while she ran her hand up and down the hot length of his erection.

Dropping to her knees, her hands settled over his narrow waist and her thumbs brushed over the enticing v-shaped muscles that led to a dark nest of curls. Kai peered up at Asmodeus as he tangled one hand in her long hair. He peered at her through glowing, red eyes and trailed one finger along the curve of her cheek. Holding his gaze, Kai ran her tongue over the rigid length of his cock before wrapping her lips around the swollen head.

He swore as Kai held the base and took him deeper with each long, slow stroke of her mouth. His entire frame was taut with restrained need and with every pass, she sensed him creeping closer to the edge. Her own body throbbed with desire and as the aching between her legs grew, she knew there was only one thing that would satisfy her.

Asmodeus, knowing exactly what she needed, linked his arms around her biceps and pulled her to her feet before kissing her deeply. He tasted like pure, unadulterated lust and Kai couldn't get enough. He tilted her head, rushing his tongue along hers before trailing hot, wet kisses down her throat as he cradled her head lovingly. Kai gripped his broad shoulders with both hands as he slid his hand between their naked bodies and backed her up against the edge of the sink.

Kai moaned when Asmodeus' talented fingers found her most sensitive spot and began to move. As he rubbed the tiny nub in slow, deliberate circles, Asmodeus lifted his head and captured Kai's gaze with his. Moaning, she bit her lower lip as wave after wave of pleasure rippled through her and brought her to the edge. A cocky grin cracked Asmodeus' face as he slid two fingers inside her hot, wet channel in a slow, deliberate pass.

Kai gasped when he took his time and applied sweet, torturous pressure in all the right spots. Grabbing the edge of the counter, Kai threw her head back as he held her hip with one hand and massaged her pussy with the other. As the beginning of an orgasm coiled deep inside her, the glow around their bodies bloomed and in that moment she knew what they both needed.

"Fuck me," Kai gasped. Sitting up, she took his face in her hands and kissed him deeply. "I want you inside me when I come," she murmured against his lips.

Asmodeus' strong hands cupped her hips as Kai wrapped her legs around him. With his intense blue eyes locked on hers, Kai reached between them and positioned the head of his cock against her swollen entrance. Kai guided the engorged length of him inside and as he filled her inch, by wickedly delicious inch, the light around them throbbed in pulsing strobes.

Gripping his shoulders their bodies joined, Kai trailed her tongue along his lower lip as Asmodeus pumped his hips with one, long, deep pass after another. Muscles straining, his tempo increased and he pounded into her time and again, rubbing against her clit with each quick, deliberate stroke. Kai's fingernails dug into his back and as the sweet, torturous orgasm crested, they cried out in unison as the world around them erupted with a flash of light.

141

CHAPTER FOURTEEN

It went without saying that Asmodeus had lots of sex in his day, but all of it paled in comparison to what he'd shared with Kai. He'd pleasured women before and had been pleasured in return, but it was limited to the flesh. What happened with Kai could only be described as soul stirring and considering he didn't have a soul that was saying something.

Making love to Kai had gone beyond a physical exchange. Looking at his hands, Asmodeus swore quietly as the glow of Kai's aura still flowed over his body. It had been two hours since he'd made love to her but so far, Asmodeus had continued to retain her light. As he stared out the window of the dining room, looking for any signs of the Brotherhood, he couldn't help but worry.

Asmodeus glanced over his shoulder at her. Sitting at the dining room table, her blonde hair spilling over her shoulders, Kai looked more like a Fae than she ever had. Her aura glowed in a deeper shade of yellow, and the look of concentration as she scoured the pages of the spell book was nothing short of fierce. Asmodeus hoped Kai was right and that by taking her light he wasn't destroying her but everything he ever knew told him he was.

"Asmodeus." Her brown eyes flicked up and she smirked as she caught him studying her. "You're staring at me again."

"Yes." He nodded and turned back to the window. "That's something you should grow accustomed to."

Kai seemed totally unscathed by their encounter and her light still glowed… but for how long? How long until it went out and she…

"I'm fine, Asmodeus," Kai whispered as she linked her arms around his waist and nuzzled against his back. Kissing his shoulder, she murmured, "In fact, I'm better than fine."

"We should leave now." He held her hands against his stomach and squeezed. "You wanted some time to rest and you got it."

"Rest?" Kai bit his arm playfully and slipped around so that she was standing in front of him. She hooked her thumbs through the belt loops on his jeans and wiggled her eyebrows at him. "I'd say we didn't do much resting in the bathroom and then when you carried me to bed…well…we didn't *rest* much there either."

"I didn't hear any complaints," he murmured. Asmodeus dipped his head low and brushed his mouth over hers as memories of their lovemaking filled his head. However, darkness edged in when he recalled the threat that their enemies continued to pose. "My apologies, Ms. Kelly. I would love nothing more than to *rest* with you time and again but we do have to leave before the Fae, or my brothers, find us."

"Okay, then where do you plan on taking me?" Kai cocked her head and gave him that challenging look that he adored before linking her arms around his waist. "Because the spell that's hiding us is going to wear off in an hour or so and when it does we'll be sitting ducks, so to speak."

Asmodeus opened his mouth to respond but Kai popped up on her toes and kissed him. As her sweet lips melded with his, and he held her in his arms, any thought to argue was driven from him and all he could think about was being inside her again. She smelled like lavender and summertime and innocence. Everything he wasn't.

Kai broke the kiss and settled her hands on his chest, pushing him gently away. Asmodeus growled when she tried to wiggle out of his embrace but he kept one arm linked around her waist, holding her to him.

"Just listen to me for a minute, okay?" Kai pressed one finger to his lips and shook her head. "Shut it and listen. Before you came upstairs and distracted me so deliciously, I was thinking a lot about the Fae and Ben."

"What about them?" His expression darkened and his hold on her tightened. "I despise the idea of you spending any time thinking about that fairy man."

"Oh please. I wasn't thinking about him like that." Kai rolled her eyes. "I propose that Ben was acting on his own, and *not* on behalf of the Fae Queen. Think about it for a second, Asmodeus. Why haven't any other Fae come after us? If they can travel using beams of light, or whatever, wouldn't a whole army of them have attacked me that night in the barn? And why haven't any others come after us since then? What if Ben wants the ring so he can use the Brotherhood to overthrow Zemi and rule the Fae?"

"I...," Asmodeus' brow furrowed as he thought about what Kai suggested. It hadn't even occurred to him that Ben was acting on his own but as Kai laid it all out in front of him, it began to make sense. "I suppose your theory holds some merit but even if what you're suggesting is true, what do you---" Kai's smile broadened and Asmodeus scoffed audibly as he realized what she was suggesting. "Are you implying that we should approach the Fae Queen for assistance the way we did with the Witches Council?"

"Yup." Kai grinned and smacked Asmodeus on his ass before going back to the spell book. "You bet I am. The witches helped me find my way to this spell book, so who knows what kind of info I could get from the Fae. Right?"

"Not a chance." Hands on his hips he turned and looked at her with nothing less than total incredulity. "Even if what you're saying is true--and I highly doubt that it is--there's no way that Zemi would help us. She hates the Brotherhood, Lucifer most of all."

"Well, maybe she does but I still say we keep it on the table as a last resort." Kai picked up the spell book and went to the front door. "I also vote that we stay right here. Running away isn't going to solve anything."

"So you just want to wait here, like a sitting duck?

"No. We'll be proactive." Kai tilted her chin as that steely look in her eye returned. "I'm going to go back up to my grandmother's altar in the barn to see what else I can find. Then I'm going to try to commit a few of these charms to memory. Besides, this place is isolated and I can practice using my magic without worrying about any regular people seeing me, not to mention, if we venture into the general public, who knows what minions could be lurking around the corner. Right?"

Before he could answer her, Kai pushed open the screen door and bounced down the steps toward the barn. Asmodeus laughed and shook his head as he realized she was absolutely right. Running would solve nothing. As he followed her outside, Asmodeus surveyed the expansive property and knew the battle would be fought here.

***

Over the past couple of hours, Kai had managed to memorize two charms and was relatively confident she'd remember them when she had to. One was supposed to turn the subject to ice or make them freeze like ice, Kai wasn't sure which it was and the other was supposed to render her opponent blind. Whether or not they were going to work was another story entirely.

She'd scoured the rest of the second story of the barn for any other item that might be able to tell her more about her grandmother or the family line, but no such luck. However, by all accounts, this space seemed to have gone untouched since her grandmother died. There was no sign that Kai's mother had ever been up here, and chances were, she didn't even know it existed.

Back at the house, she'd changed into a pair of shorts, a tank top and her purple Converse sneakers because if she was going to fight off crazies, she wanted to feel as normal as possible. However, so far it wasn't working. Learning how to cast spells and engaging in toe-curling sex with a demon, wasn't normal...*at all*.

Kai's gaze settled on Asmodeus. He hovered by the open hay-bale door in his usual battle-ready stance. She hadn't even noticed that door was there before but when they came back upstairs, Asmodeus went right over and pushed it open. Arms at his side, back straight and muscles taut, he looked every bit the demon he'd always been, with one exception.

Asmodeus now had an aura. It was faint but it was there.

Kai smiled wistfully because so far she had been right. Asmodeus may have been taking her light but it wasn't harming her.

145

In fact, she felt more alive and empowered than ever before. Her own aura wasn't dimmed at all but she did notice the color had changed to a brighter yellow—more like Ben's light.

More like a Fae.

Sitting on the edge of the bed, she flipped through the back half of the book and stilled when she came to the very last page. There was a folded piece of paper wedged into the binding. Kai pulled it gently from its resting place, careful not to tear it, and held it between shaking fingers.

"Holy shit," Kai whispered.

"What is it?" He turned toward her but Kai was already up and headed to the altar with the book and the mysterious paper. "What did you find?"

"There's a note," Kai said quietly as she laid the book on the altar.

"From your grandmother?"

"I'm not sure." With shaking fingers, Kai carefully opened the yellowed paper. She read the message that was scrawled across the page and looked at Asmodeus through wide eyes. "It's not from my grandmother. It's from my grandfather... Jacob."

Asmodeus stood by her side as they read the letter together.

Kristine,

I know your stay with me is almost over and soon it will be time for you to leave. As promised, I will take good care of our darling Katherine and I will be sure that she seeks you out when she comes of age, so that she can learn the magic of the Fae. She carries your light and though it still remains to be seen if she's one of the Chosen Ones, it's clear to me that she's as special as you are. I'm still not sure why you picked me but I will always be grateful that you did. You've given me a beautiful daughter and a world filled with magic. I will love you forever.

--Jacob

"He knew," Kai whispered. A gust of wind whisked through the large open window, making the paper flutter in her hand. She shook

146

her head in disbelief as she looked at Asmodeus, who seemed equally surprised. "Jacob knew that my grandmother was Fae?"

"She must have been a pureblood," Asmodeus said evenly. The muscles in his jaw flickered as tension radiated off him. "Your grandmother didn't die. She left. By the sound of it, she went back to the Fae dimension."

"But why? Why would she leave them and why didn't my mother go find her?" Kai ran her fingertip over the yellow, aged paper as she spoke. Memories of her mother came roaring to life. "She ran away when she was eighteen and married my father. Why didn't Jacob tell her about the Fae?"

"Perhaps he did tell her, Kai," Asmodeus said gently. "Maybe it wasn't your grandfather that she was running from all these years."

"She was running from herself, wasn't she?" Kai murmured. She lifted one shoulder and looked into Asmodeus' piercing blue eyes. "I don't suppose I could blame her. I've had the urge to run ever since this crazy shit show started."

"It makes sense. You said your mother knew about the light but she didn't like using it because she was worried about attracting the Dark Ones." Asmodeus' voice was edged with sadness. "Perhaps he did tell her but for whatever reason it frightened her. That is probably why Jacob left you this place. Maybe he wanted you to have a chance to find out who you really are?"

"Damn it. I feel like for every step forward, we take ten steps back and I end up with a hundred more questions." Kai folded the paper back up and slipped it into the spell book before locking it up again. She put her head in her hands and let out a weary sigh. "You know what this means, don't you? Now we *have* to go to the Fae."

Asmodeus started to argue with her but the loud, rumbling engine of a truck captured their attention. His eyes flickered to red as he ran to the window but the tension eased almost as quickly as it came.

"It's the company coming to retrieve your Dumpster." He leaned against the wall and folded his arms over his chest as he sliced a look in Kai's direction. "This conversation isn't over, by the way."

"Nope." Kai winked and smiled sweetly. "But I'm not going to change my mind, so there's really no point in arguing with me."

147

She spun on her heels and trotted down the steps leaving Asmodeus grumbling by the window. She couldn't help but laugh at his reaction but when she pushed the door open, her smile fell. Looking at the giant, burnt hole in the barn door, she wondered how on earth she would explain that to the guy driving the truck.

Kai squinted against the morning sunlight as she approached the loud, smelly truck that had already hooked up to the Dumpster. She waved at the guy as he climbed out of the cab. His aura was gray and musty, which told Kai he wasn't exactly the kind of person she'd want to hang around with. He was a big, burly, beast of a man with dark hair that covered his arms and crept out the neck of his t-shirt. It seemed to sprout from everywhere except his head.

"Hi." Kai waved and shouted over the engine as she backed toward the house. She flicked her gaze toward the barn but Asmodeus hadn't come out yet. "I'll grab my check book and be right out."

"Right." The man nodded as he hitched up his dirty jeans and spit onto the ground as he watched her go. "Two fifty," he yelled.

Kai ran into the house and scoured the first floor for her purse. Standing in the kitchen, she stopped for a minute, trying to remember the last time she'd even seen the damn bag. She heard the front door slam as she went into the mudroom off the kitchen.

"Hey, Asmodeus?" Kai shouted. "Have you seen my purse?" Emerging back into the kitchen empty handed, she puffed her hair out of her face. "I can't find…"

Kai stopped dead in her tracks as the cold hand of fear gripped her by the throat because it wasn't Asmodeus who'd come into the house. It was the guy who'd been driving the truck but he looked…different.

A slack-jawed expression covered his face and his eyes were completely white, as though they'd rolled back in his head. His hands were balled into fists and his enormous sweaty, hairy frame filled the doorway, blocking her exit. Trying not to panic, Kai inched her way along the edge of the counter, trying to keep the table between them because for the life of her she couldn't remember either of those stupid charms.

Awesome.

"Why are you in here?" Kai asked in a shaking voice. Her mind

148

raced as she tried to remember what Isadora told her to do. A second later, prickling heat began to gather in her chest. "I told you that I'd bring the check out to you."

"The ring," he gurgled. The man took two lurching steps forward into the kitchen as a string of drool dangled from his plump lower lip. "Give us the ring, Kai."

The voice that boomed out of this man was not natural and it wasn't one voice. It sounded like several voices speaking at once and Kai knew it was the Brotherhood.

"So," Kai murmured, while inching toward the doorway but she froze when he lurched closer. "This is one of your minions."

"Hand over the ring, Custodian," he shouted.

The screeching chorus of voices pierced the air as the man's mouth opened wide and he let out a howling wail. At the same time the engine of the truck seemed to roar even louder outside and she doubted Asmodeus would hear what was happening.

Kai slammed her hands over her ears, attempting to drown out the deafening sound of the frightening shriek. It felt like a swarm of bees were buzzing inside her head and scraping at her skull from the inside out. She wanted to use one of the charms she memorized but the sound was making it impossible to concentrate.

She shook her head, trying to get away from the sickening sensation and horrid sounds but it was inescapable. The minion lunged toward Kai, knocking over chairs and though his fingers scraped her arm, she managed to elude his grasp and keep the table between them. He let out another ferocious scream, grabbed the kitchen table with both hands and tossed it into the windows as Kai screamed Asmodeus' name.

Glass shattered around her and as the tortured creature stumbled across the kitchen and grabbed Kai by the throat, the power in her chest coiled and burned. It was the same, flickering rush of power she'd felt in the barn and in the field—and Kai knew what she had to do. Picturing the rope of energy, like Isadora told her, Kai focused on it as she placed both hands on the man's plump chest.

She gasped for air as he tightened his grip on her throat and Kai tried to fight the self-defeating effects of panic. As she pictured the tentacle of light shooting through her, a prickling rush of energy shot

149

down her arms and sent the man flying across the kitchen and into the stove.

Stunned and with smoldering singe marks on his chest, he screamed in rage as he tried to regain his footing, which gave Kai enough time to run. Calling Asmodeus' name, she burst through the front door and to her relief he was already on his way, running toward her.

"What's happening?" Eyes glowing, he held her in his arms and cradled her against his chest but the respite only lasted a moment. "Minion," he whispered, tightening his hold on her. "Bastards shielded their presence from me."

The engine of the truck shut off abruptly and Kai jumped when the screen door slammed, shattering the momentary silence. Shaking, Kai turned to see the truck driver shuffling toward them. He reminded her of a marionette and she realized that's really what the pathetic man was. The Brotherhood was using his body and he was merely a puppet on a string.

His belly, which hung over his pants, was now partially exposed as his shirt retreated up the swollen mound of flesh. His arms hung at his sides loosely and that same vacant expression covered his face as he took one lurching step after the other.

"Give her to us, Asmodeus," said the terrifying chorus of voices. "Or she will be our undoing."

"Kai is a Custodian and the ring has bonded with her. It cannot be removed." Asmodeus pushed Kai behind him as he spoke. "She poses no threat to the Brotherhood."

"She wears the Ring of Solomon." The minion's face reddened but his eyes remained white as they stared vacantly back at Kai. "You cannot hide her from us. We are everywhere." The tortured creature opened his mouth in a silent scream and his body shuddered violently before speaking again. "We will not stop until we have the ring safely in the Underworld. You must not protect her."

"He doesn't have to," Kai bit out. She was furious with herself for hiding behind Asmodeus like some helpless female. She was tired of feeling out of control and sick to death of being a victim of her circumstances. She stepped out from behind Asmodeus and as the now familiar tentacle of energy writhed beneath her flesh, she focused her rage and extended her arms toward the minion. "I can protect myself," she whispered. "I am a Custodian of the Light."

The ring glowing red, Kai pictured the light firing through her body and as the power gathered in her chest, she threw the surge of energy toward the staggering man. Kai shook as rippling waves of white light flew from her hands and slammed into the minion, sending him flying through the air. He landed on the porch with a deafening crash as the boards cracked beneath the weight of his rotund body.

Shaking and lightheaded, Kai let out a sound of relief asAsmodeus wrapped one arm around her waist. She hated to admit it, but his embrace was the only thing keeping her from crumpling to the ground in a weak-kneed pile. He kissed the top of her head and cradled her shivering form against his resolute one.

"Don't fuck with the fairy," Kai said in a shuddering voice. Squeezing her eyes shut she let out a laugh that sounded a little crazy as she hugged Asmodeus as tight as possible. Burying her face against his chest she muttered, "Or the fairy-witch, or whatever."

"Perhaps my brothers will think twice before sending more minions after you," Asmodeus murmured before kissing the top of Kai's head. His hands ran down her back and settled on her hips. "Who knows they may even…"

Asmodeus stopped speaking and his body went completely rigid. Kai's brow furrowed as she pulled back to look him in the eye, but he was staring over her head at something to his left. The expression on his face made her stomach twist into knots because it was nothing short of fury.

"What is it?" Kai turned to the left and squinted against the sun to see what had captured his attention so swiftly. In the distance, with the mountains looming behind them, Kai saw six individuals walking toward them. Ripples of heat radiated around them in the sun and as the dark figures moved closer, it was glaringly obvious who they were.

The Brotherhood had come to Bliss.

CHAPTER FIFTEEN

"What do we do now?" Kai whispered, her fingers clutching the fabric of his t-shirt. She kept her voice low and did her best not to sound completely terrified, but failed miserably. "Do we try to make a run for it?"

"Where?" Asmodeus kept his intense sights on the men as they strode closer in slow, unhurried strides. Their slow pace reminded Kai of Jason or Michael Meyers. It was as if there was no point in running because their victims could never escape. "Now that they've found you, there's no way to hide from them. Our only hope is that they'll listen to reason and give us more time."

"This is a pretty ballsy move if they think I can control them with this ring."

"True. But given the fact that you haven't tried to control me, Lucifer is taking a gamble and testing the waters, so to speak. Perhaps, he'll be willing to listen." Asmodeus' deep voice resonated through his chest as she remained in his embrace. "But...stay alert and don't let your guard down for a second."

Kai leaned deeper into Asmodeus' embrace while his brothers strode casually across the field. They were all rather tall and muscular, except for the one furthest to the right. He was shorter with a stocky, muscular build and he glared at Asmodeus with nothing short of contempt. They were all dressed in black t-shirts and fatigues and clearly ready for combat. Kai didn't see any weapons but given the extent of their powers, they probably didn't need them.

Like Asmodeus was when Kai first met him, all six of them were without light—Dark Ones.

"Who's the guy on the end," Kai whispered. She didn't take her eyes off them. "The shorter one. He's looking at you like he hates you."

"That's Levi." Asmodeus smirked and flicked his gaze to her briefly. "Leviathan the Demon of Envy. Levi is always bitching about getting screwed on one level or another."

"Leviathan?" She shuddered and tried not to look as terrified as she felt. "Great."

When the six of them were about fifty feet away, Asmodeus raised his hand and shouted, "That's close enough."

They didn't stop moving until the tall blonde one in the center stopped and held up both hands, signaling the others to follow his lead.

"You must be Lucifer," Kai said in a surprisingly calm voice. "I'd say it's nice to meet you but—it's not."

"Lucifer, Demon of Pride and leader of the Brotherhood. Charmed to meet you, Kai Kelly." Lucifer flashed a toothy, white grin and bowed his platinum blonde head. He was strikingly handsome. They all were but there was a cold, cruelty in Lucifer's pale, green eyes that sent a chill up Kai's back. "No wonder you've become infatuated with her, Asmodeus. She's feisty and you know how much I adore feisty women."

"You better behave yourselves," Kai said all too sweetly. "Or you're going to see just how feisty I can be."

"I thought you might try to use that ring against us, so a witch friend of mine cast a little spell for us. It's temporary but will last long enough to accomplish what we need to here." Lucifer jutted a thumb toward Satan. "He may have messed up our relationship with Willow and the Witches Council, but there a few witches out there who still enjoy our *charms*."

Kai tried not to look surprised but failed miserably and she didn't miss the look of triumph on Lucifer's face.

"She's not going with you to the Underworld and, charmed protection or not, I would advise against trying to press the issue." Asmodeus nodded toward the broken body of the minion. "As you can see, it didn't work out too well for him."

"That guy's soul has been tagged as mine for years." The redhead winked at Kai and jutted both thumbs at his chest. "Beelzebub, Demon of Gluttony, but you can call me Zeb. In fact, that greedy bastard's soul is down there right now with the rest of today's damned who are waiting to be processed."

"You mean...I killed him?" Kai said in a barely audible voice as she flicked a glance at the body on the porch.

"Not really," Zeb laughed. "He was gonna die of a heart attack today anyway so it's kind of a wash."

"Can we get this fucking show on the road?" Satan, a brunette with dark, almost black eyes, pounded his fist into his palm and glared at Kai. "I'm tired of all the talking because as usual, it's not getting us anywhere. Give us the girl, Asmodeus."

"Kai, I'd like you to meet Satan, the Demon of Wrath." Asmodeus let out a weary sigh. "He's never one to mince words and usually lets his fists do the talking."

"Right," Kai pursed her lips and nodded. "You're the guy who jilted Willow."

"Is that what she told you?" Satan's face carved into a mask of fury. "That I jilted her? Really? Next time you see her, why don't you ask her about that little spell she cast on me?"

Kai's eyebrows flew up in surprise and if she didn't know better, she'd swear that hurt flickered across his features. Perhaps there was more to that story than Willow had let on, but Kai knew better than anyone that there were three sides to every story.

His side. Her side. And the truth.

"Sucker." The one on the left, with long, sandy, blonde hair and an easy going smile, laughed slowly. He reminded Kai of the stoners she knew in high school. "She's still so pissed at you."

"Fuck you, Belphegor." Satan's eyes blazed red and his hands balled into fists at his side. He, on the other hand, reminded Kai of the football jocks who stuck the nerds in the garbage cans. "Shut up."

"Whatever, man." Belphegor pushed his long hair off his forehead and closed his eyes as he turned his face toward the sun. "I say we chill out and see what happens next."

"The Demon of Sloth wants to avoid a conflict? What a

shocker." Satan punched Belphegor on the arm. "You'll never change, you lazy shit."

"Cut the crap." Belphegor grimaced and rubbed at his arm. "Dick."

"Enough," Lucifer bellowed. The others immediately came to attention but Kai was still thinking about Satan's reaction at the mention of Willow. "We don't have time for your bickering."

"What about Zemi?" Kai asked innocently. "You have any time for her?"

"What?" Lucifer seethed. "You will not speak her name to me."

Eyes blazing in two red slashes Lucifer took a step toward Kai but she watched in awe as a red ball of fire materialized in front of her. Asmodeus, his arm extended, murmured, "I suggest you back off."

"Still being led around by your libido, Asmodeus." Lucifer's eyes flickered back to green as he laughed. "Last time you acted like this... it got you a half-mortal son."

"You have a son?" Kai asked, slicing a glance at Asmodeus. "You admit you're a demon but leave out the part about having a kid?"

"A discussion for another time and he's not a kid anymore," he murmured. The fireball still hovered in front of his extended hand. "Lucifer, are you willing to hear me out?"

"Of course." Lucifer extended his arms and smiled before clasping his hands in front of him. "Enlighten us and speaking of light... that's an interesting light you have, Asmodeus. I hope poor Kai is feeling alright."

"Right," Kai snorted. "Like you give a shit."

"No, Lucifer." Asmodeus shook his head. "Just you. The others go back to the Underworld or things are going to get messy. I don't want to fight all of you but I will if I have to. You'll have to kill me before I let you take her with you."

"You would fight your own brothers for this...half-breed fairy?" Satan groused. "You're pathetic."

"Hey," Kai said, feeling more than a little wounded. "I'm right here ya know."

"You say anything like that again," Asmodeus ground out, "and I'll shove this fireball right up your wrath loving ass."

"Fine," Lucifer said calmly. "They'll go."

"What?" The one with the shaggy black hair and hazel eyes

voiced his displeasure. He was the only one who'd remained silent up until this point. "Why do we have to leave? Our fate is at just as much risk as yours, Lucifer. This is bullshit."

"Because I said so, Mammon." Lucifer kept his voice calm and commanding as he waved them off. "Now go. All of you."

They all grumbled their displeasure but amid an explosive flash of flames and smoke, all of them, other than Lucifer, vanished into thin air.

"I did as you asked." Lucifer moved closer until he was only a few feet away but Kai didn't take her eyes off him. "Now start talking."

***

Kai sat at the dining room table with two demons, her spell book, and a glass of wine. She didn't give a shit that it was first thing in the morning. If ever there was a time that called for a drink—it was now. Even Zephyr knew enough to leave and had high-tailed it out of the house.

For the past hour they'd been filling Lucifer in on everything-- the inability to remove the ring, the Custodians of the Light, Kai's mixed heritage and the Prophecy. He'd tried to touch the spell book but it continuously slid out of his reach anytime he attempted it. However, his entire demeanor changed when Kai told him her theory about Ben and the Fae Queen.

"You think this Ben Flaherty, the fairy man, wants to overthrow Zemi and wants the ring so he can use the Brotherhood to do it?" Lucifer asked calmly with his hands folded on the table, making him look almost like a CEO in a board meeting or something. He was powerful, perfectly manicured and intelligent but that controlled façade wavered whenever he discussed Zemi. "He wants to harm her?"

"It's just a theory." Kai sipped her wine and noticed that Lucifer's gaze was drawn to the ring. "Do you want to try and take it off?"

She extended her hand to him but Asmodeus covered it with his

"Kai?" Asmodeus cautioned. "We don't know what kind of effect it may have on Lucifer."

"Thank you, *Kai*." Lucifer's voice was edged with irritation as he shot Asmodeus an annoyed look. "I would like to try and remove it."

"Suit yourself," Asmodeus sighed and sat back in the chair. "Don't say I didn't warn you."

"It might hurt," Kai warned as she held her hand out over the table.

"I'm the Demon of Pride," Lucifer said haughtily as he reached toward her. "I don't feel pain."

However, as his fingertips brushed the ring, a look of pure horror covered his face and he swore at the top of his lungs as he yanked his hand away. Rubbing the wounded hand absently he gaped at the ring. Kai covered her mouth to keep from laughing, but Asmodeus made no such attempt and laughed his ass off. Kai looked between the two men and wasn't sure what was more humorous, the look of shock on Lucifer's face or the guffaws coming out of Asmodeus.

"I'm sorry." Asmodeus' laughter faded and he swiped at his eyes, as tears streamed down his face. "Shit. That was great."

"It's not funny," Lucifer sniffed and folded his hands on the table again. "However, it is irritating."

"Sorry." Kai shrugged. "I'm not making it do that. It used to burn Asmodeus but not anymore."

"That wouldn't have anything to do with the fact that you have an aura now, would it?" Lucifer made a face of displeasure and pointed to Asmodeus' arms. "Your marks seem lighter as well."

"His tattoos?" Kai hadn't noticed a difference but with everything that had happened, she was lucky she remembered her own name and wasn't in a looney bin.

"Yes," Lucifer said quietly as he held his arms out for her inspection. "It's the mark that all members of the Brotherhood possess."

Kai nodded. She'd seen it clearly on all of the men earlier but hadn't noticed a change in Asmodeus'. She grabbed his arm and ran her fingers over the linked circles as the muscles flickered beneath her touch.

"He's right." She looked at Lucifer and then to Asmodeus as she released him. "Yours are lighter—a dark gray rather than the jet black circles on Lucifer."

"Strange." Asmodeus' brow furrowed before glancing at Lucifer. "But that's really not important. I'm more concerned about whether or not the Brotherhood will back off while we try to figure out what's happening with Kai and the ring."

"Yes." Lucifer smiled at Kai. "Well, I can tell you that *I'm* only concerned about the ring."

"Jeez." Kai rolled her eyes and rose from her chair. Leaning both hands on the table she locked gazes with Lucifer. "You're a piece of work, you know that? Isn't it glaringly obvious to you that I have no intention of trying to control you, or anyone else in the Brotherhood, with this ring? What the heck do I have to do to convince you? Sign a contract with my blood or something? I could have taken control over Asmodeus a while ago if that was my intention. Believe me, dude. I don't want to control the Underworld. Okay? I'd just like to get some kind of handle on my life."

"Like I said…she's feisty." Lucifer's blonde eyebrows flew up and a smile played at his lips. "I will admit that you don't seem to have world domination on your mind but what you need to realize, Ms. Kelly, is that it's not actually about *you*. It's about the Ring of Solomon. You may not want to use it for nefarious purposes against the Brotherhood but there are others, like our friend Ben Flaherty, who do."

Lucifer rose elegantly from his seat but kept his gaze on Kai and out of the corner of her eye, she saw Asmodeus stand as well. The tension level in the room went from zero to sixty in a split second.

"As long as you wear that ring, my brothers and I are at risk."

"I can take care of myself," Kai countered.

"Perhaps," Lucifer said quietly. Sadness rimmed his eyes. "You are powerful, Kai, no one will deny that, but you are not immortal. You are made of flesh and bone. You should be kept someplace safe until we can remove the ring from your finger."

"She's not going to the Underworld," Asmodeus said firmly. "That's not protecting her, it would be tormenting her. I won't allow it."

"It's not up to you," Lucifer kept his stony stare on Kai. "Kai is an intelligent woman and I'm sure she'll come to the most rational conclusion. I can't imagine Kai wants to spend her life running and fighting. Do you, Kai?"

"No," Kai murmured. She grabbed her glass and went to the kitchen door. "But you know what? I also don't want to spend it wondering. I need answers. I want to know why the hell my grandmother ditched the family and why my mother never went looking for her. I also want to know who the other six Custodians are. I want answers and I'm not going anywhere until I get them."

The sunlight streamed through the windows into the dining room and Kai let out a weary sigh as she leaned against the doorjamb. The yellow light, with dust particles drifting through it like glitter, looked almost like liquid gold.

"I want the truth," Kai whispered as she reached out and swept her hand through the rays of the sun. "I need to know."

The dust danced around her fingers as if it were alive and everything around her seemed to fall away as subtle tinkling sound filled her head. Smiling wistfully, Kai ran her index finger through the fluttering, glittering dust within the golden light. It sounded like wind chimes and as the music grew louder, the ray of light expanded as though the sun were rising at a rapid pace.

Kai could hear Asmodeus shouting her name but he sounded far away and the enticing, gentle sound of wind chimes consumed her. The golden light covered Kai, making her feel weightless. It was like being wrapped up in the arms of her mother and soon all she could see was light.

***

It happened in a split second.

One instant Kai was standing in the doorway of the kitchen and the next she vanished. Asmodeus screamed her name and lunged toward her as the unnatural swath of light swallowed her up --but he was too late.

Shaking with incandescent rage, Asmodeus turned slowly toward Lucifer who stared at him through a furious, burning gaze. Neither of them had to say a word. They knew exactly what happened.

Kai had been taken by the Fae.

159

CHAPTER SIXTEEN

The veil of sleep lifted and a smile played upon Kai's lips while recalling the beautiful dream. She'd been swimming through golden, glitter filled air. It was the most liberating sensation she'd ever experienced and her body still hummed from the energizing memory.

Stretching her arms over her head, Kai let out a sound of pure contentment. She hadn't felt this rested in years but it was probably because the bed was as soft as a marshmallow and the blankets were so luxurious, Kai likened it to being inside a cocoon of cashmere.

Bed? How did she get in bed? Oh shit, not again.

"Asmodeus?" Kai murmured.

Her eyes flew open as she shot up in the bed and scanned the unfamiliar surroundings. She was in a bedroom, albeit a beautiful one, that conjured up images of a quaint B&B she once went to in New Hampshire. It wasn't that place exactly, but the feel was similar to be sure.

Asmodeus was nowhere to be seen and Kai was totally alone in the massive, lavender and white bedroom. She lifted the covers to find she was no longer wearing her clothes, but a simple white nightgown.

"What the heck is going on now?" Kai whispered to the empty room. Was this the Underworld? Had Lucifer pulled a fast one and tricked them somehow? She pursed her lips while surveying the pristine condition of the room. "If this is the Underworld then sign me up. This place is nicer than my old apartment."

Kai could tell by the feel of the air that it wasn't the witch's lair beneath Larrun Mountain. The energy in that place had a distinct vibration that she didn't feel here and it was probably because the witch's lair was underground. No. This place, wherever it was, had a vastly different feel than anywhere else she'd ever been.

Scanning the spacious room for any clue to where she might be, Kai's attention was captured by a familiar object on the nightstand. It was her grandmother's spell book. Kai frowned. She was here and so was the spell book, but there was no sign of Asmodeus, or anyone else.

Kai was alone.

Heat bloomed in her chest as panic began to creep its way in and right about now, she'd even be happy to see Lucifer's smug face. She scrambled to recall what happened but the last thing Kai remembered was being in the dining room of her grandfather's house talking to Asmodeus and Lucifer.

And a glittering ray of light.

Flashes from the dream flickered through her mind. She remembered standing in the doorway of the kitchen and running her finger through the beam of sunlight as it streamed in through the window. Beams of light and wind chimes. That was the very last memory Kai had before she woke up here.

"But where the hell is here?"

Pushing the covers off, she swung her legs over the side of the bed and shivered when her bare feet touched the cool wood floor. She spotted a gauzy bathrobe draped over the white wicker rocking chair in the corner and quickly pulled it on. The shades were drawn but sunlight streamed in around the edges, giving the room an ethereal glow. The walls were trimmed in lavender but everything else was a pristine shade of white. The bed, a large wardrobe on the other side of the room, the side tables and even the loveseat, was stark white.

Kai tiptoed over to the door but the glass handle wouldn't budge and heat prickled down her arms as she realized she was locked in. She stepped back and closed her eyes, wrestling for control of the volatile energy as it rippled beneath her skin. To her great relief, the power recoiled and though it still hummed in Kai's chest, she knew there was no longer a threat of blowing anything up.

161

Kai's breath caught in her throat and she froze when the familiar sound of wind chimes jingled on the other side of the door. She tiptoed over and pressed her ear to the cool surface. Straining to listen, Kai's heart began to pound as she heard the sound of footsteps.

Someone was coming.

Kai ran over to the bed, dove beneath the covers and immediately pretended to be asleep. Her heart thundered in her chest and she struggled to keep her breathing steady. The sound of the door opening shattered the quiet of the room and Kai stilled

"I know you're not asleep." The teasing, singsong tone of a woman's voice drifted through the room along with the enticing aroma of pancakes and bacon. Kai's stomach growled loudly. "Why don't you stop playing possum and sit up and have some breakfast."

Kai, with the covers pulled up to her chin, steeled her courage and opened her eyes but nothing could have prepared her for what she saw. A woman she'd seen only in a few old pictures smiled at her lovingly.

It was her grandmother, Kristine.

***

Twelve hours had passed since Kai vanished into the beam of sunlight, but it felt like an eternity and Asmodeus thought he'd go mad with worry. Lucifer, who was equally unsettled by Kai's departure, assured Asmodeus that he could get him to the Fae dimension.

Asmodeus had his doubts because no member of the Brotherhood, other than Lucifer, had ever traveled to the Fae realm. Given the fact he and Zemi were still in their off-again phase, getting there seemed next to impossible. But Lucifer muttered something about a potion before leaving for the Underworld in a flash of smoke and fire.

Standing on the porch of Kai's house, Asmodeus looked out over the moonlit property and swore. For the first time in his bleak existence, he felt remarkably out of place. Not having Kai by his side gave him a heightened sense of uneasiness and nothing would soothe him except being with her.

Zephyr meowed loudly at his feet as she wove her way around his ankles, rubbing against him seeking affection. He let out a sigh before scooping up the persistent Siamese and scratching her behind her ears.

"I miss her too," Asmodeus murmured as the cat purred loudly in his arms. "We'll get her back."

"Since when did you start talking to cats?" Lucifer's irritated voice floated out of the darkness. "How mortal of you."

The cat leapt from Asmodeus' arms as Lucifer strode up the steps, looking every bit the arrogant bastard he was.

"Did you get it?" Asmodeus asked impatiently. "Did you get the potion?"

"You can relax." Lucifer smirked at the cat as it hissed at him before running off. "Whoever has Kai, obviously hasn't gotten the ring or we'd be dancing around like a couple of drooling minions by now."

Pure, unadulterated fury fired through Asmodeus. Quicker than lightning he grabbed Lucifer by the front of his shirt and slammed him up against the wall, sending splinters of wood flying through the air.

"Careful, or you'll break Kai's house," Lucifer quipped. Asmodeus held him there, eyes burning, he kept Lucifer pinned but all the son of a bitch did was smile. "To say nothing of my waning patience."

"How many times do I have to tell you that I don't give a shit about that ring?" Asmodeus seethed, his face just inches from his brother. "Not anymore. All I care about is getting Kai back here safely. Do you understand that you selfish bastard? Can you possibly comprehend caring about anyone or anything more than your own miserable ass?"

"Careful, brother," Lucifer said in a barely audible tone as his eyes flickered to bright red. "Given that I'm the one who has your ticket to fairy land, I suggest you let me go. Otherwise, I might change my mind about helping you."

"Helping me? That's a fucking joke." Asmodeus' jaw clenched and he growled as he shoved his brother one more time before releasing him. Stepping back, he fought to keep his anger under control because like it or not, he needed Lucifer's help. "You don't give a shit about Kai. All you care about is getting the ring away from

163

the Fae. The only person you're concerned about helping is yourself."

"Love has blinded you, hasn't it?" Lucifer smoothed the fabric of his shirt before reaching into his pants pocket and pulling out a small, black bottle. Rolling it between his fingers, he leaned casually against the wall and leveled those sharp, green eyes at Asmodeus. "It's actually not *just* me I'm concerned about, brother. I'm surprised at you, Asmodeus. Allowing a woman to take priority over the Brotherhood?"

"I'm sure you are." Asmodeus folded his arms over his chest and met Lucifer's intense gaze. "Zemi knows better than anyone that you would never allow a woman to interfere with you duty. Doesn't she?"

Lucifer stilled and his mask of arrogant calm wavered briefly as he closed his fingers around the precious potion in his hand. Fighting to keep his cool, the muscle in his jaw clenched, but Asmodeus knew him well enough to know that he'd touched a nerve.

"Drink this." Lucifer tossed the bottle at Asmodeus, who caught it in mid-air. "It's my last dose and you're on your own once you get there. Kai will have to figure out how to get you back but since she's part Fae, the woman should be able to use their light travel."

"Where did--?"

"It's left over from my momentary lapse of judgment with that woman," Lucifer groused, referring to Zemi. "Women are nothing but trouble. Love and emotions are a sure fire way to fuck up your existence and something tells me you're going to find that out the hard way. Stand in a beam of light and drink that. It will take you the Fae dimension, but I have no idea where you'll end up or who'll you find there. When I went it was always to see…well, for all I know, you could land in Zemi's castle and then you're really screwed"

"You're not coming?" Asmodeus asked with more than a little surprise. "You've literally been raising hell about getting the ring back and now you're sitting this part out? I thought you would want all seven of us to go."

"First of all, that elixir will only take one of us at a time and secondly, showing up with the entire Brotherhood would be nothing short of a call to war. Besides, our presence there would be of little help," Lucifer murmured. "Your only hope is that Kai was correct and Zemi doesn't want that ring in the first place."

"I'll get Kai and bring her back with the ring." Asmodeus clutched the bottle tightly and kept his sights on Lucifer. Back straight and hands at his side, his brother always looked ready for a fight. He brushed past Asmodeus and strode down the steps before stopping in the driveway. "I'll fix this," Asmodeus called after him.

"And then what?" Lucifer asked quietly. He turned around slowly and leveled a stern stare at Asmodeus. "What do you plan on doing with her? Will Kai work side by side with you in the Underworld ushering the damned to their eternity of torment? You can't stay here and if you are foolish enough to attempt it, then you'll destroy her. Even that ridiculous prophecy in Kai's spell book confirmed it."

Asmodeus opened his mouth to respond but snapped it shut because he had no idea how to answer that question. He tightened his grip on the potion, a sense of foreboding crawling up his back. Lucifer was absolutely correct.

"It's brutal isn't it?" Lucifer whispered.

"What is?" Asmodeus snapped as frustration and helplessness swamped him.

"The moment when you realize you're not worthy of love."

Heavy silence fell between them as Lucifer looked up at the moonlit sky and the leaden truth of his statement fell over Asmodeus like a shroud. For a moment, just a moment, he'd allowed himself to believe that Kai could be his and that love, real, pure love was within his reach but nothing could have been further from the truth.

When Lucifer finally turned his attention back to Asmodeus, he could swear he saw something akin to sadness in his brother's eyes.

"We were created to oversee the damned for all eternity. Nothing more. Nothing less. Love is not a sin. It is not an abomination. It's the kindest, gentlest part of humanity and we were not made to experience it or bask in its glow." He lowered his voice to almost a whisper. "And if you try to capture it, you will turn that love and anyone who touches it, to ash."

Before Asmodeus could respond, Lucifer vanished in a flash of fire. As the last wisps of smoke dissipated, Lucifer's warning ran through his mind but he pushed the hopeless message back. All that mattered was making certain Kai was safe.

165

Ripping the cork out of the bottle, Asmodeus ran down to the driveway and stood in a ray of moonlight that shone through the trees. Drinking down the sweet liquid, he kept one thought in the forefront of his mind…. *I may not be worthy of love but Kai is.*

An odd tingling sensation spread across Asmodeus' chest, and radiated through his body as he watched the beam of moonlight grow. The pale light washed over him slowly, like water spreading on a smooth surface and the odd tingling sensation grew with it.

Out of nowhere, gut wrenching pain flashed around him and it felt as though his chest were being pinned in some kind of invisible vice. The crushing pressure stole his breath and his fists clenched, turning the bottle to dust as the throbbing agony surged. Asmodeus screamed with rage and blinding pain as the world around him exploded in a luminous blaze.

He landed facedown, on the marble floor with an audible grunt and immediately pushed himself up onto all fours. Asmodeus' vision blurred and he shook his head, trying to bring the room into focus but everything was spinning. Muscles straining, palms pressed against the cool stone, he heard the faint sound of a woman laughing.

"Who's there?" Something wet spilled into his eyes, further blurring his vision. Asmodeus shoved himself to his knees, and though his body wavered, he managed to stay upright. He pressed the heels of his hands against his eyes and when he pulled them away, he saw his right hand was covered in blood. "What's going on?"

Squinting, he looked up and found himself face to face with Zemi, the Fae Queen. Asmodeus looked around and swore under his breath because he was in what looked like Zemi's bedroom. But he didn't see any sign of Kai.

If he ever got out of this he was going to beat the shit out of Lucifer.

"Sorry, demon," she said, with a wicked grin. "You're in my dimension now."

Asmodeus, struggling to get to his feet, raised his hand to conjure up a ball of fire in an attempt to have Zemi keep her distance. However, much to his surprise, no magic came. Swearing, he tried again but still…nothing.

Asmodeus was powerless, bleeding, and mortal.

166

Zemi must have seen the look of confusion on his face and it only made her laugh harder. A sudden wave of dizziness swamped him but despite his best efforts to remain upright, he dropped to the floor like a stone.

"Didn't Lucifer tell you?" Zemi's amused voice was the last thing he heard, as the darkness closed in. "Demons have no power in the Fae dimension. Welcome to you own personal hell."

167

CHAPTER SEVENTEEN

Dressed in a long sapphire colored gown of chiffon and silk, the woman who looked just like Kai's grandmother, placed the tray of food onto a small table. Kai, not quite sure she was actually seeing what she thought she was seeing, pushed herself up to a sitting position while she watched the woman unfurl a napkin and arrange the food.

"Y—you're my...I mean you look just like my..." Kai's voice trailed off as she struggled to make sense of the latest development. "This is nuts."

"I'm your grandmother." The elegant woman dressed in blue turned to face her. "You can call me Kristine and to be quite honest, I'm surprised by your reaction. You already know that you have Fae and Witch blood. You're sleeping with one of the Brotherhood and you wear the Ring of Solomon. Really, Kai, I thought you'd be happy to see me."

Large dark, brown eyes and wavy, sandy blonde hair framed a heart shaped face that was strikingly similar to Kai's mother. Tall, and with the lithe, elegant body of a dancer, she was luminous, beautiful and young. By all accounts, Kai's grandmother should be eighty or so years old but this woman didn't look a day over thirty.

"You should really eat it before it gets cold." She gestured to the lovely breakfast she'd set out on the table. "Come sit on the loveseat and have some breakfast. I believe I made your favorite."

Unmoving, Kai stared at Kristine like she'd just sprouted wings. Clutching the sheet between her fingers, her stomach rumbled again from the delectable smell of bacon.

"You did." Kai laughed nervously and shrugged. "Pancakes and bacon is my favorite breakfast."

"See? I'm not so bad at this grandmother thing." Kristine winked and clapped her hands. "Come on, now. We have a big day ahead of us, so come, sit and eat."

"That's it?" Kai asked with more than a little incredulity. "You show up, back from the grave, looking more like my sister than my grandmother, and you want me to eat breakfast? What's going on? Where's Asmodeus?"

"He's in the mortal dimension or maybe he went back to the Underworld but wherever he is, I'm sure he's pitching a fit as we speak. Now have something to eat, Kai." Kristine smoothed the chiffon of her long dress and swept over to the rocking chair before making herself comfortable in it. She waved toward the food. "Come on."

"You're a piece of work, lady." Kai shook her head as she got out of bed and went to the couch because crazy or not, she was hungry. "I tell you what. I'll make you a deal. I'll eat this if you'll tell me what in the hell is going on. For starters, where am I and where have you been all this time?"

"I've been here," she waved her hand around, "in the Fae dimension."

"I'm in the Fae dimension?" Kai looked around the room and when her gaze drifted over the sunlight peeking in around the shades, it came together. "My dream..."

"It wasn't a dream. I brought you here using our light travel but you fainted along the way." Kristine lifted one shoulder. "I would have come for you sooner but you hadn't tapped into enough of your Fae power and I had to wait and see if you and Asmodeus would...connect."

"Yeah, we connected but I hope you haven't been peeking through any keyholes." Kai's face heated with embarrassment. "As for the fainting thing, apparently magical travel makes me pass out. Who knew?"

169

"At any rate, you have to understand that time doesn't pass here the same way it does in the human dimension." Kristine pointed at the food. Kai let out a sigh before sitting down, grabbing a piece of bacon and taking a big bite. "Thank you. Now. Where was I? Oh yes, the time discrepancy. Time in the mortal dimension passes rather quickly compared to time here. The mortals exist in dog years compared to the Fae."

Kai's forkful of pancake came to a screeching halt. "Are you saying that we're dogs?"

"No," Kristine laughed and began to rock slowly in the chair. "I'm just trying to help you understand. One Fae year is like twenty of your mortal years. As far as you're concerned, I've been gone for a little over fifty years but from my perspective it's only been about two and a half."

"Okay," Kai said slowly between bites of the remarkably delicious breakfast. "That's all fine and dandy but why did you leave? Why didn't you come back and teach my mother or me? It would have been nice to have some guidance through this freak show that I now call a life."

"I tried. I came back for your mother when she turned eighteen." Her eyes lit up as she recalled the memory. "I was so excited to show Katherine the altar I created for her in the barn and Jacob had kept it up so beautifully. I'd hoped it would please her to see me but it didn't." The smile faded from her eyes as she let out a slow breath in a clear attempt to get a handle on her burgeoning emotions. "When I told your mother about being Fae and a Custodian of the Light, she was enraged, furious with me for staying away. She blamed the Fae world for robbing her of a normal childhood, for taking her mother away and for the pain I caused Jacob. Katherine wanted no part of the magical realm. I was, as you can imagine, saddened by her decision and when I saw that she hadn't discovered the ring *and* that she wanted to marry that mortal…"

"Watch it, Grandma. That mortal was my father and he was awesome. As for my mom, well, I can't really blame her for being pissed." Kai wiped her mouth with the napkin before tossing it onto the plate. She pulled her feet up on to the loveseat and looked at Kristine with thinly veiled disgust. "You left her, Kristine. You didn't

170

die like she thought you did. You weren't taken…you chose to leave your own daughter. That's shitty, lady. What kind of mother leaves her kid like that?"

"You don't understand, Kai." Kristine's voice wavered and she looked down at her hands that were folded in her lap. "I didn't have a choice. I had to stay away until Katherine was of age. That's how it's done…how it's always been done. Zemi is quite firm on that rule."

"How what's done?" Kai scoffed. "Being a crappy mother?"

Kristine flinched but sucked in a calming breath and for a split second, Kai actually felt sorry for her.

"When Fae produce Halfling children, we aren't permitted to participate in their upbringing. It's the only way to determine if they truly possess the light of the Fae and Katherine was not only Fae but, part Witch as well. Jacob didn't know it but he had Witch blood running in his veins." Kristine looked down at her hands and her voice dropped to a whisper. "That's why I chose him."

"Okay. What do you mean chose him?" Kai rolled her eyes and grabbed the mug of coffee off the tray before taking a sip. Part of her wished it that was a shot of bourbon. "And why are you running off to earth and making Halfling fairy babies or whatever."

"The Prophecy. Zemi has always been obsessed with it," Kristine whispered as her large, dark eyes latched onto Kai's. "It could not be set in motion until the arrival of the first Chosen One who we knew would be a Fae Custodian with Witch blood. Though several Halfling children have been born over the years, none had discovered the ring…until now."

"The Prophecy?" Kai swallowed the lump of dread in her throat and gripped the mug. "Right. I read about that in the spell book," she said with a gesture toward the nightstand. "How did the book get here anyway?"

"It will always remain with the one who wears the ring."

"Weird, but okay." Kai sipped her coffee and stared at the book. "So when I stumbled across that crate and put the ring on, then I kick started this Prophecy. Right?"

"Yes, but you didn't just stumble across it. You are the first of seven Chosen Ones. There will be one for each member of the Brotherhood." Katherine rose from the chair and sat next to Kai on the loveseat. She brushed Kai's hair off her shoulder and trailed one finger down her cheek in a heartbreakingly tender gesture. "You are the first, Kai and we have been waiting for you for three thousand years."

"To do what? What the hell am I being chosen to do exactly? Because Asmodeus and I were reading that Prophecy and I have to tell you, it sounds kind of sketchy." Kai's gut clenched, terrified of hearing the answer but at the same time desperate to find out. "Do you know what Asmodeus and the rest of the Brotherhood think? They are under the impression that Zemi, and the rest of the Fae, wants to use the ring to turn them into slaves or something."

"No," Kristine said quietly. "That is not what the Prophecy foretells."

"I didn't think so," Kai said triumphantly. "It didn't really make sense to me given what's happened or, more to the point, what hasn't happened. So, I was thinking—"

Kai was about to tell Kristine about her theory regarding Ben Flaherty but the familiar tune of wind chimes could be heard in the hallway. Kristine stilled as though she was listening to something Kai couldn't hear and then nodded curtly. The wind chimes jingled again briefly before silence fell over the room.

"What does that sound mean?" Kai asked slowly as she set the coffee mug down and looked from the door to Kristine. "That wind chime noise. I heard it right before you beamed me here, or whatever."

"It happens when we use light travel. That was Bentley, the queen's advisor, and I thought he would come in and introduce himself but he was in far too much of a rush." Kristine forced a smile and patted Kai on the arm before rising to her feet. "We will be leaving shortly for Zemi's palace. You must get ready to go now."

"But, how were you talking to him?"

"Telepathy," she interrupted. Kristine's entire demeanor had changed. She went from being loving and concerned, to cold and uptight in a split second. "You don't possess that ability because you aren't pure Fae. Please, Kai. We have to go."

There was something about the way Kristine referenced not being pure Fae that sent a chill up Kai's spine. Without looking at Kai, she went over to the massive white wardrobe, opened it up and pointed to an array of colorful dresses.

"You may select whichever one you like. They are all in your size." Kristine swept over and opened the door, which led out to an empty hallway that reminded Kai of a hotel. "I'll be right out here but please hurry as Zemi doesn't like to be kept waiting."

"Kristine, wait." Kai hopped off the loveseat, ran over and grabbed her grandmother's arm before she could leave. "If Zemi doesn't want to enslave Asmodeus and the others, then what does she want? I mean, why did you bring me here?"

"To destroy the Brotherhood," Kristine whispered. "The Chosen Ones are the only ones capable of doing it."

"Me?" Kai let out a sound of total incredulity. "No way. This is crazy. She wants me to kill them? Asmodeus? Well, forget it. I won't do it."

"Yes, you will." Kristine lowered her gaze briefly before looking Kai dead in the eyes. Her voice dropped low but she held Kai's stunned gaze as she repeated the Prophecy. "She who wears the ring holds the light for the dark. When the circles of seven are dark no more, the prophecy will be fulfilled and keepers of the damned will roam the earth."

"I know," Kai said wearily. "Asmodeus and the rest of the Brotherhood will steal the Custodian's light and roam the earth. Blah blah blah. I don't see how that's destroying them."

"Kai." Her eyes, rimmed with sadness, stared earnestly at Kai. "Please, just get dressed."

"This is crazy." Kai almost laughed out loud. "If you ask me there's a lot of room for misinterpretation with the whole Prophecy deal. I can't get a straight answer out of anyone."

"Zemi will explain it further to you. My cousin is well versed in the Prophecy."

"Wait?" Kai stilled. "Zemi is related to you? Er—to me?"

"Yes," Kristine said quickly. "She's our cousin and a Custodian of the Light as well, like all women in my clan."

"Well you and our cousin have it all messed up." Kai ran over and grabbed the spell book. Using the ring, she opened it and flipped to the correct page. "All this time and you'd think you'd have a clear explanation. Geez"

"Kai, we don't have time for this," she said impatiently. "Your destiny was laid out thousands of years ago. Please don't fight it or you'll only make it worse. Now, we must go."

"What's the rush?" Kai grabbed Kristine's arm before she could leave. "I mean I know Zemi's got a bug up her ass about the Brotherhood and everything but Asmodeus isn't even here."

"Yes, he is." Her mouth set in a grim line. "Zemi is holding him prisoner."

***

White-hot pain fired through Asmodeus' head and he grit his teeth against the unfamiliar and unpleasant sensation. He had no idea how long he'd been chained up like a dog but it seemed like forever. He'd been trying, to no avail, to use his powers but it was futile. He was completely void of all of his abilities.

Talk about being screwed.

Arms stretched over his head, he was chained and shackled by his wrists and ankles to the wall of what could only be described as a dungeon. His shirt had been removed at some point, as well as his shoes, and the jeans he was wearing were bloody and torn.

The dank room was about thirty feet square with various torture chamber type devices scattered about. Light flickered through the cracks of a massive wooden door that was directly across from him and the only other light came from a window to the left that was about ten feet up with iron bars cutting through it.

He could see that the sky was a vibrant shade of lavender and had pink clouds floating in it that conjured up images of cotton candy. Asmodeus let out a wry laugh but winced as bone rattling pain fired through him from head to toe. It was fascinating that so much discomfort could be generated from such a small movement.

A jingling sound of keys and the click of the lock opening caught Asmodeus' attention. Biting through the vicious pain ripping through his head, he forced himself to stand as tall as possible. The last thing he wanted to do was show weakness because he knew that's exactly what Zemi wanted.

Two of Zemi's guards, both men dressed in full silver armor, carried long spears of about seven feet. They stepped in the room and immediately stood at attention on either side of the door. A moment later, Zemi whisked into the room, looking as beautiful and deadly as ever.

Adorned in a medieval style ivory dress with intricate gold embellishments, she emitted a distinctly royal air, which was accentuated by the gold and pearl crown she wore. A mass of springy, black, curls spilled down her back and bright, blue eyes stared at him from a stunningly, lovely face. Zemi may have been one pissed off Fae Queen but there was no denying her beauty. It was no wonder Lucifer was so hung up on her.

"Are you enjoying your stay with us, demon?" Zemi asked. Hands clasped in front of her, she walked around slowly but didn't take her eyes off him. "I was hoping these accommodations would make you feel right at home."

"The name is Asmodeus," he seethed. "And I think your accommodations suck ass. Is this how you treat all of your guests, Zemi? Because so far, I'm not impressed."

"Well, first of all, Asmodeus," she murmured. Her blue eyes narrowed as she moved closer. "You aren't my guest. You are an interloper who arrived in my dimension, to say nothing of my quarters, unannounced and uninvited. Now, why are you here? It wouldn't have anything to do with the Ring of Solomon, would it?"

"I don't give a crap about that ring. You know damn well why I'm here. You took Kai. Where is she?" He tugged on the chains and shouted, "What have you done with her, Zemi?"

"Kai?" Zemi asked with feigned ignorance. "Whomever are you talking about?"

"You know exactly *whom* I'm talking about, you crazy bitch," he seethed.

Quicker than a snake, one of the soldiers ran over and whacked Asmodeus across the mouth with the shaft of his spear, making his teeth clatter. Pain ricocheted through his head and had him seeing stars but Asmodeus refused to flinch.

"Not bad for a fairy," Asmodeus ground out before spitting blood on the ground. "But I've been hit harder by an elf."

The soldier went to hit Asmodeus again but Zemi raised her hand, immediately bringing him to a halt.

175

"Enough." Zemi waved the soldier back. "We wouldn't want to wear him out before the big event this evening. He is, after all, not exactly himself."

"Yeah," Asmodeus licked the cut on his lip and adjusted his stance as the shackles dug into his ankles. "Lucifer failed to mention that demons turn mortal in the Fae dimension. I'll have to remember to give him a kick in the nuts next the time I see him."

"Yes. Soulless demons are quite powerless in the Fae realm." Zemi's lips lifted at the corner. "I'm sure omitting that little fact was an oversight because I can't imagine your trusted leader would intentionally send you here so horribly unprepared."

"So, what's going on tonight? Have a big feast prepared in my honor?" He wrapped his fingers around the chain, wishing he could rip them out of the wall, but knowing he couldn't. "What time should I be ready? I hope it's not a dressy event because I left my tux on Earth."

"So nice to see you've kept your sense of humor." Zemi laughed loudly and clapped her hands. "I'll be meeting with your girlfriend in a just a little while so I can explain it all to her. She might not be on board right away but once I tell her how you've been lying to her all this time...well...I'm sure she'll see my side of things."

"What are you talking about?" A sense of foreboding crawled up his back. "I haven't been lying to Kai."

"Yes, you have." A smile cracked her face as she inched closer. Zemi trailed one silver fingernail down his cheek but he jerked his head away. "She's really quite lovely, Asmodeus. Too bad it won't work out for the two of you but then again it never could, could it?" Her smile faded and a cruel look glimmered in her eyes. Zemi's voice dropped to a whisper. "The Brotherhood never chooses a woman over duty. Do they? You boys lie through your teeth to get what you want and then once you have it, you toss us aside as though we mean nothing."

"You'd know that better than anyone, wouldn't you, Zemi?" He leaned closer, meeting her challenge. "Lucifer really fucked you up, didn't he? What happened between the two of you?"

Zemi's mouth set in a tight line as her hands curled at her sides. Asmodeus saw that cool exterior falter and in that moment, she actually reminded him quite a bit of Lucifer. They were both arrogant leaders, obsessed with duty and obligation and neither wanted to admit being wounded by the other.

The only weakness Lucifer and Zemi seemed to have was each other.

"Leave us," Zemi shouted to the guards. She glanced over her shoulder. "Now."

When they didn't move, she swept both arms wide and in a flash, a hurricane strength gust of wind rushed across the room and tossed the two men out like rag dolls. The door slammed shut behind them as Zemi smoothed her windblown hair and folded her hands delicately in front of her once again.

"You will not speak of him to me." Zemi attempted to keep her voice calm but it continued to rise as she spoke. "All of the members of the Brotherhood are cut from the same cloth. You're all liars. You seduced Kai's heart and body just so you could get the ring from her and once you have it, you'll toss her aside as though she means nothing to you at all."

"Listen, I don't know what went down between you and Lucifer and to be honest, I don't give a shit. But I can tell you that I care about Kai. All I want is for her to be safe and to get that ring off her hand so everyone will leave her alone. So you can go ahead and do whatever you want to me. Kill me. Draw and quarter me. I don't give a shit." Muscles straining, he yanked on the chains but barely felt the metal as it cut into his flesh. "Just get that ring off Kai's finger and send her back to the mortal dimension safely. That's all I want."

"Is that so?" Zemi smirked and walked away from him toward the light of the window. With her back to him she continued speaking. "Am I supposed to believe that you, a member of the Brotherhood, would put a woman's needs above your own?"

"Believe what you want, lady." Blood dripped down his arms from the gashes along his wrists. "I love Kai and I'll do whatever I have to in order to protect her."

"Love? You love her?" Zemi spun around to face him. Eyes wild, she flew toward him, grabbed him by the chin and smashed his head against the stone. "Don't you dare speak to me about love," she seethed. Her face just inches from his, he saw silver tears glimmering in her eyes and her voice shook with emotion. "Demons know nothing of love or tenderness. You have no right to use a word when you have no comprehension of its meaning."

Zemi's hand fell away from his face as sterling tears fell over her cheeks. She backed away from him and into the beam of golden light that streamed into the room through the window.

"You shall be dark no more, demon." A jingling, musical sound filled the space and as the sunlight consumed her, Zemi murmured, "The Prophecy has begun."

CHAPTER EIGHTEEN

Kai tried not to fidget with the green, silk and chiffon dress she chose but it was a far cry from her cut off jeans and sneakers. The silver trimmed concoction was beautiful but Kai felt like an escapee from a Renaissance fair or something. At least the silver slippers were comfortable and easy to walk in—or run in-- if the situation called for it.

Walking along the empty hallway with Kristine, Kai couldn't stop thinking about what she had said. Zemi brought Kai here so she could kill Asmodeus? Not a chance. Aside from the fact that she wasn't in favor of running around killing people, she also happened to be in love with the big brute.

I'm in love with a demon.

A smile played at her lips. Asmodeus may be a demon but he was the kindest, most thoughtful man she'd ever been involved with. Demon or not, she loved him. Kai clutched the spell book to her chest as she followed Kristine. There had to be something, some kind of spell or whammy, in this damn book that would help her and Asmodeus get out of this mess. She just needed the time to find one so she could figure out how to get back to her own dimension.

About a hundred more questions rattled through Kai's head but when Kristine opened the door at the end of the hall, and Kai caught a glimpse of the world outside, her mind went blank. She stood at the top of a set of marble steps and gaped at the stunningly gorgeous

179

world before her. It was like something out of a storybook from her childhood and everything someone would expect from a fairy dimension.

The sky reminded her of a watercolor painting she'd seen once. It was rippling waves of lavender and purple as far as the eye could see. Aside from the two yellow suns, the swath of violet sky was marred only by the occasional dots of pink, tufted clouds. The trees and grass were green but everything was brighter and seemed more alive than at home. The sleek, paved streets were bustling with people who blinked in and out of the sunlight, going to and from God knows where.

All of that aside, it was the towering castle in the distance that truly took Kai's breath away. Zemi's castle looked like it was made of diamonds and a glittering prism of colors wavered around it, almost like a rainbow colored aura.

"I'm definitely not in Kansas anymore," Kai murmured.

She watched a family stroll by on the sidewalk and when the pigtailed girl waved, Kai instinctively waved back. Yet, as beautiful as the world was, something seemed amiss and it took a moment for Kai to realize what it was. The people here didn't have auras. Kai trotted down the steps, holding her skirt so she wouldn't trip, she met Kristine who was standing at the bottom of the steps.

"No one here has an aura," she said breathlessly.

"Well, we do but you can't see them when we're in our own dimension. Our auras are only visible in the mortal plane," her grandmother said impatiently. "You can sight see later on but we have to keep moving."

Kai nodded her understanding and went with Kristine, even though all she wanted to do was find Asmodeus, get out of this place and go home. She decided that her best tactic right now was to smile and just go along with it until she could figure out what to do next.

They walked toward the castle in silence and Kai glanced at Kristine from time to time but she continued to stare straight ahead. But as they got closer to the diamond like structure, the ring on Kai's hand burned against her skin with a now familiar warning. She curled her hand into a fist and held the book closer to her chest as dread crawled up her back.

They approached a clear beam of sunlight that was streaking through the clouds. Without a word, Kristine grabbed Kai's arm with her left hand and dipped her right hand in the beam of light. Kai held her breath, knowing what was next. The light flashed over them in a prickling flash and an instant later they were standing outside the towering gates of the castle.

"Whoa." Kai wavered a little but managed to stay on her feet while the lightheadedness subsided. "That's wild but how did you get it to work? I mean do you just stick your hand in a beam of sunlight? Then boom, you're there."

"Yes." Kristine kept her sights on the gate as it swung open slowly.

"No magic words?"

"No," Kristine laughed. "The power is in your mind, Kai. All you have to do is think of where you want to go and the light will take you there."

"That's not all that different from the witches' magic. Isadora told me the same thing, she said my mind holds the power," Kai said murmured. "But the witches use spells and potions." She brushed her fingers over the cover of the spell book as some of the pieces started to come together. "The Fae don't use spells. Fae magic, the Power of the Light, is just kind of there, inside of us. Wait a minute…. this spell book isn't a Fae book. Is it?"

"Not exactly," Kristine said quietly. She sliced a nervous glance in Kai's direction. "Come on."

"Wait." Kai followed her through the gates. "But, if it's not a Fae spell book…?"

"It belongs to the Custodians of the Light," Kristine said firmly. "And the Custodians are Fae. That's all you need to know."

"Hang on." Kai stopped walking and looked at the book in her hands. "Are the Fae somehow related to the Witches? Is that why the first Chosen One, had to be both Fae and Witch bloodlines?"

Kristine stopped dead in her tracks but kept her back to Kai and she didn't miss the tension in her grandmother's body language.

"Holy crap." Kai closed the distance between them as she spoke, keeping her voice low. "The Fae and the witches….you guys are related aren't you?"

181

"Shhh." Kristine grabbed Kai by the arm and pulled her close. Keeping her voice down, she kept talking so no one else would hear. "Thousands of years ago, yes, Fae and Witch lived together as one people but then we divided over differing ideologies. Most Fae wanted to remain here, free from the constraints of the mortal world, but there were others who desired nothing more than to live among humans."

"Holy shit," Kai shouted louder than she expected. She clapped her hand over her mouth and looked around but luckily no one was in sight. "So you're part of the same race?'

"We were until about a thousand years ago." Kristine released Kai's arm and a pained expression flickered across her face. "But living in the mortal realm, for any length of time, robs us of our light."

"For how long?"

"After a few days, we begin to see the effects and within a month, our light disappears."

"So about a thousand years ago, there were Fae who stayed on earth and lost their powers and then they became witches?"

"To put it simply, yes. They lost their light but they weren't entirely powerless." Kristine looked past Kai toward the gate where two guards were now standing by and watching. "Over time, they learned how to parlay their abilities into spells and potions."

"Okay, fine." Kai rolled her eyes. "So what's the big deal? Why are you acting so secretive about it?"

"Because we don't speak of it." Kristine clasped her hands in front of her and squared her shoulders. "We live separately. That's simply the way it is."

"Why?"

"Because the rift between them has never been repaired." Kristine lowered her voice. "The betrayal was too great."

"Rift between who?" Kai asked. "The Fae and the Witches?"

"No." Kristine's mouth set in a grim line. "Between Zemi and her sister."

"Kristine," Kai asked in a barely audible voice. "Who's her sister?" Silence hung between them and Kai thought she'd scream with frustration if Kristine didn't just spit it out. "Who is it?"

"Willow," Kristine said through a shuddering breath. "Willow is Zemi's sister and they haven't spoken in over a thousand years. In fact, none of us are permitted to have anything to do with the witches unless Zemi first approves it.

"Oh shit," Kai breathed. "Except when you need to find some poor, unsuspecting, part-witch-human guy to have a baby with." Kai shook her head and looked Kristine up and down. "You people are fucked up."

Without another word, Kristine spun on her heels and waved to the guards. As the gates opened, Kai stayed close to Kristine but kept note of her surroundings. Her situation was getting more precarious by the second and Kai didn't trust anyone-- except Asmodeus.

Every single aspect of the castle was made of diamond or crystal but the color changed as light hit it. The prism of colors made the building seem as though it was breathing or had a heartbeat or something. Enormous doors, that had to be two stories high and looked to be made of sapphires, swung open and two more armored guards jumped to attention as Kristine and Kai strolled past.

Holding the book against her chest, she flinched when the sound of the closing doors ricocheted through the cavernous entry hall. Kai let out a whistle as she surveyed the lush surroundings. The ceilings, the walls, everything, it was all made of the same crystal as the outside of the building. It was like being inside fishbowl made of diamonds and they were the fish.

Her slipper clad feet brushed along a bright, pink carpet. It stretched out in front of them and along various adjacent hallways but she and Kristine were heading toward another set of doors.

"I'm feeling more like Dorothy with every passing second." Kai fiddled with the ring and stayed close to Kristine as a few different people walked past them. Each person smiled and nodded but nobody spoke. "What's the deal, grandma? Where's the great and powerful Oz?

Kristine cast her a doubtful look but before she could answer, they were interrupted by one of the most unusual looking men Kai had ever seen. Standing in front of the arched doorway, he was dressed in a gold doorman's uniform. He looked to be almost seven feet tall, was rail thin and had the darkest skin of any person she'd every laid eyes on.

183

"Welcome, ladies," he said in a deep baritone. Giving them a wide smile, he bowed deeply and kissed both of their hands in the true fashion of a gentleman. Even given how tall he was, his most striking feature were his bright, blue eyes that sparkled with humor and intelligence. "Lovely to see you again, Kristine."

"Murdoch, it's always a pleasure to see you." Kristine curtsied and gestured to Kai. "This is my granddaughter."

"Kai Kelly," Murdoch said with a wink. "I've heard quite a bit about you, young lady. The queen is thrilled about your arrival and we have spent the past several hours setting up for tonight's event. And of course, we have your guest quarters within the palace prepared for you as well."

"Guest quarters?" Kai flicked a wary glance to Kristine. "But I thought I was staying with my grand—with Kristine—at her house."

"That wasn't my house. It was our equivalent of a hospital, Kai." Kristine gave her a tight smile. "We had to assure that your transition into our realm would be safe for everyone. Not all Halflings survive in our dimension and given the power of the ring...well...we had to be sure that..."

"The queen was safe," Kai said quietly. She studied Kristine closely. "So, you brought me to your world even though there was a chance I might die? Is there anything else you'd like to spring on me, lady?"

Kristine said nothing but looked at Kai with something that looked a lot like regret. Before she could respond, Murdoch interrupted.

"Now, now, my dear. That's neither here nor there." Murdoch waved his hand and the doors opened revealing a long, crystal corridor. "All is well and you are a cousin of the Fae Queen. Therefore, you will be staying here in the palace as her guest. Follow me."

Kai and Kristine walked behind Murdoch in silence. A knot of anger coiled in Kai's chest, as heat rippled over her arms and the ring burned. She wanted nothing more than to zap the crap out of Kristine because any illusions Kai had about a loving relationship with her grandmother were vanishing with each passing second.

The woman brought Kai here knowing it might kill her. Nice.

"Are you excited for tonight's event?" Murdoch asked as they approached the end of the corridor. Stopping in front of the glistening red doors he looked down at Kai with an eager smile and pointed at the spell book in Kai's arms. "I do hope you've picked a good spell to use on him."

"Him? Do you mean Asmodeus?" Kai asked with more than a little dread. She looked from Murdoch to Kristine and didn't miss the look of warning her grandmother gave him. "Is he in there?"

Kai tried to push past Murdoch but Kristine grabbed her by the elbow and pulled her back. Murdoch laughed loudly and clapped his hands, clearly misunderstanding Kai's motives.

"I'm glad to see how eager you are and I'm sure it will make for a fine display."

"What display?" Kai tugged her arm out of Kristine's grasp. "Cut the crap, Kristine."

"That's quite enough." Kristine interrupted. Kai didn't miss the look of warning she shot Murdoch. "As the queen's secretary, I'm sure Murdoch knows that Zemi would like to tell Kai all about it herself."

"Yes." Murdoch bowed and a contrite look covered his face. "My apologies."

He waved one hand and the doors swung inward, revealing an enormous silver and ivory hall that brought to mind the gladiator arenas of ancient Rome. The ruby red door closed silently behind as the three of them walked along sterling silver floors into the center of the hauntingly, silent arena.

When Kai looked back the doors were gone and she felt as though they had been entombed. The circular space was lined with ivory colored walls made of marble that were about twenty feet high. Directly above it were several rows of seating, which would give an audience a clear view of whatever happened on the arena floor.

Gauzy, red bunting hung around the edges of the domed ceiling and at the center was a massive crystal sunroof that cast a colorful, glittering beam of light into the center of the room.

Murdoch led them around the beam of light so that they stood to the left of it. Kai noticed that neither, Murdoch or Kristine attempted to touch the light. In fact they avoided it entirely.

185

Perched high above them there was a gilded balcony fit for a queen. Beneath a canopy of flowing fabric was a massive sterling throne encrusted with jewels and Kai had no doubt that's where Zemi would be sitting. Just as Kai was going to inquire about the queen, the wall behind the throne vanished and four women scurried out. All of them were dressed in dresses similar to Kai's but their hair was coiled on top of their heads. They stopped, two on either side of the door, and bowed their heads.

Kristine and Murdoch dropped to their knees as one of the most beautiful women Kai had ever laid eyes on, emerged onto the balcony. Her coffee colored skin stood out against an ivory and gold dress that fit her curvy body to perfection. Thick, curly, dark hair flowed over her shoulders and as she placed her hands delicately on the edge of the balcony, her piercing, blue gaze landed on Kai.

"Don't you think you should kneel before your queen?" Zemi asked. "Clearly, you didn't learn any manners on Earth."

"Really?" Kai laughed as Kristine and Murdoch rose to their feet. She knew it was probably unwise to mouth off to the queen but she was tired of all the bullshit. "Well, you may be *a* queen but you aren't *my* queen."

"Kai," Kristine warned. "Mind your tongue."

"You certainly have the spirit of a Fae woman," Zemi said, her voice echoing through the cavernous space. She clapped her hands. "Murdoch, you are dismissed. Please tend to the rest of the details for tonight's gala."

"As you wish." Murdoch bowed regally and winked at Kai before leaving. "Until tonight."

"Kristine, bring the girl up here."

Laying one hand on Kai's arm, Kristine waved the other in the beam of light. The familiar sound of wind chimes filled the air and when the light spread over them, that warm fuzzy feeling rippled through Kai.

A split second later, the two of them were standing on the balcony in front of Zemi, who was seated in her throne. Kai swooned with dizziness but fought the lightheaded sensation, clinging to the book like her life depended on it. Fainting in front of the queen would definitely make her look like an idiot.

186

"For a Chosen One, you seem to get woozy rather often," Zemi, said, with mild amusement. She waved her hand and two small silver chairs appeared behind them. "Sit. We have much to discuss."

Kai and Kristine sat down and within a few seconds the four servant girls scurried over with gilded glasses of wine. Kai smiled but politely refused. Even though she wanted a drink—badly—it seemed a wise idea to keep a clear head.

"Do you like the stage we have set for you? I wanted to show it to you so that you'd be familiar with it before this evening," Zemi said before sipping her wine. The queen's intelligent gaze studied Kai intently over the rim of the gilded chalice. "I thought it only fitting that you eliminate him in a grand setting for all to see."

"Yeah, about that," Kai began, "I'm not eliminating anyone." Kai placed the spell book on her lap. She folded her hands on top of it but kept her calm expression focused on Zemi. "Sorry to disappoint you."

"It's really not up to you, Kai," Zemi said sweetly. "You are the first of the chosen Custodians. You have been given the Ring of Solomon and that spell book so that you can eliminate Asmodeus. Once that is complete, then the duty will go to the next Chosen One and so on. The cycle will continue until all seven members of the Brotherhood are dark no more." She sipped her wine and smiled. "Until they're destroyed...and then we will be free to roam the earth."

"What do you mean...we?" Kai swallowed the lump of dread in her throat.

"Keepers of the damned? Well, that doesn't refer to the demons, my dear." Zemi laughed and took another sip of wine. "It's a reference to us. The Fae Custodians....*we* are the keepers of the damned. We hold the light for the Dark Ones--the light that will destroy them."

"Oh my God." Kai, completely agog, stared at Zemi as the ring burned against her flesh. "You can't be on Earth for more than a few days without losing your power."

"Not without becoming like my sister," Zemi seethed. "That traitorous wretch and her pathetic coven living beneath Larrun Mountain like insects. They may live in the mortal world but their

187

magic is weak. However, if we destroy the Brotherhood and bring an end to their evil, then all of the Fae can roam the earth freely without any danger of losing our light."

"You crazy bitch," Kai whispered. "I won't do anything to help you harm Asmodeus or his brothers."

"You forget yourself," Zemi spat. She rose to her feet and tossed the chalice of wine aside, with little care that it almost hit one of the servant girls. "You may be the Chosen One but I am your queen and you will not speak to me with that insolent tone. Perhaps too much time with that filthy demon has made you lose your senses?"

"Zemi, please," Kristine begged. "She has had much to adjust to in a very short time. I beg you to be patient with Kai while she learns our ways. I fear her judgment has been clouded by her feelings for the demon."

"Leave us," Zemi whispered. Holding Kai's gaze, she waved her hands at the servant girls. "All of you." She turned her sharp, blue stare to Kristine. "Now."

Kristine and the four ladies-in-waiting scurried silently out of the room. Her grandmother sliced a worried look in Kai's direction before she left but didn't do a damn thing to help her. Fear oozed off all of them but Kai couldn't blame them because she was feeling more than a little anxious herself.

"You love him, don't you?" Zemi asked calmly. "And you are a foolish enough child to believe that he loves you."

"I'm not foolish or a child. I may not be a million years old like you are but I know what it feels like to be loved." Kai straightened her back and curled her hands around the edges of the spell book. "But maybe that's your problem. You don't know what it feels like to be loved do you?"

Zemi's smile faltered and her body stiffened. Kai knew she'd hit the nail on the head.

"Asmodeus doesn't love you, Kai." Zemi's tone grew cold and her eyes glittered with bitterness. Letting out a cruel laugh, she rose from her chair. As she spoke, she walked around the balcony but kept her attention on Kai. "He wants you to love him, though. Oh, yes. He desires nothing more than to have you weakened by your love for him because then, how could you possibly destroy him? Mark my words, child. Asmodeus will use your love and tenderness, against you before betraying you and laying you wasted. He'll leave you barren, broken, and alone. Trust me," she whispered in a quivering breath. "That is the only future possible with a member of the Brotherhood. Therefore, it is your duty to use your light to destroy them before they can do it to us."

Sadness edged her voice and sterling tears glittered in Zemi's eyes. And that's when everything fell into place. The woman standing in front of Kai wasn't a Fae Queen obsessed with freedom on earth. Her motive was far more personal.

Zemi was a woman scorned.

"This isn't about the Fae getting freedom on earth at all. Is it?" Kai gripped the book tightly as she studied Zemi. "This is about taking out your revenge on Lucifer for whatever went down between you two. Listen, I don't know what happened but I can tell you that Asmodeus is different. He loves me. You want to worry about someone betraying you, then how about Ben Flaherty?"

"Who?" Zemi looked at her with obvious confusion. "I know no one by that name."

"Ben Flaherty is Fae." Kai's attention was caught by a single beam of light that shone past her and reflected off the jewels on Zemi's throne. She rose to her feet slowly and inched toward it, but all the while kept her eyes on the queen. "He attacked me at the farm and tried to steal the ring. Based on your reaction, I'm guessing you didn't send him to steal the ring from me."

"Why would I do that? It cannot be removed." Zemi rolled her eyes and gave Kai a bored look. "All of the Fae are aware of how important the Ring of Solomon is to the Chosen One and to the future of our people."

"Well, maybe, but I think you better watch your back, Your Highness." Kai moved casually toward the beam of light and prayed Zemi wouldn't notice. "This Ben guy tried to take the ring. He seemed to think it was pretty valuable and since his little attack wasn't sanctioned by you...well...I'd say you've got a traitor in your midst."

"A traitor?" Zemi scoffed. "Let me tell you about traitors. The members of the Brotherhood are nothing but that. Demons know

189

nothing of love. They lie, deceive, and toy with the hearts of women as a means to an end." She looked at Kai as though she were a fool. "I used to be naïve like you. I believed in love…until Lucifer betrayed me with my own sister."

Kai stilled. Lucifer and Willow? But didn't Asmodeus say that Willow had a thing with Satan? She shook her head and let out a sound of frustration.

"I'd love to sit here and listen to the Real Housewives of the Fae Dimension." Kai flicked her gaze to the beam of light, dipped her finger in it and focused her thoughts on where she wanted to go, as she whispered, "But I've never been into that kind of drama."

As the familiar jingling sound filled her head and a tingling sensation flashed over her body, Zemi's shocked face was the last sight Kai saw before she vanished.

CHAPTER NINETEEN

Through inky darkness, a whisper of warmth washed over Asmodeus' cheek and he imagined that velvety soft lips brushed over his. He moaned as pain mixed with pleasure and his imagination tormented him with what he knew couldn't be real.

Dreaming, he thought, I must be dreaming. Demons didn't dream but at the very least, Asmodeus knew he had to be hallucinating because he was still bleeding and chained to the dungeon wall.

"Asmodeus." Kai's voice sounded painfully real as she murmured his name. "Wake up."

"Kai?" Fingertips fluttered across his chest as a clean, familiar scent filled his head. Asmodeus peeled his eyes open to see the Kai's smiling face. Dressed in the garb of a Fae woman, she looked luminously beautiful and remarkably self-assured. He licked his dry, cracked lips and rasped, "How is this possible?"

"No time for explanations." Kai kept her voice down and glanced over her shoulder toward the door. "I've got to get you out of here. You might want to close your eyes because I have no idea if this will work and I could blow your head off."

"I trust you," he rasped.

Asmodeus watched as a fiercely, determined look covered Kai's face and the ring began to glow. She held up her hand and aimed the blooming light toward the chain where it was latched to the wall. A

191

blast of heat and a blinding flash flew from her body and a split second later the chains were shattered to bits.

As bits of stone and metal rained around him, Asmodeus dropped his arms. He bit back the pain that fired through his stiff, tortured muscles and sagged against the wall while Kai used her magic to vaporize the chains that shackled his ankles.

"Come on." Kai wrapped her arm around his waist, encouraging him to lean on her for support. "We're getting out of here."

"There's nowhere to hide from Zemi. She knows every nook and cranny of her own dimension." He did his best not to put too much weight on Kai but, much to his dismay, the mortal body he was bound in was far weaker than expected. The sound of guards in the hall captured his attention and he tried to push Kai away. "Leave me."

"Are you kidding?" She raised one eyebrow and shuffled with him into the ray of light that streamed in through the window. "After all of the crap we've been through, do you really think I'd leave without you? And who said we were staying in this dimension?"

Light seeped over their bodies just as the door of the dungeon burst open. An instant later, Kai and Asmodeus were consumed by the sunlight.

***

The clean scent of lavender and ivory soap drifted over Asmodeus, along with the crackling sound of fire. His eyes drifted open to see Kai, barefoot and clad in a pair of cut off shorts and a tank top. She had her back to him and was speaking quietly in the corner with Isadora.

They were back at Larrun Mountain.

Asmodeus pushed himself up to a sitting position in the bed, bracing himself for the pain he'd become accustomed to over the past few hours, but none came. He lifted his hands and saw that a subtle aura glowed over his flesh and while the tattoos of the Brotherhood were there, the lacerations from the shackles were not.

He was completely healed and with any luck, all of his powers were restored now that he was back in the mortal plane. Testing his theory, Asmodeus he held his hands in front of him and called up the power of fire. An instant later, energy pulsed through him with a familiar and comforting surge. He smiled while when a red and orange ball of flames materialized in the air.

"You're awake," Kai said with a smile. Asmodeus pulled the power back inside him, making the fire vanish just before she climbed up and kneeled on the bed next to him. She placed a warm, welcoming kiss on his mouth and murmured, "How do you feel?"

"Is that a trick question?" He teased. Asmodeus curled his hand around the back of Kai's neck and brushed a kiss on the corner of her mouth before she snuggled up against to him. "Because the only thing I want to feel, right now, is you."

"Good to see you back in the land of the living. You've been passed out for hours but given the extent of your injuries, I'm not surprised. You got your ass kicked by a bunch of fairies." Isadora, who once again looked young and beautiful, folded her arms over her chest and wiggled her eyebrows. "But you're feeling as horny as ever, I see."

"Only for Kai." Asmodeus kissed Kai again and brushed his thumb over her cheek. "How did you get us back here?"

"Well, I am a Fae you know," Kai, teased. He knew she was mimicking him and it only made him adore her more. "I used the light travel, and you'll be pleased to know that I didn't faint for a change. Anyway, I figured this was the safest place to come while we planned out what our next steps would be."

Asmodeus kissed her again and pulled her into his arms as he breathed in the clean, shampoo smell of Kai's hair. The woman embodied purity and goodness and it killed him to know that he'd have to let her go. Eyes closed, he kissed the top of her head and peered at Isadora who gave him a knowing look.

"I can see that you two need some time alone and besides, I have to deliver our message." Isadora opened the massive wooden door but stopped before leaving. "You're a smart woman, Kai. It's no wonder you are the first of the Chosen Ones. I'll see you in three hours at the rendezvous point but don't be surprised if Zemi doesn't show up."

"What rendezvous?" He asked with more than a little concern but Kai didn't answer him. "Kai? What is this nonsense about meeting with Zemi?"

The door closed quietly behind Isadora and, without a word, Kai hopped off the bed. She moved to the windowsill and opened the spell book. Swinging his legs over the side of the bed, he pushed the covers aside and stood up, uncaring that he was stark naked.

"Do you love me, Asmodeus?" Kai asked quietly. She peered at him over her shoulder before looking back at the book quickly, as though she couldn't bear to look at him. "Do you just want to get the ring and take it back to Underworld, like Zemi said? Or do you love me and want to spend your life with me?"

"It's not a matter of what I want. It's not possible," he murmured. "If I stay with you…"

"I didn't ask you if it was possible." Kai squared her shoulders and kept her voice steady as she stared out the window. "I asked you if you loved me."

Every single instinct he had told him to push her away, that Kai would be better off without him in her life. What kind of life could he give her? His choices were either offer Kai an eternity in Hell or her destruction on Earth. An ache bloomed and throbbed deep in his chest as he went against nature and spoke the words he had no right to utter.

"Yes," he whispered. "I do love you, Kai."

Kai let out a slow breath and nodded her head, but still, she avoided his gaze.

"Why do you think you've been taking my light, Asmodeus?" Kai asked quietly. She kept her back to him and ran her fingertips over the Prophecy that was written out on the ancient page. "The Prophecy says… holds the light *for* the dark…*not from* the dark."

Unsure of what else to say, he sidled up behind her and brushed her long hair off her shoulder. Kai turned to face him and linked her hands with his and even though his body instantly responded to being so close to Kai, he held his desires in check. As the Demon of Lust, his first reaction was to soothe or comfort with pleasures of the flesh, but Kai was asking for something far more intimate.

"Do you know what I think it means?" Kai lifted his fingers to her lips and placed a tender kiss on his knuckles while holding his stare. "I think it's about love, Asmodeus. Love and light. You and your brothers are chained to Hell by the tortured souls who abuse the gifts of the mortal world. Aren't you?"

194

"Yes." His body rigid, he fought for restraint as Kai inched closer.

"I have a theory. I suspected this before I went to the Fae dimension but after talking to Zemi, I think I'm on to something. Want to hear it?" Kai unlinked her fingers from his and a sexy smile played at her lips just before she pulled her tank top off and tossed it aside. She unhooked her bra and let it drop to floor as she spoke to him. "I've always thought that Hell would be the absence of love. Hell is darkness and loneliness. Would you agree with that?"

Asmodeus, rendered speechless by the sight of her gorgeous flesh in the firelight, simply nodded curtly. Hands curled into fists at his side, every inch of him hardened as she drifted just inches from his aroused state.

"Every time you touch me, each brush of your flesh against mine, makes your light glow brighter." Kai unbuttoned her shorts and pushed them past her hips along with her panties. Asmodeus watched with rapt attention as the garments slid down her legs and she kicked them aside. Kai ran her fingers up the taut muscles of his arms before trailing them down his chest. "You keep saying that taking my light will harm me but it doesn't. In fact, I'm more empowered and alive now, than I've ever been."

Kai slid her hands down to his waist and inched closer still, so that his erection was pressed between their naked bodies. Asmodeus shook with restrained need as her fingers wandered over his ass and her warm breath puffed enticingly over his chest.

"I don't think you're taking my light," she murmured. "I believe you're taking my love, Asmodeus. That darkness, the absence of love you've lived with, is vanishing and being replaced by love and light."

"What if you're wrong?" His voice, tight and gravelly sounded more like growl.

"What if I'm not?" Kai arched one eyebrow and a smile lingered on her sweet lips. "Enough talking."

Before he could respond, Kai captured his lips with hers. Asmodeus groaned and wrapped her up in his arms as her tongue tangled enticingly with his. Need, stark carnal need, fired through him as her soft, sexy body melded against his flesh. Kissing her deeply, he scooped her up and carried her to the bed while reveling in the silky, soft feel of her skin.

195

This couldn't be wrong. Being with Kai was, by far, the most perfect act he'd ever participated in and he would no longer be convinced otherwise. He laid her on covers and she stretched her arms over her head as he settled himself between her legs. Propped up with his elbows on either side of her head, he tangled her long locks between his fingers and took his time, licking and suckling those sweet, plump lips.

Kai giggled and captured his lower lip between her teeth briefly. Wrapping her arms and legs around him, Kai urged him to turn onto his back, so that she was straddling him on the bed. She grabbed his wrists and pinned them over his head while rocking her hips in slow, tantalizing strokes, brushing her hot, wet center over the rigid length of his cock.

Asmodeus almost lost it while he watched Kai pleasure herself as she rubbed her clit against him. She threw her head back and moaned and that erotic sight was more than he could take. Asmodeus tore one hand from her grasp, reached in between them just as she lifted her hips, and inserted the head of his erection in between her slick folds.

Kai gasped and remained on her knees, hovering above him. Holding his stare, she sank down onto his rock hard shaft, inch by wickedly, hot inch. Asmodeus groaned when she impaled herself on the entire length of him and took all of his cock inside. He swore and grabbed her hips with both hands as she began to move with the rhythm of pure desire.

Gazes locked, Kai raised her arms over her head as she rode him.

Slowly at first, she rolled her hips and arched her back with every pass, making her breasts jut toward him temptingly.

Wrapping one arm around her waist, Asmodeus sat up and flicked her nipple with his tongue as she rode him. He couldn't get close enough or deep enough and as though reading his mind, Kai wrapped her legs around his waist and took him deeper still.

She fucked him faster and cried his name as the orgasm crested and the most intimate part of her shuddered around him in tiny spasms. Asmodeus held her close and buried his face in her neck and as the orgasm ripped through his body, with Kai curled around him, he whispered, "I love you."

***

Kai and Asmodeus stood on the porch of her grandfather's house ready and waiting. The early morning sun was already making the air feel hot and sticky which was just one of the reasons Kai refused to wear one of Isadora's get ups. If she was going to face down supernatural crazies then she was gonna do it in her own clothes. Nothing beats a pair of Levi cutoffs, her tank top and Converse sneakers. Comfort was paramount at this point.

Even though he'd agreed to come with her, she could tell that Asmodeus still wasn't convinced that Kai's plan would work. He stood at attention, scanning the property, with a laser sharp intensity that put all of his other efforts to shame. The man, demon or not, was a tension filled bundle of nerves and he was beginning to stress Kai out.

"Where are they?" Asmodeus seethed. He sliced an annoyed look in Isadora's direction. She was sitting on the steps of the porch with Zephyr in her lap, looking totally unconcerned. "I've tried communicating with them but I can't seem to connect with the collective consciousness of the Brotherhood."

"Relax. Maybe it's a left over side effect from your time in the Fae dimension? They'll be here." Isadora rolled her eyes at his impatience. "I told you. We've got it all set up. They're coming and so is Zemi, although I'm sure she'll bring an entourage with her."

"I cannot believe I let you convince me this was a good idea," Asmodeus said with an annoyed glance in Kai's direction. "There is no way this will end well and I find it hard to believe that Zemi agreed to this meeting with Lucifer."

"Well, at least here, in the mortal realm, we are all on an even playing field here. Anyone who's got magic will be able to use it." Kai shrugged. "We've all got a weapon to use, so maybe no one will use it. It's kind of like the world super powers and their nuclear weapons. Everyone's got nukes but they don't use 'em. Get it?"

"Perhaps," Asmodeus murmured. "But Zemi is not exactly stable and she's even less stable when it comes to Lucifer."

"Who said she even knows that he's gonna be here?" Isadora smirked. "My message asked her for a temporary truce and to meet

197

you and Kai here. Willow should be here soon as well. A neutral zone, so to speak."

"Let's hope so. Now, I can understand how you got a message to Willow but how did you get a message to Zemi?" Asmodeus asked, without taking his eyes off the horizon. "If memory serves, she doesn't like you very much."

"Murdoch," Isadora said causally. "He's Zemi's secretary but he also happens to be an occasional lover of mine. Damn if he isn't one fine lookin' fairy man. Anyway, he and I take a tussle in the sack from time to time. I had him meet me for a quickie at my place and then he took the message back to Zemi. Ain't nothin' that man won't do for me if he thinks he's gonna get some nookie."

Kai laughed and shook her head at Isadora's typically frank commentary but the moment of lightheartedness was cut short by a sudden burst of smoke and fire. Seconds later Lucifer and the other five members of the Brotherhood stood in Kai's driveway. Dressed in black from head to toe, they looked like a squadron of super-secret government soldiers or something.

"Glad to see you made it back from the Fae dimension unscathed, Asmodeus." Lucifer winked at Kai. "And you too, of course, Ms. Kelly."

Zephyr hissed and fled Isadora's lap before she rose to her feet and stood by Asmodeus' side.

"I knew my cat had good taste," Kai said with a triumphant glance in Lucifer's direction.

"I'm hurt, Ms. Kelly," Lucifer simpered. "Why so angry?"

"You conveniently forgot to tell Asmodeus that he'd lose his powers in the Fae dimension." Kai glared at him and moved closer to Asmodeus. "That was a shitty thing to do."

"Must have slipped my mind," Lucifer shrugged. "Apologies. Besides, he looks no worse for the wear and in fact, one could say you're positively glowing, brother."

"Dude, what's with that bright ass light you've got?" Belphegor asked Asmodeus with genuine interest. He pushed his long blonde hair off his forehead and hooked his thumbs in the pocket of his pants. "You've got a full on aura man and your girl, here, still has hers. I thought she'd be almost dark by now but she's still way luminous. That is some freaky shit."

"Shut up, Belphegor," Satan hissed. He flicked his ebony eyes to Kai before turning to Lucifer. "I don't give a crap if he can light up an entire fucking city, right now I just want to know what's going on."

"Asmodeus," Mammon interjected, "Lucifer said you have some news regarding this Prophecy and the Fae."

"Patience, gentleman," Isadora purred. She sashayed down the steps, bewitching all six demons with her youthful beauty. Kai couldn't help but wonder what they'd think of good old Isadora without her youth spell. "Good things come to those who wait."

"Well, sweet thing," Satan said with a wink. "Why don't you come over here and wait with me?"

"No." Isadora stood at the bottom of the steps and leaned on the stair railing. "I think it would be wise if I kept my distance from you. Willow is a High Priestess and I don't think she'd appreciate it if I let you get a whiff of my wiles."

"Willow?" Satan shifted his weight and squared his shoulders. "What's she got to do with it?"

Satan's tirade was interrupted by the familiar sound of wind chimes.

"Fae," Lucifer seethed, turning his furious sights on Asmodeus. "What the fuck is going on, Asmodeus?"

Kai watched as the eyes of all seven demons flickered to bright red and, as though it were a carefully coordinated dance, Lucifer and the others backed up and formed a circle. Facing out, arms at their sides and bodies taut, they looked ready to turn everyone around them into ash.

"Zemi's coming," Kai said quietly.

"No shit," Lucifer spat.

"Just trust me, okay? We've got to face this situation head on. There are too many miscommunications flying around and I will not live my life on the run from anyone. Fairy. Demon. Witch. No more bullshit." Kai looked at each of them in earnest. She knew there was a chance they would split but curiosity must have gotten the better of Lucifer because they didn't leave. Moving in, next to Asmodeus, she rubbed her thumb against the band of the ring and threw a silent prayer to the universe that her hunch was right. "Just keep your cool and let me do the talking."

Lucifer cast her a doubtful look before turning his attention back to the pulsing ray of sunlight that shone over the roof of the barn and into the driveway.

"If Zemi makes one move toward you, the last thing I'll be doing is talking to her." Asmodeus' body hummed with tension and the muscles in his arms flickered beneath the faded tattooed rings. His eyes glowed red and heat wafted off his tall frame in thick waves but the tension in his voice made his feelings clear. "She's going to find out just how much of a demon I can be."

The wind chimes jingled louder and in a pulsing flash of light, Zemi and Murdoch materialized in front of the barn. Dressed in a turquoise and silver dress, she looked every bit the queen she was, but a mask of fury swiftly replaced a smug smile once she spotted Lucifer and the rest of the Brotherhood.

"You," Zemi seethed.

She raised her hands to, undoubtedly, throw her light at the Brotherhood but Kai ran down the steps and stood between them, using her body as a shield. Asmodeus, of course, was right there with her and the two of them stood back to back, with their magic at the ready. He faced his brothers while Kai aimed her power toward Zemi and Murdoch.

"Please wait." Kai's voice sounded remarkably strong and she prayed Zemi didn't know how terrified she actually was. "I asked Lucifer and the others to come here so we could all talk and straighten this whole mess out. And before you have another royal size temper tantrum, Willow is coming soon too. At least, she's supposed to. You're all wrong about the Prophecy."

Shaking like a leaf, Kai's heart hammered in her chest and she started to sweat as the power coiled and swirled inside of her. Light glowed from the ring that burned against her flesh as Kai held out her palm toward Zemi. The only person who hadn't moved was Isadora. She was standing at the foot of the steps with her hands on her hips, looking at all of them like they were a bunch of idiots.

"So are you gonna blast the shit out of each other or what?" Isadora snapped. She folded her arms over her breasts and walked causally between Kai and Zemi while looking them all up and down.

200

"I could cut the tension in the air with a knife and the buzz from all the magic is making me feel a little stoned. Now, as much as I love a good high, I have a feeling that no one is gonna win if you all start zapping each other's butts."

"She's right," Kai said firmly. With a deep breath, Kai lowered her hands slowly but all the while kept her sights on Zemi. "Please, Zemi. Give me five minutes to explain why I brought you all here."

"Your majesty," Murdoch whispered. Hands raised, he was ready to fight but clearly had no interest in doing so. "I beg you. Please hear what the girl has to say."

"You knew that he would be here and that Willow was coming?" Zemi asked without taking her furious gaze off Kai. Her mouth set in a grim line and her voice dropped to dangerous tones while she slowly lowered her hands. "I'll deal with you later Murdoch, but right now I want to know why *he* has been brought into my presence."

"Actually, I was here first, darling," Lucifer teased. "So technically *you* came into *my* presence."

"Shut up," Asmodeus barked. "You're not helping matters."

"Typical," Zemi simpered. She brushed her long, curly hair off her shoulders and folded her hands in front of her before turning her bright, blue eyes to Kai. "Fine. I will hear what you have to say, Kai. Unlike a demon, I am capable of controlling my urges. I realize my sister isn't here yet but I have matters to attend to in my own realm and cannot dally here all day."

"Fine. I'll get started," Kai said with relief. She let out a sigh and leaned against Asmodeus' strong frame for a just a second before finding the strength to continue. "Lucifer?" Looking over her shoulder, she smiled when she saw all members of the Brotherhood had relaxed their position. Though their eyes glowed red, they weren't poised to douse everyone with fire. "Okay, good. This is…progress."

"Get on with it, Kai," Satan groused.

"I'd watch the way you speak to my woman if I were you," Asmodeus growled.

"Anyway," Kai said, giving Asmodeus a look that pleaded for him to give the macho stuff a rest. She took his hand in hers and shifted her body so she could look easily from Zemi to the

Brotherhood. "I asked you to be here so we could clear up the confusion about the Ring of Solomon and the Prophecy. This ring does not have the power to control Hell or command demons...at least, not for me." She gave Asmodeus a small smile before continuing. "There have been several times since I put this damn ring on, that I wanted Asmodeus to do certain things and he didn't. So, let's put that rumor to rest."

"I don't buy it," Mammon scoffed.

"Really?" Kai arched one eyebrow held up the hand with the ring and shouted, "Dance like a clown, Mammon."

"No way." Mammon folded his arms over his broad chest and made a sound of derision. Squaring his shoulders he looked awkwardly from Kai to his brothers and said, "I'm not fuckin' doing that."

"See? No commanding of demons over here." Kai looked at each of them earnestly. "I *cannot* control you boys and I have no desire to do so."

"I don't get it," Belphegor interjected. "Solomon was able to control us with it. So why can't you?"

"I don't know and neither do you." Kai looked fondly at Asmodeus. "And that's the problem. All of us have a lot of a little bit of information but none of us have the whole story. From what I understand, like a million years ago, King Solomon suddenly had this ring one day and started controlling all of you. It didn't stop until he got drunk, took of the ring and gave it to Asmodeus who then tossed it into the ocean. Right?"

The boys in the Brotherhood nodded and Kai didn't miss the looks of discomfort that passed between them while recalling unpleasant memories. Asmodeus' body tensed at the mention of it but Kai gave his hand a reassuring squeeze. Zemi, however, stifled a giggle at the mention of their unfortunate experience and Kai caught Lucifer giving her a look that could kill.

"Zemi?" Kai turned her attention to the queen who'd been staring at Lucifer. "Right around that same time, something big went down with the Fae didn't it?"

"Yes." Zemi lifted her chin as though she was trying to rise above the difficult memory. "That was when my sister and the others

202

walked away from the Fae dimension to reside in the mortal world and live as witches."

"Fine." Kai nodded and put her hands on her hips. "I have another question. If this ring is part of the Custodian legacy then how the heck did old Solomon get his hands on it?"

"I haven't the foggiest notion." Zemi smiled. Even though she acted clueless, Kai had a sinking suspicion that she knew exactly how Solomon got it. "Just a stroke of luck, I suppose." She winked at Lucifer. "Or bad luck, depending on how one sees it."

"You?" Lucifer seethed. He lifted his hands but Asmodeus countered and gave him a warning glare, which made Lucifer lower his hands. "You gave Solomon that ring. Didn't you?"

"I don't recall," Zemi said, while twirling a lock of hair around her finger. "It was an awfully long time ago."

"Actually, it might not have been Zemi." Kai looked at Lucifer and then to Satan. "Willow would have enjoyed seeing you suffer a little. Wouldn't she, Satan?"

"Son of a bitch," Satan spat. "How could she do that to me?"

"Witches can be bitches," Isadora said with a wink to Satan. "But I suppose you can ask her that for yourself, if she ever gets here."

"Anyway," Kai said, with a warning look to Isadora. "I have another question for you people. Where did this spell book come from?"

Kai extended both hands and an instant later the spell book flew off the wicker table on the porch with wicked speed before landing in her hands with an audible slap.

"Be careful with that," Zemi cautioned in an oddly gentle tone. "It possesses more power than you could possibly fathom, Halfling."

"I'm sure it does." Kai held it against her chest and studied Zemi closely. "I haven't had time to read all of it but there are some spells in here that can do serious damage to every one of the members of the Brotherhood, not to mention anyone else who pisses me off. Now, I'm the one who's losing patience, so how about you cut the crap and tell me where this book came from and who wrote this Prophecy?"

"Why?" Zemi's voice quivered with something that sounded like fear. Her blue eyes flicked from Kai to Lucifer. "It is of no importance who wrote it or why."

"I beg to differ," Lucifer said in a surprisingly calm voice. "If our destruction is at stake, I'd say that the origin of this so-called Prophecy is of the highest importance."

"Please," Zemi whispered. Her eyes glimmered with silver tears as she stared at Lucifer. "There are some wounds that are best left alone. I'm sorry but once the Prophecy has been set in motion there is no way to stop it."

Kai looked from Zemi to Lucifer and saw that the anger and frustration that flowed between them so freely before, was replaced with sadness and regret. Lucifer stepped away from his brothers and walked slowly toward Zemi. Asmodeus went to stop him but Kai grabbed his arm and held him back. "Let him go."

"Zemi?" Lucifer moved closer, until he was only a few feet from the queen. "How long are you going to punish me for one foolish mistake?"

The unusually tender moment was interrupted when Murdoch, who was standing behind Zemi, started to make an odd gurgling sound and what happened next, went by in slow motion. Kai watched in horrified fascination as Murdoch's eyes rolled into the back of his head and his body shuddered before erupting in an explosive flash of light. The look of surprise on Zemi's face as she spun around, was swiftly replaced by rage when she saw her secretary disintegrate into nothingness.

An instant later, Kai noticed disruptions in the air around them and it became very clear that their party was getting crashed.

In a split second, chaos erupted and a supernatural war came to Bliss.

Flashes of fire and white light exploded from every angle and through the smoke she saw an evil smile on a familiar face as it emerged from the light.

Ben Flaherty.

The smell of burnt flesh and smoke filled Kai's head and made her stomach roll. Somewhere in the background, Kai heard Isadora scream but she sounded so far away that Kai wasn't even sure that's who was screaming. For all Kai knew, the scream may have come from her.

A blast of heat and otherworldly power knocked Kai through the air and slammed her into the trunk of the massive elm tree by the driveway. The book fell from her hands and she dropped to the ground in a gasping, writhing heap. Pain fired through her body as she struggled to get to her feet, while dirt and gravel dug into her palms. Coughing and gasping to find her breath, she squinted but could only make out ghostly figures in the smoke.

Through the chaos, Kai heard a woman's voice chanting. It was quiet at first but as it was repeated, the chant grew louder and Kai stifled a scream.

Someone was casting a spell and it wasn't Isadora. And Kai had no idea how to stop it.

Bound and frozen, solid as stone.
Bodies fall still, blood and bone.
No sound, no breath, no whimpers or pleas.
The wicked will halt and their magic shall cease.

"Kai!" Asmodeus screamed her name but she couldn't see him. He started to call her name again but was cut off and horrid silence followed.

"Asmodeus! Lucifer....Isadora?" She called and called but no one answered.

The world around her was burning. Blinded by smoke and submerged in darkness, Kai stumbled forward, held up her hand with the ring and though the power swirled violently in her chest, she was terrified to use it because she had no idea who she might hit.

Then, as suddenly as it began, the explosions and the chanting stopped. A haunting, unnatural quiet fell over the property and Kai shuddered with blood curdling fear. Hands raised, the ring glowed while she held her ground and tried to calm her rapid breathing.

A gust of wind came along and in one fell swoop, all of the smoke was sucked away but a pall of darkness covered the sky, blotting out the sun. Kai's hands flew to her mouth in horror when she saw the scene before her.

All of them were frozen. Everyone. Zemi, Isadora, all of the Brotherhood...and Asmodeus. Frozen in time and space.

Isadora was standing with her arms in the air attempting to call up a spell and her long, black hair whipped around her, suspended in mid-air. Five members of the Brotherhood were in various positions, all of them charging toward a perceived enemy. Trails of fire shot from their hands but they were frozen, like a snapshot in time.

Asmodeus was just a few feet from Kai and was immobilized like the others. Rage stamped into his features, he was reaching toward her, trying to protect her, no doubt. Zemi and Lucifer were back to back and looked like they were fighting a common enemy as opposed to each other.

Kai looked back at Asmodeus and when she captured his gaze with hers, she stifled a cry. He may have been frozen but he was totally aware of what was going on. Bodies frozen but minds alert, she could only imagine how tortured they all were and the cruelty of it fueled Kai's rage because in the middle of it all were two frighteningly familiar faces. Ben Flaherty wasn't alone. Standing next to him was one of the secretaries to the Witches Council—Rosalyn.

CHAPTER TWENTY

Asmodeus watched in helpless fury as Kai threw her light toward their two attackers. However, Ben and Rosalyn matched Kai's magic with their own, creating a mid-air explosion that was almost as deafening as it was blinding. Kai staggered backward as the power bounced back into her and when she found her feet again, Rosalyn was standing in front of her with a jagged, ancient looking dagger pointed at Kai's throat.

Kai had been visibly weakened by the exchange of magic and Asmodeus watched her attempt to call up her light, but nothing happened. The ring's light sputtered and Rosalyn laughed cruelly at Kai's failure to rejuvenate her power.

"Seems you shot your load," Rosalyn laughed. She leaned close and grabbed Kai's jaw, while pressing the knife against her throat. "I'm not surprised to see you out of gas so quickly. An inexperienced half-breed like you doesn't deserve the power of the ring or the glories hidden within the spell book."

Kai's body shook and she looked at Asmodeus through wide, frightened eyes. Rosalyn was going to kill Kai and there wasn't a damn thing Asmodeus could do to help her. A scream echoed through his head but wouldn't escape his lips. All he could do was watch the horrific scene play out in front of him.

"Now, I know you can't remove the ring," Rosalyn hissed. "But I could cut off that pretty little finger, couldn't I? I was wondering if my immobility spell would work on you but that damn ring seems to be protecting you somehow."

"Quit fucking around, Rosalyn," Ben shouted. He was behind Asmodeus and most likely right next to Zemi and Lucifer. "I've got the queen, kill that girl and get the damn ring off her hand. Don't forget to grab the spell book. We have to get out of here and take Zemi to the others before your damn spell wears off or her magic rejuvenates."

"Fine." Rosalyn moved with the speed of an ancient witch, and in a blur, had Kai pinned up against the tree. "I never liked you much anyway."

Asmodeus, his body burning from the inside out, watched with disbelief as Rosalyn raised the knife high in the air. Kai's frightened gaze met his, and as the scene unfolded, a fire erupted inside of him. With a bone shattering bellow of outrage, Asmodeus burst free from the constraints of the spell and charged toward Rosalyn.

"Get away from her." Asmodeus called up the power of fire and incinerated Rosalyn when she turned around to charge him. Rosalyn's body exploded in a flash of fire and smoke.

Weakened from breaking through the spell, Asmodeus stumbled and fell to the ground at Kai's feet. She immediately squatted next to him and rained kisses over his face. He couldn't help but smile because even in the midst of all the death and destruction, she still smelled like ivory soap and lavender.

"No!" Ben, red faced, screamed with indignation while Rosalyn's ashes rain down like snow. Stalking slowly toward Kai and Asmodeus and with ashes covering his face, he whispered, "I will avenge you, my love."

The look in his eyes was nothing short of ice-cold revenge.

"Why are you doing this?" Kai huddled behind Asmodeus and wrapped her arms around him protectively. "The ring won't do you any good, Ben. You're not a Custodian or a Chosen One and good luck opening that book. It won't even let you near it, let alone allow you to open it."

"Do you have any idea how long I've been searching for that ring? I spent countless hours, weeks, tearing this shit hole upside down and you come in here after a few days and find it."

"It wasn't yours to find," Asmodeus said, between halting breaths. Heat flickered along his arms but still his powers remained just outside his reach. "It's not yours to possess. It's not your place."

"Not my place?" He seethed. "My *place* is on the throne not being her *advisor*. The woman never listened to a damn thing anyway. She has driven our people to the edge of extinction with her obsession over this Prophecy and her ridiculous infatuation with that demon." He gestured toward Lucifer who was still frozen next to Zemi. "She's had the finest Fae women breeding with half-warlock humans in an effort to create the Chosen One. She doesn't deserve to rule our people and now she rules no longer."

"You're Bentley?" Kai asked quietly. "Zemi's advisor."

"Her *advisor*?" He let out a sound of disgust and threw another bolt of light above their heads, which made the leaves of the tree burst into flames. "I'm her *son* and her dirty little secret. A Witch-Fae offspring who just didn't fit the bill for her precious Prophecy. She prohibits the Fae from having contact with the Witches so how would it look if the queen herself mated with one and had a little half-breed boy? I made the mistake of being born with a dick and we all know the Chosen One had to be a girl."

"Listen, it's a shitty gig," Kai laughed. "I don't want to be the Chosen One and I'd gladly pass the baton to you or anyone else but I can't."

"You can if you're dead." Ben's body shook with unbridled rage and he stalked toward them, throwing rippling bolts of power one after the other but he wasn't aiming at Asmodeus…he was aiming at Kai. Yet every strike of light he threw landed inches on either side of them, always close but never hitting their mark. Kai's body shivered against Asmodeus' as Ben toyed with them time and time again.

He stopped when he was just a couple of feet away and leveled a deadly glare at Asmodeus.

"Say good-bye to your girlfriend," Ben leered.

Ben roared with fury and raised his hands for the final, deadly blow. Asmodeus, with his last shred of strength, scrambled to his feet, pushed Kai back and took the strike of lightning point blank in the chest. Agonizing pain seared Asmodeus' torso and his arms flew out to his side as every muscle in his body hummed with white-hot

209

agony. The entire world seemed to explode around him in a luminous blaze before the darkness closed in.

***

Asmodeus was dead.

That was the first thought that ran through Kai's mind when she watched Ben's light slam into his hulking form. Asmodeus sacrificed himself for Kai and while she watched his immortal body shake with otherworldly power, her heart shattered in a million tiny pieces.

The only man she'd ever truly loved---was dying before her eyes.

And that's when it happened.

Ben's light consumed Asmodeus in an incandescent flash just before it ricocheted back out and slammed into Ben. The power threw him head over heels through the air across the property. His limp body landed with a sickening thud just before it skidded to a halt at Zemi's feet. Kai held her breath while his aura sputter violently before finally going dark.

Shaking and sweating from fear, relief, and pure adrenaline, Kai scrambled over to Asmodeus' unmoving form. At first glance, someone else might think he was dead, but Kai knew better.

Asmodeus' aura glowed brighter than it ever had but something else was different as well.

The tattoos on his arms were gone.

Kneeling next to him, Kai wiped at the tears that fell down her cheeks. Placing a warm kiss on his forehead, she brushed his stubble-covered jaw with the back of her fingers. She whispered his name and laughed through her tears when his eyes fluttered open before staring into hers. Sobbing with relief, Kai rained kisses all over his face as he sat up and pulled her into his arms.

"You did it," she said in between kisses. Sitting in his lap, she linked her arms around his neck and hugged him tightly. "And I hate to say I told you so...but I told you so. I was right."

"What are you talking about?" Asmodeus held her face in his hands and pulled back so he could look her in the eyes. "Right about what?"

"Look." Kai stood up and pulled Asmodeus to his feet. Holding his hand in hers, she lifted his arm and ran her fingers over the unmarked flesh. "The mark of the Brotherhood…the chains…they're gone. *And* you still have an aura. Like I said, baby. Light and love. You haven't been taking my light, Asmodeus. You've been taking my love and that fed your soul."

"This can't be possible," he murmured. Asmodeus stared at his arms and shook his head in disbelief. "I don't understand. I still have my powers." He conjured up a fireball briefly before reabsorbing the energy. "I'm still a demon, so how can I possibly have a soul?"

"You were willing to sacrifice your life for mine." Kai made a wide sweeping gesture with her arms. "What could be more loving and soulful than that?"

A clinking sound caught Kai's attention and she noticed her hand felt markedly lighter.

"Holy shit," Kai gasped. She pulled her hand in between them and they both stared at her now naked finger. Smiling broadly, Kai murmured, "The ring came off."

Asmodeus' smile was short lived as he looked around them. "Where is it?"

Just as the words escaped his lips, a rumbling and cracking sound filled the air. The pall of darkness vanished and in a swirl of light the others were freed from the spell.

A chorus of grumbles, a considerable number of f-bombs, and a few explosions of localized fireballs filled the air while the others emerged from their restraints. Kai leaned into Asmodeus' embrace and rested her head on his shoulder while Lucifer tended cautiously to Zemi. The two of former lovers huddled together and spoke in hushed tones, and Kai could only hope they were on the road to an on-again phase.

They had all witnessed what had happened so there was no need to fill them in and Kai couldn't help but smile as she watched Isadora snuggle with Zephyr. It was a glimmer of normal behavior in a sea of weirdness.

"Where's the ring?" Satan asked with his usual impatience. He rolled his shoulders and straightened his back as he stalked over to Asmodeus. "Right before the spell wore off, I heard Kai say that the ring came off. We've gotta find that damn thing and take it to the Underworld where it can't do any more damage. No offense to you two and your weird lovey-dovey-soul-creating-union, but I like my darkness, thank you very much, and I don't need some woman taking it away from me. It keeps my head clear."

"I second that emotion," Belphegor murmured. He was doing some kind of yoga stretch before rising to a standing position. "Dealing with the souls of the damned is hard enough without adding a chick into the mix."

Mammon and the others all started talking at once and voicing their displeasure at the idea of losing their darkness. Kai peered up at Asmodeus who said nothing but simply pulled her into his arms and kissed her as he murmured, "I do love you, Kai Kelly."

"You're such a horny fucker, Asmodeus," Satan muttered. "Can you stop pawing at her for two seconds and answer my damn question."

"I said *no*, Lucifer," Zemi's angry voice rose above the din, capturing the attention of the group. Lucifer had his hand firmly around Zemi's wrist but she was struggling to get free. Kai knew she couldn't go to the Fae dimension without taking him with her but it was curious that Zemi wasn't using her magic to get free either. "Please, don't ask me to do this."

"You see, Zemi," Lucifer's eyes burned red as he tugged her up against his much larger body. "That's where you're mistaken, my love. I'm not asking."

Zemi's aura gleamed a blinding shade of white but it was the glow on her hand that caught Kai's attention. As the rest of them looked on with rapt fascination, Lucifer and Zemi vanished in a plume of smoke and fire.

"Well, put a spell on my ass," Isadora said, in a genuinely awed tone. Turning to the others she jutted her thumb toward the fading cloud of smoke. "Did that son of a bitch just take the Fae Queen to the Underworld?"

"What the fuck is he thinking?" Mammon shouted. "Abducting the Fae Queen and taking her to the Underworld? Why would he do that? I mean, I know he's still hung up on her, any fool can see that, but why would he take her there against her will?"

Kai looked up at Asmodeus through wide eyes before turning to Satan and the rest of the Brotherhood. "Because Zemi is wearing the ring."

The End

212

DEMON OF PRIDE

PRINCES OF HELL
BOOK 2

Coming 2015

SARA HUMPHREYS

ABOUT THE AUTHOR

Sara is a graduate of Marist College, with a B.A. Degree in English Literature & Theater. Her initial career path after college was as a professional actress. Some of her television credits include, A&E Biography, Guiding Light, Another World, As the World Turns and Rescue Me. In 2013 Sara's novel UNTAMED won two PRISM awards--Dark Paranormal and Best of the Best. Sara has been a lover of both the paranormal and romance novels for years. Her sci-fi/fantasy/romance obsession began years ago with the TV Series STAR TREK and an enormous crush on Captain Kirk. That sci-fi obsession soon evolved into the love of all types of fantasy/paranormal; vampires, ghosts, werewolves, and of course shape shifters. Sara is married to her college sweetheart, Will. They live in New York with their 4 boys. You can find information about upcoming books on her website: www.sarahumphreys.com

CPSIA information can be obtained
at www.ICGtesting.com
Printed in the USA
LVHW040030100420
652901LV00002B/417